The Art of Murder

T0159603

Also by Walter Reutiman:

Blood on Elkhorn Mountain
Lake Effect
Murder at Christmas Lake
Melt Point

THE ART OF MURDER

WALTER REUTIMAN

NORTH STAR PRESS OF ST. CLOUD, INC.
St. Cloud, Minnesota

Cover Design: Liz Dwyer

Copyright © 2014 Walter Reutiman

All rights reserved.

ISBN: 978-0-87839-725-9

This is a work of fiction. Names, characters, places, and incidents are the products of the author's imagination or are used fictitiously. Any resemblance to actual events or persons, living or dead, is entirely coincidental.

First Edition: June 2014

Printed in the United States of America

Published by
North Star Press of St. Cloud, Inc.
P.O. Box 451
St. Cloud, MN 56302
northstarpress.com

Prologue

Spring had been struggling to make its appearance at Excelsior on the plains of central Minnesota. Winter clung on with icy tendrils. Finally as June neared, cold finally yielded to southerly breezes, and spring, with summer right on its heels emerged in the suburban Minneapolis community. The softball season began, contributing to widespread activity on the Excelsior Commons. This thirteen-acre lakeside park, located on a point of land at the north side of town, separated Excelsior and Gideon Bays of Lake Minnetonka, and had been a fixture in the community since the 1850s.

An evening game was in progress, with attentive fans rooting for their favorite athletes skillfully laboring under the lights. Young children, still confined to strollers, longed for the freedom that older siblings enjoyed, their squeals of joyful glee blended with the shouts of encouragement for the gladiators on the field.

The ball field, however, was not the only center of activity this evening. Boats, coming into use from a long winter hibernation, traversed the adjacent bays, giving birth to breakers that beat against the rocky shoreline. The nearby swimming beach was well attended now that school was over for the season, and young Olympians splashed and played to exhaustion under the watchful eyes of parents. Bikers, skateboarders, and joggers shared use of the sidewalks in pleasant conviviality.

A soft breeze blew onshore, lending to the public's comfort, while puffy, white clouds spattered a blue sky, painting a picture of serenity and well being. This indeed was an ideal place to enjoy a warm summer's eve.

While most attendees at the game closely followed the action, one man was singular for his inattention. At first glance he appeared no different from his compatriots, dressed as he was in khaki shorts, a knit shirt, and a baseball cap that covered his dark hair. Sunglasses shielded his eyes. He merely acted differently. His eyes nervously scanned the crowd, seemingly less interested in the game's final outcome than in his search for something or someone.

The concrete viewing stands he occupied had been pressed into a large knoll behind the batting screen, and could be accessed either from field level or by way of a sidewalk that climbed the knoll from either the north or south ends of the park. The beach lay to the north, the downtown district to the south. Coolers and chairs were scattered across the small green space that separated the sidewalk from the seating area.

Before long another inning had played to conclusion when a late arrival strolled across the grass strip and stood atop the bleachers, scanning the enthusiastic crowd. Then, nodding recognition, the new fan moved laterally before carefully descending the bleachers. This fan moved two steps down before stopping on the same level as the inattentive fan. Pausing momentarily, the new arrival inspected the concrete platform for any sign of detritus before sitting. This person had yet to acknowledged anyone. After watching the action on the field for half an inning, the late arrival stood and brushed off his dark denims before cautiously climbing down the remaining steps to field level. A large manila envelope was casually left behind near the afore mentioned inattentive spectator.

The man who had been left behind surreptitiously glanced to his left at the package without reaching to pick it up. A nervous hand played with the cement deck as if afraid, nervous at the idea of reaching out to the abandoned folio. Instead, the man looked up at the departing figure, who circled behind the backstop and strolled over to the refreshment stand, mixing with the crowd awaiting a turn at the concessions.

After a short interlude, and a successful purchase of an ice-cream cone, the short-term visitor walked away from the ball field, past the restrooms, and on south, away from the festivities, and back toward the downtown business center.

The man who had been watching these proceedings, now glanced around himself, hastily picked up the abandoned envelope, and with it securely tucked under his arm, hurried up three levels of seats, across the grass berm and to the sidewalk beyond. There he turned left and followed the walkway downhill toward the departing fan. His goal was to head off the visitor who was sauntering along the walk, while enjoying the newly acquired refreshment.

Fifty yards separated the two at the start, and now the pursuer had to scramble to close the gap. His flushed face registered both his excitement and level of concern. Finally catching up with his quarry many yards away, and gasping to catch his breath, the pursuer grabbed at a free elbow. Then he wheezed, "I need to talk to you."

Strong fingers pried away the man's fingers, while a look of distain was the only reply. As would be expected, others along the shared pathway eyed the two of them to determine what was taking place. The two men silently stared at one another.

Catching his breath, the second man looked at his hand and dropped it to his side before saying, "Really, this is important." He reached for his companion's shoulder in an effort at camaraderie.

Pulling away, the first man hissed, "What are you doing? You aren't even supposed to know me, you idjit. People shouldn't be seeing us togedder. Christ, you're breaking da rules." Then the messenger turned and once again began to walk away slowly, ignoring the still puffing first man, who stood frozen for a moment, watching the other man leave, before following with less exuberance.

Catching up once again, he said excitedly, "Okay, okay. I know. I know I'm not following procedure, but this is really, really important." This time he had whispered, cognizant of the surrounding environment.

A sigh and a slow shaking of the head was the only response the other gave him. The crowds, bent as they were on their own pursuits, ignored the two men. The whistle of a nearby boat unexpectedly bleated its call, momentarily drowning out all else nearby.

Frustration mixed with concern in the man's face as he whispered to the man with the accented speech. "Listen, please. You have to tell them I want out."

The other stopped and turned with a look of contempt. A sneer crossed his darkened face. "Dat's easy, brother, just pay the money back, then."

A forlorn look distorted the distressed man's features. Shaking his head, he said with a wimper, "I don't have it. You must know that. They for sure know that. It's all invested in the project. Can't they just get someone else . . . you know . . . like a replacement for me?"

The messenger narrowed piercing eyes, while thin eyebrows lowered in warning. "Look, brother. I know nottin' of the finances, nottin' of your personal . . . situation. Nottin'. Quit your whining. I don't see what you're worrying about," the stranger said softly, before taking a final bite of the sugary cone.

"Well, yeah, you're not me. How can you understand?" He threw up his hands in exclamation. "Well, if you don't know anything, they know my situation, then. You can pass it along."

The envoy raised two hands outward, palm side up. "So, they know. What's your point, guy, huh?"

"I . . . I need to get out. Can't you understand? I can't do this anymore. I'm a nervous wreck. I'm not cut out for this. I have to think of my family." The man seemed close to a breakdown.

The other man paused a few seconds as if collecting his thoughts. He meticulously wiped his hands on a napkin. "You shoulda thought a dat when you decided to join the team. I imagines yous was plenty happy to be involved when yous got the money, got all set up in business. Man, oh, man you have short-term memory problem."

The courier put a hand on the dejected man's left shoulder and looked him in the eyes. "Look, fella. You're talking to wrong guy here. I just messenger."

"Then tell them for me, won't you?"

This entreaty caused man to turn away from the distraught man. Looking back over their shoulder, the reply came in a soft whisper. "There are two ways out. Pay back dough or . . ."

A frightened expression contorted the man's face. "Or what?"

"I thinks you can figure dat out. Somebody pays yous a visit."

Panic overwhelmed him. "No! I don't . . . you can't. I've done everything you wanted."

"Then shut the fuck up and do yous fuckin' job. Stay out of my face. That's not the deal. You got nuttin' to worry about dat I can see. Yous a lay-gitimite businessman. Yous in da clear, fella."

At that the man turned and walked away, tossing his crumpled napkin into a trash container, leaving the troubled man standing alone on the sidewalk in front of the boat docks.

Chapter One
Party Time

By the time I stepped out the rear door of my lakeside town home, the brilliant afternoon light had begun yielding to dusk. Pausing momentarily on my deck to survey the lake, I watched a fog of shadow slowly flowing along the water surface. It began swallowing those docks closest to shore, blending them into the surrounding dark water and shoreline. Boats moored furthest out appeared to be on an island oasis. They too soon began fading into the gloom as if swallowed by the lake itself as they gently bobbed on the tranquil surface.

The contrast between the air conditioning inside and the humid night air was shocking. Although it had been clammy earlier in the day on my walk home from work, I would have expected it to have cooled somewhat by now. I swear I could almost see water droplets hanging in the air before me. High humidity was quite unusual for Minnesota. Nonetheless, we got so few warm nights that those of us who lived here appreciated every last one. I was not complaining.

Nighttime boaters have few opportunities where they don't have to bundle up after dark to enjoy time on the water. I regretted I would not be able to venture forth for this night. That is, of course, unless I went later, which still was an option, though only a remote one. The weatherman was predicting the chance of a storm.

I laughed at that probability, since the purveyors of atmospheric conditions were wrong more often than they were right. However, with this high humidity and the forecast of a cool front moving in, chances of something severe were elevated. Be prepared was what I always said.

My name is Michael Connelly. I am native to the area, having only left for a short while pursuing higher education. I was uncertain if it said something about my personality that I gravitated back to my old stomping grounds after school, but I supposed some shrink might have an opinion, one I was not so sure I'd like to hear.

I attended the home state university, the U, but went to law school at Michigan. Consequently, that was one football game I usually attempted to attend. For once, I had to be on the winning side no matter who won. For the remainder of the season, I followed my high school team, the Skippers. They were plenty competitive, and provided a nice Friday night's entertainment.

I watched as boats piled one after another into Maynard's Restaurant, like ducks into a prairie pothole. All signs said their outdoor deck would be busy tonight, as I was sure every lakeside restaurant would be.

During these warm spells, I normally left my air on during the day while I was away at the office, but I kept the thermostat elevated to eighty degrees. That took care of the humidity, without breaking the bank on energy costs. I could be as conscientious as the next guy, though it was less about going green than an attempt to save money.

Opening up my place to fresh air this evening before I left home would have been preferable, but the humidity level was just too high for that, and it wouldn't be good for sleeping, at least not for me. My preference leaned to forty percent humidity, sixty degrees, and a cool breeze. Most summer nights here lakeside were like that. Not tonight though.

I looked at my watch. Time to go uptown. I walked back inside, locked my patio door and headed out the front entrance along Lake Street. With the possibility of a storm, I checked the sky as I hit the sidewalk. White, billowing clouds were mounting high in the western sky, foretelling an active atmosphere. For once the weatherman might have gotten it right, but then I hadn't planned on being out long, and I wasn't far from my shelter. Not to worry.

My humble abode overlooked Excelsior Bay and fronted Lake Street, just down the block a short walk from Water Street, the main thoroughfare through town. This location isolated me from most of the business district noise. Even a sleepy little burg like Excelsior had its moments.

I stopped momentarily to catch a breath. The air was suffocating. I'd gone only half a block, and already I was feeling awash with moisture. My earlier shower quickly was being negated. I lifted one arm to gauge the degree of dampness, and wasn't surprised at the dark circle forming. At least my deodorant was doing its job, I hoped.

Dressed casually in a blue knit shirt, a pair of khaki cargo shorts, and tennis shoes sans socks, I was ready for my night on the town. Unfortunately, my shirt already had darkened and was beginning to stick to my back. But as I said, I was the last one to complain about warm weather. I hoped to retire down south some day if I had the opportunity. If so, I had better get used to damp shirts.

As I strolled along, I noticed that every parking spot along my street was taken, which certainly was not unusual for weekend summer nights here. Our little town was a big draw for nearby folks looking for a good time, and there certainly was plenty here for them to do. Not many clunkers among the parked cars, either. Money was what it took to partake in our local pleasures.

My journey took me across Lake Street near the corner bar and liquor store, which as usual was a major magnet for activity. The outdoor tables were jammed with revelers on most any night found no exception tonight. What was different tonight was the number of people just hanging around on the sidewalks. This locale usually was busy, with its proximity to the lake, the boats, and a ready supply of liquid merriment on sale within, but tonight exceeded normal.

The large crowd had spilled out into the street, taking over nearly half of the right-of-way. No one seemed to care. I wended my way through the sea of humanity toward my downtown destination, taking in the sights and sounds. It was a lively, though seemingly well behaved crowd. Maybe the police car parked across the street in front of the theater had some effect on the situation.

So far on my short sojourn I had not seen anyone I knew. That wasn't surprising, though, since the pub was more of a draw for the out-of-town revelers looking for a good time in our quaint lakeside village. The townies probably were safely ensconced in their own yards grilling and masticating cow. I was sure to find acquaintances later on my walk.

Pausing briefly by the pub's parking lot entrance to light my cigar, I scanned the immediate area. Most people appeared to be in their twenties, and women outnumbered men roughly two to one. Those were my kind of odds. On any other night, I might have just remained here. Not tonight, though. I had other things in mind.

Lines of folks were both entering and exiting the bar. There was a good deal of cheerfulness about tonight, and that gave me a lift. A person would have to be in a foul mood, indeed, not to be carried along by the crowd's bubbling enthusiasm.

I gave my Tobascos Baez a deep draw and slowly blew out the smoke. The cigar tip glowed red as I twisted the cylinder between my thumb and index finger. The lighter clanged into my house keys when I dropped it back into my pocket.

I generally tried to confine my smoking to the out of doors to preserve the pristine interior of my place. Women friends did not care for the smell of stale tobacco, and I acquiesced to their demands, having grown tired of the complaints. Thus, my deck held a wide assortment of ashtrays.

My motivation for going out tonight was the street dance hosted by Excelsior in conjunction with Minnetonka High's all school reunion. I knew the main drag would be a zoo, but I wanted to at least make an appearance. One trip up the street and back down the other side was my plan. This I could manage. Maybe I would even get lucky and meet some young woman who could profit from my wisdom and sage advice. Plus my boat always was an attraction.

The real impetus for the journey was that I practiced law in this small city, and I counted this sortie as public relations. I knew I was getting too old to get involved in the high spirits that would occur later tonight when the beer took hold. I'd leave that to the younger graduates. By then I'd be safely situated in my place with my old friend Crown Royal. That was plenty good company on a night such as this.

Thirty-seven shouldn't be considered old, and I tried to convince myself of that, but then I asked myself why I felt that way. It was nineteen years since my own graduation, and I had not been doing much physically to ward off the advancing years. That was one thing I would have to rectify when the weather cooled. There was only so much time in the day, and right now my time was spoken for.

I had taken one step along the sidewalk to continue my journey when a young reveler staggered into me from the left, and jostled my arm. After taking the brunt of the assault, the cigar in my left hand quickly gave up its ash, showering sparks over the adjacent sidewalk. Though I was knocked a short step sideways, that fortuitously allowed me to be in a better position to grab my assailant by the back of his collar with my right hand, which probably saved him from going face first into the gutter. Without giving it a thought, I dropped my cigar and grabbed the poor guy's available arm with my left hand, at which time I attempted to pull him upright.

That was easier said than done because the young man's legs seemed to be made of rubber. If I could have brought him upright, I was guessing he would have stood almost a foot shorter than my six foot three. From the ease with which I hefted him, I imagined I must have outweighed him by a hundred pounds.

The florid face and glazed eyes that stared uncomprehendingly at me spoke of him being unwell. My hope was that he would be able to control his stomach. I was not sure what to do with the baggage. The guy was dressed casually in a cotton shirt and shorts. He has no hat, which allowed me to see his crimson-colored skin. It was obvious where he had spent his day in the sun. Perhaps too much so.

Before I could decide what to do, I become aware of a young woman rushing up, screaming, "Don't hurt him. Please don't hurt him."

The distressed woman was a petite, dark-haired beauty, casually attired. She appeared to be relatively sober by my quick appraisal. The anxiety displayed on her continence forecast tears.

"You big bully. Can't you see he's not well?" she squealed.

My face certainly must have exhibited my astonishment that she thought I was the offender here, because she momentarily paused. Indecision was reflected in her eyes. I could see she was truly upset. She was clenching and unclenching her hands in an attempt to remain in command of her emotions. She was barely succeeding.

The nearby throng had quieted and was paying some attention to our performance, lending uncertainty to the situation. It was anybody's guess as to where I stood in their collective view. The last thing I wanted was trouble. I looked at my hostage, gave a sigh, raised my eyes toward the heavens, and released my grip. The young man slithered to the ground like a balloon that had lost its air.

"Why did you do that?" the girl screamed, hysterically. She knelt down and threw her arms around her friend drawing a hand through his hair. She gently rocked him against her chest.

"Lady, you and your friend need to go home and sleep it off," I stated, with a good deal of restraint.

"He's just had too much sun," she wailed, looking up at me with pleading eyes.

"Then get him hydrated and out of my face," I hissed at her, as she closed her grip on the young man. Kids.

Her response was a shocked look, which left me to wonder if she comprehended much in her current state. I wasn't about to wait and find out.

I looked for my cigar, but gave it up. It had been stepped on several times. What a waste. I pushed through the assembled throng, making my way between two parked cars and into the street. I moved along quickly. I did not want any part of the drinking masses. Drunks were too unpredictable. Glancing over my shoulder, I saw that the young couple seemed to be drawing some attention. That was a relief.

Looking ahead, I saw a cop step out of his car, looking toward me. It was Joe Dupont. Joe's older brother Bob and I attended school together. I waved and hollered. "They're okay," before continuing on. Joe looked at me and returned my wave before walking toward the milling crowd, which left me to my own pursuits. I moved along quickly.

I can take care of myself in a fight, but it never looked good for an attorney to be seen brawling downtown. The suspicion would be I was drunk and that wasn't good for business, at least not the kind I preferred.

It was necessary for me to remain in the street to bypass the throng assembled in front of Licks Ice Cream Parlor. There was such a demand for that refreshing treat tonight it would be difficult to pass through the mass of humanity waiting there with eager anticipation. The thought of an ice cream cone just now did sound good, but the line looked way too long. I demurred.

This part of Water Street was not blocked off to traffic, but the street was terminated ahead at the intersection with Second Street, so no traffic was moving through right now. Those who earlier had found parking here were not likely to give it up until much later tonight.

I had practiced law in Excelsior now for twelve years, and I had enjoyed my life here in this community. I liked both the town and the people who resided here. The stability and constancy appealed to me. I guess I had become set in my ways, but I wasn't fighting it.

A feeling of contentment washed over me as I approached the intersection. Looking up, I spotted a large cloth banner strung across Water Street at store-top height. It welcomed the Tonka Alumni in bold blue and gold lettering. The banner was attached to a wire strung from buildings on either side of the street.

I smiled as the sight above brought back a memory from my younger years when it had been my job to take down a similar banner after our annual town celebration. I had been a member of the Jaycees, and it was our project to hang the banner.

Somehow the large metal rings attached to the canvas and strung on the wire had jammed when the banner was part way across. We repeatedly tried to free it from the building's roof with no success, and we didn't have a pole long enough to reach up from the ground. After much deliberation, we found the longest extension ladder available and extended it up against the wire. It had barely reached the cable.

Then I had volunteered to climb up and see what I could do. The ladder was placed in the middle of the street right at the intersection, and cars were going both ways past me and my companion at the foot of the ladder. I was not sure what good he was doing, but it had given me comfort to have him there. At least drivers would hopefully have seen him where they might not have seen the ladder. To reach the banner, the ladder stood almost vertical to the ground. This made climbing it difficult.

The wire had not seemed very high from the ground, but once I had reached the top and looked down, I changed my opinion. I felt very shaky, indeed, being pushed back and forth by the breeze. I had grabbed the wire with one hand, although I had been uncertain what good that would do if I had lost the ladder. I could just see myself going hand over hand to the nearest roof, especially with the banner in the way. Of greater concern, only a foot of the top of the ladder extended above the wire. A good stiff breeze and . . . Why had I ever volunteered for that assignment?

But I had untangled the banner, and my compatriots on the roof of the building had successfully pulled it across. On the other hand, the now non-weighted wire rose relative to the ladder's top, eating up most of my safety margin on the ladder, leaving only three inches of aluminum still holding me in place. I wanted to scream, as I held onto the ladder with one hand and the wire with the other. I made it no secret I was shaking. Holy shit was I scared.

I could stay holding the wire to the ladder, hoping maybe for a helicopter rescue, or I could go down, and I figured the helicopter thing was unlikely. With the ladder nearly vertical, I quickly calculated that, if it began to fall, I could slide down, minimizing my drop distance. Oh, the follies of youth. Fortunately, I made it down without mishap. I smiled at the remembrance. Now I looked back up at the wire as I walked underneath. It looked plenty high. I wonder how I could have been so crazy.

The block ahead had been cordoned off since morning and was devoid of cars. Partiers covered the area from sidewalk to sidewalk, milling about in small groups, dancing or just scouting, as I was doing. Two amplified bands played, one near each end of the block. Conversations would be strained, but that didn't seem to bother anyone.

I nodded at a couple people I knew, but saw no need to engage in dialogue. I saw them frequently. Stores were closed for the night, but a few had decorated their windows and backlit them. Cheap advertising.

Near the middle of the block I ran into my old friend Pat O'Neal. I'd known Pat since second grade. We didn't see each other much anymore, just an occasional e-mail. Pat lived in Apple Valley, so at least he still was in the area. A shock of red hair was Pat's most noticeable feature. I waved, intending to move on by.

Pat waved back, and hustled toward me. He said. "Hi, Mike."

"Hi, Pat. How've you been?"

"Good, you?"

"Finer than frogs hair," I replied.

Pat stuck his hands in his pockets. "Nice. Been down here long?"

"No, I just walked up the block," I said.

Pat looked around. "I've been here over an hour and have seen damn few people I know."

"All burned out from last night, maybe?"

"Maybe," he answered. "Sure is warm. Feels good, though."

"I agree, but tough on the old power bill."

"Man, you can say that again. I'm glad I'm on budget."

I nodded.

Pat stood just under six feet tall and had a stocky build. His round face was pale complexioned and sported numerous freckles. He had soft features and looked Irish through and through.

Neither of us had much new to say. There was a short pause before Pat said, "There's someone you've got to see."

"What? Who?"

"Over here. Follow me," and Pat started to walk across the street and through the crowd. He turned and waved me to follow. Little did I know I was about to enter a very troubling episode in my life.

Chapter Two
Out of the Past

Pat O'Neil moved with singularity of purpose, and I momentarily hesitated, wondering what mischief he was up to. But then I shrugged and followed him, wending my way through knots of people toward the far sidewalk. The band was playing a crowd favorite and some in the nearby assemblage were whooping it up as they danced all over the street.

Pat's destination appeared to be two women talking together on the sidewalk away from the throng. I could tell by the manner of the brunette facing me they were enjoying themselves. The woman seemed familiar, but I couldn't place her. Maybe I had seen her around town at one time or another. Her companion, a blonde, had her back turned toward me, but there was something familiar in her demeanor.

Pat moved right into their space. With the noise, I could barely hear him say, "Hi, girls," interrupting their conversation. "There's someone here I want you to see."

By this time, I also had arrived, but was blocked off from their view by Pat's back.

The blonde turned her head toward Pat, and I saw who she was. I almost choked. I finally managed to breathe, though it took a conscious effort. The event had become a surreal moment for me. I stood frozen in my tracks, and time seemed to slow down. There no longer was any significant sound around me, just a continuous din. My face felt as though it was on fire.

Yes, I knew this woman. I recognized every feature, every nuance of her face. Granted, her hair now was cut in a different style and her makeup was different, but I was intimately familiar with everything else. Fine lines showed here and there on her face that had not been there nineteen years ago, but they did little to detract from the overall splendor. The face was not quite as thin, as I had remembered it, but the nose was just as straight. It was a beautiful face. A face I once had loved.

I must have looked the fool, staring as I did, but I didn't care. I wanted to reach out and caress her fine skin. Somehow I resisted the urge. The woman's hair was parted to one side and brushed across her brow. Blue eyes sparkled in the night as they always had for me.

The woman, Grace, had been smiling as she turned toward Pat's voice, but then she appeared befuddled. She'd seen me. Her smile quickly returned, however, and she said something I couldn't quite hear.

Suddenly Pat jabbed me in the ribs with his elbow and I was back. "Excuse me," I said, lamely. "Sorry, I didn't hear," motioning toward the band.

"Look what the cat dragged in," Grace joked.

My three companions laughed, and I generated a weak smile.

"What a surprise," I managed. I felt awkward, like a teen on a first date.

"Good to see you too, Mike," Grace replied.

"You too, Grace. You look wonderful." *Is that the best I could do*, I thought?

Grace was dressed in a blue skirt and a white sleeveless blouse. She had a white ribbon in her hair and blue, dangling earrings. It took me a minute to realize she was dressed in the school colors.

"You're taller, Mike."

"I guess I grew some after we last saw one another." I stood as erect as I could, and we both laughed. "I think I've put on a few pounds since high school, too."

Grace smiled and said. "It looks good on you."

I was unable to tell if I was blushing, I was so overwhelmed by the moment.

Grace wore sandals and the top of her head came only to my chin. She seemed shorter than I had remembered.

Before I could make a complete ass of myself, Pat said, "Mike this is, Jill."

Turning to the other woman, I reached out my hand and said. "Pleasure to meet you, Jill. I don't remember you from school. Did you go to Tonka?"

Jill put her small hand in mine, and gave it a light squeeze. "I was a couple of years behind Grace. Grace and my sister used to hang out."

Jill was a pretty woman, I noted, with a round face, full lips and nice figure. I stared at that maybe a little too long while I wondered if it was all her own. My attention must have been obvious because Jill looked first at me and smiled, and then to Grace said, "Well, I've got to be going. I'll call you next week, Grace." Then she said, "Look me up sometime, Mike."

That statement brought me back to reality, and I found myself scanning her hand for a ring. I had no good answer to her solicitation, but lots of thoughts raced through my head.

"I'll look forward to seeing you," Grace answered Jill, looking slightly peeved. Was it directed toward Jill or me? What did it matter?

I watched Jill's graceful figure as she moved on down the sidewalk. She looked back and smiled, then disappeared into the crowd.

There was an awkward silence finally broken by Pat. "That went well. If I can trust you two to be alone, I've got to head home. Promised the wife I'd be home by ten or so."

I looked at my watch, and said. "That late already? I'll see you then, Pat. Take care."

"Good to see you, Pat," Grace seconded.

Pat gave each of us a smile and walked up the street in the opposite direction Jill had taken.

I had recovered some of my usual aplomb and looked at Grace. "Gosh Gracie, its been a long time."

"Yes it has, hasn't it? I see you still have an eye for the ladies."

I bit my lip so as to not reply. Grace paused and looking down at the sidewalk said. "I understand you have an office in town."

"That's right, a small law practice."

"Nice. You always wanted that."

Things were more awkward than they should have been. What do you say to someone you haven't seen for nearly twenty years?

Grace had been rail thin in high school. She had filled out now and it appeared the years had been good to her. "You look great, Gracie."

"I think you said that, but thanks. You look good yourself, Mike. You've grown. What's that thing over your lip?"

I reached a hand to my face, and then laughed.

I wasn't the best looking guy in town, but I did have a full head of brown wavy hair and kept a small mustache over my lip. I'd never had a problem getting a date, so I must not be that hard to look at.

"Did you come back just for the reunion?" I asked.

"No, we live here now."

Hearing Grace say "we" jolted me, but what did I expect, that Gracie was going to remain celibate for me, waiting for my return?

"You're married, then?" I managed.

"Yes. My husband owns the art gallery there." She pointed to a storefront a few feet down the block.

"I saw that it had opened," I said. "But, I've never made it inside."

"We've been open since last November."

I shrugged. "I've never been much of an art guy."

"Never too late to learn," she said with a smile.

Her even, white teeth shone. Grace had just gotten rid off her braces when we started dating back in high school.

I wanted to reach out and touch her, once again to feel her soft skin. She smelled awfully good too. The humidity was carrying her scent to me. It was making me crazy.

My brain was spinning, looking for a way to prolong this meeting. "Ahm, where do you guys live, then?"

"Over in Chanhassen. You?"

"I have a place down on the water."

"No kidding. You mean those nice ones at the end of the street?"

"Yeah."

"Sweet. I've always wanted to see those. Maybe I can stop by sometime?"

"Sure, That'd be great. I'm in 116. But give me a month's notice so I can shovel out the debris."

Grace laughed. God, I loved that laugh.

Just then I was slapped on the back so hard I nearly fell forward. "Hey, you two. Just like old times."

I recognized the voice without turning around. It was John Brooks, another Tonka graduate.

"I didn't see you around tonight, John," I said.

John was wearing a pair of khaki slacks, loafers, and a knit shirt. He was slightly overdressed for this crowd.

"At the office working late," he replied. "You two still make a nice couple. I don't suppose you're thinking of leaving your husband, Grace?"

"Only for you, John," she said, smiling.

"Touché," John said with an extravagant smile. "Well, have fun. I have a rendezvous with the beer tent."

"You take care too, John," I said.

Grace and I both smiled, and John moved on down the street blending into the crowd.

"Same old John," I said.

"He hasn't changed much, personality wise. Just a little dumpier," Grace suggested.

I thought of my own middle-aged gut and said, "Maybe too much time behind the desk?"

"Maybe."

Before I could say anything else, the band came back from a short break and began playing an upbeat tune. I took Grace's hand and we walked a few paces away from the noise.

Her hand felt good in mine. When we stopped walking, I kept her hand. Then we both pulled away at the same time.

"Are you ever at the store?" I asked.

"No. My husband and his associate handle that. I take care of our home, and work a little at the library. Volunteer stuff."

I asked. "The one here or Chanhassen?" Chanhassen is another small suburban town just a hop, skip and jump south of here.

"Chanhassen," Grace answered.

"You said you just moved here?"

"Yes, that's right."

Grace waved to someone walking past. I didn't bother to look. My attention was solely on her.

I leaned in a little. "Where were you before?"

"We were living in San Antonio."

"Texas, huh? Nice place?"

"Very."

I noticed the small scar on her neck. It was barely discernable now, but I remembered the night she got it, running through the woods and being scraped deeply by a dead branch. She had bled all over her blouse. I had been really frightened that night.

I returned to the present. "Why'd you move here?"

"Marshall got the store opportunity, so we came," she said, pointing up the block.

"What are the odds?" I said.

There was a pause, and then Grace said. "This is almost Texas weather we've got tonight."

We both looked up the street to the west at the building thunderheads. It was so hot and humid moisture was collecting on the storefront windows from the cool inside air meeting the hot humid outside air against the glass barrier.

"Awfully warm for here, as you know."

I looked back over Grace's shoulder at the sky. The set sun still reflected off the back of the billowing thunderheads. The bottoms were looking darker. "Looks like it'll rain before the party's over."

Grace turned back to me and said, "I missed the rain when I was in Texas. We didn't get much down there. Not like here, as I remember."

"I guess not. Dry, huh?"

"Yes. Pretty, though, in its own way."

"Yeah. Say, let's you and your husband meet me some night for a boat ride. I've got a boat."

"That'd be nice. Thanks."

I was lost for something else to say, and neither of us spoke. Then, the nearest band began playing a slow number and I asked Grace to dance. There weren't a lot of people around us so we danced where we had been standing.

With my arm around her waist, I held her close, but not too close. Her breasts brushed my chest as we moved, and I had the urge to pull her closer, but resisted. Just before the number ended, Grace placed her head against my chest. The moment was too brief. I could feel the heat between us, which had nothing to do with the weather.

I wondered where I could take her? Then I chastised myself. This was just like being back in high school with one thing on my mind, to score. I had to quit thinking with my pecker and grow up, even if I did not want to.

When the music stopped, we stepped apart, looking into each other's faces. Our eyes locked. I smiled and Grace returned the smile.

She spoke in a soft, inviting tone. "Thanks for the dance, Mike. It was nice. Brought back old memories."

"For me too, Gracie."

I struggled for something more to say. Something to prolong the encounter. Nothing came to mind. It was useless. My brain was locked down. Finally, at a loss for words, I offered. "Okay, then, maybe I'll see you around. Give me a call sometime."

"Sure, Mike. I'd like that."

Grace looked so tiny, so vulnerable as she stood before me. I wanted to pick her up and carry her away. Instead, I leaned in to give her a peck on the cheek. She turned her head and our lips met. Hers were soft and inviting as they welcomed my touch. They lingered way too long. My body began to respond to the contact. My head was swimming. I was blind to my surroundings. I pulled away. It was as if we had never been parted for those many years.

My eyes were watering. "Gracie . . ."

"It's been nice to see you, Mike."

"Yeah, for me too. Bye, Gracie."

I turned and walked toward home, wondering what had just taken place. It felt as though my well-ordered life was about to change.

Chapter Three
Surprising Visitor

I left Grace and began a slow walk home. My face felt flushed. Was it from the heat or my brief encounter? I was uncertain. I took out a handkerchief and wiped my face. It didn't seem to help. Following my reunion with Grace, I was so unnerved I little noticed what was taking place around me for the last block. People were scattered everywhere and I had to weave my way through the crowd until I got past the intersection with Second Street. If there were people I knew in the crowd, I had ignored them. If so, I probably would hear about it later.

My mind was occupied with chewing over the very brief exchange. What more could I have said? How could I have acted less like a dweeb? I just was too shocked at seeing my former girl to have known how to respond properly. Her appearance back here in town was a bolt out of the blue, though I had to admit, a pleasant occurrence.

I walked on past the movie theater and then stopped. There I stood with my back against the building watching the crowd across the street at the bar. The throng seemed to have thinned somewhat. Maybe because of the impending storm.

Placing one foot against the wall, I stuck both hands in my pockets and sighed. I could not get the thought of Grace being back here out of my head. Our lives together back in high school had been pure bliss.

Grace had been my first true love. We began dating in high school when I was a junior and she a sophomore. We had a marvelous summer together before my senior year. Looking back now, I could not recall much if any disharmony. We had been kindred spirits then, both easy going and free, as only high school kids could be.

Then, there had been the venture into the wonderful world of sex. She was my first as I was hers, and I didn't think there ever was anything to compare to that first coupling. Unfortunately for me and for every woman I had met since, they got compared to Grace. How totally unfair that had been to them.

Why then had we drifted apart? I had asked myself that a million times over the intervening years, and still had no answer. Youth, I guess. The young always figured things would only be better tomorrow. Without experience, I could not have known I already had the best thing ever. I tossed it aside for something else that had never materialized. I shook my head at that realization, since I never in all those years since had admitted the fact to myself. What a dumb ass I had been.

I did know one thing, though. There never was anyone after Grace to whom I felt I could allow myself to become vulnerable. Maybe that was another one for the analyst. If I had one, he could make plenty of money off me.

It was getting late. The breeze had freshened, and rain would soon follow. I decided to get on home to my sanctuary. Like I needed to rush home to four empty walls. Reaching the corner with Lake Street, I paused to watch the charter boats making their way to safe harbor. Standing and watching the waves on the bay, I saw that the wind had picked up in the short time since I'd left Grace. It was out of the west and blowing straight out onto the lake from this shore. At least it would be bow on, as the boats pulled into these docks.

I looked at my watch, since it seemed a bit early for the cruise boats to return. Maybe they were trying to beat the weather. Being caught on the lake in a thunderstorm was no picnic. One boat already had safely tied up, and people were meandering ashore.

With the hot and humid conditions, it definitely was not a night to hurry. Conversations were lively from the animated gathering. Obviously there had been plenty of liquid refreshment aboard. I smiled at their apparent cheerfulness and reached into my pocket for a cigar. Then I remembered I was out of tobacco. One more reason to get on home.

While the people from the boat were mingling in the dock area, a bus pulled up. The crowd moved as one onto their conveyance. For this night only the proprietors wisely had arranged to transport their passengers by bus to and from the Shorewood Shopping Center. Any other plan would have contributed to the nightmarish parking situation in the city. For the reunion party, people likewise were being shuttled from the high school.

As I watched, a second boat maneuvered toward the dock. Then I become aware of the degree that first party boat was tugging at its restraints. When I had left earlier to go uptown, the lake had been like glass. Now there was a nice chop building on the waters of the bay. The breeze was to my back, and the hot wind was picking up. I knew I had better check my own boat, though I thought it was secure.

Walking around the loading busses and on down the block, I walked up the front steps of my home. Inside, even with the thermostat set at eighty, I felt a chill. Apparently I had become somewhat acclimated to the heat, if that was possible. I would hate to sleep in these sweltering conditions, though. I did it as a kid and remembered finally falling asleep in the wee hours of the morning when it nearly had been time to get up. Air conditioning was a godsend.

I momentarily stood in my small foyer. There was a disquieting sense tonight about my living alone in this place, coming home to nothing but rooms of furniture. No people, no relationships, no emotion. Oh, hell, it was tough for anyone to be alone anywhere. I did not have a corner on that market. That was why I had my pal, Crown Royal. *Come here to me, my good friend.*

But first I needed to check on the boat, so I walked downstairs to the lower level. Drawing open my vertical blinds, I opened the sliding glass door, which accessed my deck, and I stepped outside. With the wind picking up, it felt somewhat cooler than it had earlier in the evening. Maybe the storm would bring cooler temperatures.

I studied the lake. Not many boats were cruising about. Most were holed up at the four nearby eateries. Maybe their plan was to remain there until after the storm passed. Why not? What better place to be then where food and drink were plentiful?

Hurrying on down to the docks, I made sure everything was safe and sound. A single overhead lamp lit the area, but that was more than enough light for me to see. I decided to hurry before it began to rain. The ropes looked good and the cover was properly snapped on. I had two automatic sump pumps so I felt confident there.

Several boats had vacated their slips for the evening. Those sailors had better watch the weather, because looking at the sky to the west I could see the tail end of sunset backlighting billowing thunderheads. They looked much more threatening than they had a few minutes earlier. A flash of lightening suddenly lashed upward from the nearest cloud. We were in for a patch of rain, if not an all-out blow.

Satisfied with the boat, I strode off the dock. Over the water I felt the humidity now more intensely than ever. I could cut the air with a knife, and it nearly was a struggle to breathe the heavy air as I climbed the steps up to my deck. I briefly considered remaining outside, but discarded the idea, feeling that soon I would have to move indoors anyway with the immanent storm.

It was comforting to get back into air conditioning, even if at first it felt bone-chilling cold. Once inside, I climbed to the upper level and my bedroom to remove my damp clothing, including underwear, throwing it over the side of the bathroom tub to dry. I considered a shower, but decided to hold off on that till bedtime.

Naked now, I leaned momentarily on the sink to survey my continence in the mirror. I decided I wasn't bad looking, certainly not handsome, but ruggedly male. My nose was a little too large, and had a couple if zigzags, but the mustache somewhat minimized that. At least I didn't have taxicab door ears. I was grateful for that. I pulled at my cheeks, but the skin there remained firm. Hazel eyes had always been my best feature. They were still clear, since I had not imbibed as yet this evening. I did an abbreviated pirouette and decided my body had not yet totally gone to seed. I would have to start working out, though, if I were going to compete with father time.

I threw on fresh clothes. Now with a dry shirt I was not so chilled. Sitting on the edge of the bed, I wondered at myself. I realized seeing Grace I had made me act more like an over-sexed teen than a mature adult. I could not go around living in a fantasy world as far as Grace was concerned. It was long past time to move on.

Move on? Hell, I *had* moved on. I had not seen the woman in, what, nineteen years, and had not thought about her in ages. That must count for moving on. Besides, she was married. She said so herself.

I realized we'd had our moment. It had passed, and now she had made a life for herself, and I had made a life, and we just had to leave it at that. Even if I secretly wanted to get together with her, it would have been unfair to both her and her family. I did not know her husband, but I realized he was one lucky guy.

Fortunately, I had neither Grace's phone number nor her address. Hell, I did not even know her last name. I could find all that out if I truly wanted to, but I thought I'd better leave it alone. I was certain she wouldn't be searching me out, so there was little to fear in that regard. Of course, we all could go for a boat ride. That would be innocent enough. What a lame excuse to get into her pants. I shook my head.

Standing there, I surveyed the room. It was a mess, so I picked up my dirty clothes strewn around and threw them in the hamper. I also pulled the bedding into a halfway decent configuration, though nothing was tucked in. I had neglected to make it earlier. Since there was no one to check up on me, I sometimes neglected those easy tasks.

Maybe I should go fishing in the morning and then afterwards do the weekly laundry, followed by my grocery shopping for the week. That would fill my day and get me set for the workweek. This was going to be a busy week at the office, and work would get me back into the groove and help me forget my recent encounter. I slapped my thigh and left the bedroom with a new resolve.

Down in the kitchen, I still was uncertain if I wanted to sit inside or outside. With the threat of a storm, I had not wanted to take out the boat, but I thought perhaps I might sit on the deck for a bit and enjoy a smoke. Boats would be crisscrossing the bay and it always was an enjoyable sight to watch the red, green, and white lights moving about. Crown Royal, a good cigar, and beautiful scenery—that was why I lived here.

There was a nice breeze, even if it was a hot one. Based on my uncertainty, I removed an insulated plastic tumbler from a kitchen cabinet, broke some ice loose from a half empty tray in the freezer, and plopped in some of the cubes. The remaining ice went into a bowl and back into the freezer. I filled the empty tray with tap water and replaced it in its proper spot. One of these days I would have to upgrade to a new refrigerator with an automatic icemaker. Some day.

I had pulled my scotch bottle out and was about to pour my drink when the doorbell gave off its familiar three-tone ring. I looked in that direction, but then went ahead, pouring three fingers of amber liquid over the ice. This was not the first time kids had played with the bell, so I found it best to ignore it unless I had been expecting someone.

Then the bell tolled a second time.

"Oh, damn," I thought as I walked up the stairs to the front landing. "Some drunk thinks he's home or needs a bathroom. Just pee in the street like always."

I wrenched open the door, ready to give someone a scathing rebuke. She was standing there. A coquettish smile left her looking vulnerable. I remained motionless, both shocked and inwardly pleased at the same time.

"Hi," she said. "Remember me?"

"Oh, hi," was all I could manage in return.

"You going to let a girl stand out in the heat all night?" She turned her head and looked up at the threatening sky.

I awoke from my daze and said. "No, of course not. Come in. Yes,come on in."

I stepped back in front of the open door, motioned with my arm, and Grace breezed into my small foyer.

"So this is where you live," she stated, looking around.

"Yup, it's all mine."

She gave me that same smile and said. "You gave me your address and I didn't have anything to write it down with. So, I figured I'd forget it by tomorrow and came here while I remembered it. That okay?"

"Sure, Gracie."

She smelled good even with a glow of perspiration on her skin.

"I think it's going to storm. The wind's picking up. People are leaving the party. Can I wait it out here? Traffic's terrible."

"No problem," I said, as I took in her appearance.

We stood very close to one another.

I hadn't really remembered much about my old girl from our earlier encounter. Now in the brighter hall illumination, I noted that her blonde hair was more raspberry than I remembered from our youth, and was cut shorter, just off the shoulder. Grace wore more makeup now. She always had worn eye makeup, but I could see some on her face, which I had not remembered from years earlier.

"What's with the two stairways?" she asked, interrupting my inspection.

I was brought back to attention. "Oh, two levels. Downstairs is the living room, laundry, bath, and kitchen, while up is two bedrooms and two baths."

"Want to give me a tour?" she asked, as she took my hand. She took the discretion away from me by leading me up the stairs. "Nice maple railings," she said.

"Yes."

"What's here?" she asked as she looked into the front bedroom. "Guest room."

She walked over to the window. "Nice view of town from here."

I nodded.

Then Grace turned and walked down the hall into my room. I could see her eyeing the stark decorating of my bedroom and general untidiness. I wished now I had done a better job with the bed.

"Sorry for the mess. I don't do well picking up after myself."

She smiled. "What do you do well?" she asked, as she looked about my Spartan quarters. Then she turned and faced me. We stood only a foot apart and looked at one another for a brief moment. Instinctively I reached out my arms and Grace leaned in and put her arms around my neck, pulling down my head to her height. Our lips met and stayed together. I felt my body going into hyper drive as we began to press together. My hands slid down her back to settle on the fabric of her skirt. It felt good.

Suddenly, Grace pulled away and went over to the bed where she lay down in a provocative pose. That was when I knew I was lost. I followed her and we succumbed to our needs. Our lovemaking was much less frantic than it had been years earlier. Today it was slow and pleasurable. I enjoyed removing her clothes, and then I explored every inch of her body. Time held no meaning, as we both were lost in the moment. As I reached climax, I willed this not to be over. I lost out on that wish.

Later when we were relaxing, lightning flashed outside my window, followed by a loud clap of thunder. Rain battered against the glass. Grace lay with her head on my chest, her hair in my face. God, this was good. When I had started the day, I never would have imagined it would end this gloriously.

"Here comes the rain," I whispered, stating the obvious.

"Good thing I stayed."

"Yeah, good for me too."

We lay quietly coupled together. My fingers traced a path along her backbone.

Then I broke the silence. "What about, I mean . . . home," I asked. "Can you stay?"

"No. I'll have to leave."

"Why did you . . . I mean we . . . ?"

Grace was silent for a minute. "Let's just leave it at that." She said as she sat up, her back to me.

I reached around her placing my hands on her soft belly. I fingered a scar. I assumed she must have had a cesarean birth. Then I moved my hands up to her breasts, rubbing them softly. She leaned back against me, turned her head and kissed me long and hard. Suddenly, she broke free and stood before me in all her nakedness.

"Mind if I take a shower?" she asked. "I don't want to go home with the smell of sex on me. It might cause a problem." She smiled as she spoke.

"Go ahead. Clean towels are in the cabinet."

When I heard the shower running, I was tempted to join Grace, but was uncertain how that would be perceived, and she did say she had to go. I opted to accept my good fortune and not push it.

When she was finished and dressed, I said. "I'll drive you to your car."

"Thanks."

We left my house together in my car. This turned out to be one hell of a school reunion.

Chapter Four
The Morning After

Returning home after seeing Grace safely to her car, I plopped into a living room chair and stared out into the darkness of a stormy night. I had the blinds for the patio windows open with the interior lights off so I was able to gaze out over the water at red, green, and white lights passing like ghost lights in the night. A steady drizzle continued. Though there was not much to see, I cared little.

My living room, which occupied half of the lower level of my dwelling, was arranged with two furniture groupings. A couch and chair faced the three-panel glass exposure, with a small coffee table placed before them. Recessed lighting met that area's needs. Behind me on the adjacent wall stood a fireplace, and on the back wall was mounted a large flat screen TV. Easily moved chairs accommodated both centers of attention. A bumper pool table sat near the remaining wall. It was a guy's room.

After finishing a watery Crown Royal, I continued to freshen my glass until three in the morning. All the while I was having a battle with myself over what had happened earlier in the evening, and what if anything I was going to do about it going forward.

On the one hand, I could do nothing, and let Grace drive any potential future entanglement, or I could be proactive and pursue her. Either way I figured to lose, because no matter what, the endeavor would be fruitless. I had to get real because I was not ready to become a family man, so unless Grace left her family for me, it would be no deal. I was foolish to think otherwise.

Did I want that to happen? Her leave her family? No. I guess not. What kind of person would break up a family? I was like a dog chasing its tail. There were no good answers for my questions. The more I thought about it, the more befuddled I became. Or was it the booze? Finally, I gave in to my malaise and hit the mattress.

When finally I woke late Sunday morning, it was too late to go fishing. Dawn had broken hours earlier to a clear sky, cooler temperatures and a steady breeze out of the northwest. Sunshine pierced my bedroom window like a laser beam where I had not quite closed the blinds. I squeezed shut my eyes and turned my head to avoid the glare.

Shaking sleep from my head, I tossed off the covers and pulled my legs around to the floor. There I sat on the edge of the bed, my head bent forward, supported by my hands. Tympani were holding practice on my brain, and I believed I knew the cause. I cranked my neck around a few degrees and listened to it bark in protest.

After a minute or more, I stood before the window in my boxers and jerked the cord that opened the blinds. Bright sunshine overwhelmed bloodshot eyes. I stepped slightly to the right and out of the direct glare, still allowing a view of the lake. Glistening blue water greeted me. At this hour it remained devoid of traffic. Perhaps I had not been the only reveler last night.

The thermometer mounted outside the window said fifty-nine. I blinked and looked again. Little wonder no one was about. There also was a nice chop on the water. That wind had to be chilly. I decided to watch the lake activity from afar with a hot cup of coffee and a nice cigar. So much for good intentions. The fish would still be there next week. I could always go some night after work.

I reread the thermometer and was having difficulty calculating the temperature drop from the previous day's high to this morning's reading. My brain needed rebooting. Then I remembered the old saw. If you were not happy with the weather in Minnesota, wait an hour, and it was bound to change.

I moved my tongue around the front of my upper teeth, and they felt like sandpaper, so I stumbled into the bathroom and brushed them. My mouth did not feel much better after that effort, more like cotton. I needed to hydrate. I guess I had stayed up too late drinking after Grace had left.

Grace. Had she really been here? Yes, I could attest to that. Her scent had lingered in the bed overnight. It had not been a dream.

Now my stomach felt queasy. What did I eat last night? Aw, shit, nothing, just booze. No wonder I felt the way I did. I decided to start the coffee before I showered. I made it good and thick. That was my first good decision. A long hot shower was what was needed.

Since I had blown off fishing, I spent the day doing chores. Fishing would not be good anyway with the big temperature drop, and I had other things to do. I started a load of laundry then sat enjoying my coffee. Finally I felt like breakfast. Sausage links and scrambled eggs topped with Picante did the trick. That meal maybe didn't quiet my stomach, but it tasted delicious. Then I left the house and do some grocery shopping. With all those chores completed, I would be set for another week.

I hoped the activity would keep my mind off Grace. I was wrong. Thoughts of her kept creeping into my head all day long. Each time they arose, I shoved them aside. Time would tell who won that battle.

I must have been tired on Sunday because I fell asleep that evening during the Twins game, never seeing the conclusion. That was all right since I needed the sleep, and it was just another loss. At least I felt more refreshed on Monday morning.

When I drove to work, Grace still was on my mind. I figured what the hell, why try to ignore what took place Saturday night. Several times during the day I found myself daydreaming about what we had done and why. How many Commandments had I broken that weekend? Then once again I would rehash the same old argument, never reaching a conclusion. This was not healthy behavior.

The biggest question for me was did I want anything to happen again? Of course, I did on one level, but also I did not like her cheating on her husband. Or at least I didn't want to be the cause of it. If she had been doing it all along with others, maybe it was okay to include me. Wait, would I want her playing the field? Grace wasn't that kind of girl, or was she? She hadn't been that way nineteen years ago.

Man, I was screwed up. If I did want to see her, which I did, should I approach her or let her come to me? She had given me no indication we would be seeing one another again, did she? I had no recollection. I was one mixed up dude. I had to smile at that appraisal, accurate as it was.

I decided to let things run their course, and see what played out. But I did not see any harm in visiting the gallery her husband owned. Scope out the place. Here it had been open for nearly ten months, and once I found out it had something to do with Grace, I was about ready to get right over there.

I chose to visit the gallery on Tuesday over lunch hour. I first had intended to check out the establishment from the outside to see what kind of art they showcased. Armed with that knowledge, I could study a little and sound halfway educated when I went in. Since I knew zilch about art, I thought I could find out enough on the Internet to be educated.

It had been slowly warming since Sunday's cold front had passed, and today had lots of sunshine. Since I generally did not wear my suit coat in the office, I left it there and took my tie off, as well, venturing forth casually attired.

Main Street was bustling. Most street parking spots were taken, and a number of people were window shopping. I waited for my chance and then ran across the street between cars.

As I approached the front of the gallery, two women were exiting. They were busy in conversation. I dodged them and looked over the storefront. The brick façade encased large show windows, and the main door was recessed four feet toward the interior of the store, about the depth of the window displays. The door was painted in a collage of bright colors.

Looking in through the front windows, I saw something totally unexpected. There were paintings, yes, I had expected those, but there also were figurines, and wood bowls, and ceramics of all types and styles. A real eclectic mix of art. Besides that, none of the paintings were what I had expected. I realized there was no way I could educate myself on all that was on display. I wouldn't know where to start. I'd just have to show myself for the boob I was, so I decided to go on in as long as I was there.

A bell rang over the door when I pushed it open. Upon entering, I noticed a man seated at a small desk near the back. The desk was partially hidden by a false wall showcasing a modernistic painting. As I stepped forward, the man rose and took two steps toward me. He had a medium build, a thin face accentuated by having long, dark hair pulled into a ponytail. A small mouth sat beneath a long thin nose. I couldn't imagine Grace married to this man. But then, that might just be my ego.

I forced a smile and received a poor representation in return. I cautioned myself not to be judgmental. Not every smile looks the same. Then I considered my appearance and saw the light. I was just some slob wasting the prick's time. Now I knew why I avoided places like this.

"Good day, sir. Can I help you?" the proprietor said.

That was a little better, I guess. "Thanks. You the owner?"

"No. My name is Ray Singer. I'm an associate of Mr. Adams."

That statement alone was a relief. I thought, okay, Adams. So Grace's name is Adams. I'd never thought to ask. I only remembered her as Summers. I had learned something already. This was not going to be a total waste of time.

I said, "Thanks. I've never been in here before, but the gallery comes highly recommended."

"Thank you." The smile was a little better. "Can we show you anything in particular?"

I shook my head. "No. I'm just looking around to see what you have. I do have to admit, though, that it's not at all what I expected."

"How so?"

"No pictures of Tuscany or the Cotswold's or Provance. I thought those were the staples of all galleries."

This time I got an even larger grin. "Thank goodness not here. We try to give people a choice of many art forms."

"I see that. Mind if I just wander about?"

"Not at all. Feel free. In the room back here on the left we have paintings, watercolors, and sketches by local artists."

Ray had turned his back and was pointing to the partitioned area I had thought was a back office.

"Then in the room to the right we have prints of things you would expect in Minnesota."

I must have looked uncertain because he said. "You know, Splitrock Lighthouse, the streetcar boat, that sort of thing. We don't sell frames, but any frame shop will do that for you. Of course we do frame all the finer work we sell."

"Of course," I replied.

Ray went back to his desk and I began looking about. The space itself was austere. The false ceiling had been removed which gave the room a feeling of endless height. Everything above about ten feet was painted black. Lighting was suspended, so nothing up above showed.

Eight-foot high partition walls, painted white, were set at angles around the room as backdrop to the art. Paintings were hung on those, and the open space was broken by their location. Pedestals were creatively placed showcasing statuettes, or bowls of various kinds.

I wandered through the store for forty-five minutes, and was about to leave when I stopped at a painting I thought was of somewhere in the American Desert. It looked like Arizona or New Mexico. I squinted to see a signature but had difficulty reading it. I was curious because I had seen a similar painting earlier this very spring in a friend's house. I looked for Ray Singer, but he was busying himself at the desk. I took out my phone and shot a picture of the work.

I waited a bit, but Ray still appeared occupied, so I interrupted him and asked. "Could you tell me who did this desert painting?"

Ray came to me and looked at the work, turning it over to see the back. He seemed to be stalling, and then he suddenly said, "Let me look that up. I'm not very familiar with that piece.

Ray went to a large book on his desk and flipped some pages before looking up at me and saying, "I remember now. The work is by Zola Jimenez. We could let you have it for $800."

I nodded, while internally gulping. "That sounds fair enough. Let me think about it. Do you have any more of the artist's works?"

"No. I'm afraid not at the moment. I believe this artist recently died and what he had in stock is tied up in probate. There aren't many works of his around. You wouldn't be hurt to snap up this one."

"Died? I bet that'll cause the prices of his work to go up."

"It sometimes works that way."

"Do you know if this artist does multiples of the same work?" I asked.

Ray hesitated before asking, "You mean paint the same scene over and over?" Ray looked mildly upset at the suggestion.

"Yes," I answered.

"I don't know for sure. I don't think so. Why would you ask?"

"That would diminish the value wouldn't it?" I inquired.

"If someone did that, yes it would. That's the biggest reason I don't think any artist would choose to repaint the same scene. Certainly not if he or she wants to sell well. Of course they might do similar scenes. Often times these western scenes don't change much from location to location."

"No, I suppose not, and that's good information to know. I'm not educated in the art world so I had no idea. If I bought this work, I would like to think I got value for my money."

Ray nodded with a satisfied look on his face.

"I'm looking for a piece for my office and that just might do it."

"We'd be happy to work with you on that. Are you local?"

"Yes. I have a small law office."

Suddenly Ray seemed more attentive, but I brushed him off and left.

Chapter Five
Following a Lead

I left the gallery and stepped out onto the sidewalk into bright sun-shine. Shading my eyes with one hand, I squinted to adjust my eyes to the glare. Then I jaywalked across the street, cut through the alley, and headed back to my office in the lower level of a large office building fronting Second Street. Our offices are reached from the parking lot side, on the lower level. My law practice was not retail so I did not need public exposure with my office location. Plus, the rent was more affordable in this out-of-the-way location. My work mainly involved banks and insurance companies. Pretty bland stuff.

Walking through the lot, I realized I had not learned anything relevant about Grace's husband. All I knew was that his name was Adams. Maybe I could Google him.

When I entered the office, my right-hand man, Janet Brown, was hard at work.

"Anything going on?" I inquired.

"Almost finished with the last Worldwide Insurance processing."

"Good."

Janet had been with me roughly ten years. She was married, but her kids were grown and scattered across the country. Her husband, Dick, was her sole concern besides running my life. She was in her fifties and had chosen to return to work when the children no longer needed her constant attention. I was lucky to snatch her up at the time. I'd describe her appearance as matronly. She was pleasingly plump, wore her graying hair in a perm, and had the sweetest personality. She was a constant ray of sunshine in the office.

Our office was little more than one big room, and the entire front wall facing the parking lot was glass. We had shades for the afternoon sun, which could get quite intense, even in the winter. There was a small waiting area near the door for clients, and a partitioned glass area, which I called home. Mostly my door was open so I could converse with Janet, but we could close off the space if either of us needed privacy. A row of file cabinets lined the back wall, but they were used less and less as we moved almost entirely to electronic data storage.

After chatting briefly with Janet, I went into my office where I sat at my computer and downloaded the picture I had taken at the gallery. Then I uploaded my e-mail and composed a note to my friend, Paul Johnson of Colorado Springs. In my note I asked him what he knew about the painting he recently had acquired by Jimenez, and if he could send me a photo of that painting.

Paul had shown me that particular work when I visited him at his home this past April. He was quite proud of obtaining it. At that time, I learned that Jimenez was recently deceased, and that Paul was trying to acquire all his unsold work. In light of that, I wondered how one lone painting had ended up in Excelsior.

If I was imposing on Paul for this favor, I didn't mind because I thought of him as something of an art expert, knowledgeable particularly on Jimenez's works. After becoming better acquainted with Paul, I had found out he'd studied art in college and also for a period in Paris. He currently was the owner of a well-known art store in Colorado Springs. I could not think of anyone better from whom to garner information.

A few years earlier Paul and I had met when I was on a vacation in Colorado. When I journeyed down from Denver to visit the Air Force Academy, someone there had suggested I should see an outdoor presentation of the Stations of the Cross at a Carmelite Monastery near Littleton. I was touring those grounds when I chanced to speak to Paul, also touring the site. We talked for a while about the exhibit and then lunched together. Over time we had become fast friends.

There was no urgency in my request. I was merely curious about the similarity of what I saw in Excelsior and previously in Colorado.

Paul answered my inquiry the next morning. I set about comparing the picture of his painting with the one I had taken at the gallery. They were not the same work. Both were of natural stone arches, but were different in shape. The colors in each work also were dissimilar, and the background skies were totally different. So the artist liked stone arches. Nothing sinister there. I was uncertain what I had been looking for, but the gallery seemed to be on the up and up. Dead end.

I suppose I had been anxious to discredit Grace's husband to justify my actions. What an analyst would say to that one?

I still had not met the man. For all I knew, he was a great guy. Of course he would be. Why else would Grace marry him? End of subject.

I went about my work, trying to keep Grace out of my head. I figured with each passing day it would become easier. But there was more to it than that. I began to realize that, if I didn't drop this crusade, I'd slowly go nuts. Let me see how I did with that resolution.

The remainder of the day dragged for me. I was suffering a letdown after my visit to the gallery. When I tried to get back into the groove, I began to think of it more as a rut. I began to think maybe I needed to shake things up some. Maybe take a vacation. Paris would be nice.

Everyone was going to Europe these days, why not me? With my luck, though, some rouge volcano probably would trap me there. I guess I'm just a glass half-full kind of guy. I would have to find some way to get myself back onto firm ground.

Chapter Six
A Hot Night on the Town

The very next evening I went out to dinner with two good friends, Steve and Cindy Anderson. We supped at the Irish pub located on the corner of Second and Water streets in downtown Excelsior. We had eaten there together fairly often. Each time we were there our goal had been to sample a different beer label. Sometimes I was with a date, though not tonight.

The establishment was crowded, as usual. We were seated in a booth along one wall that isolated us from some of the noise. The place had a real pub feel to it, making our visits lively and enjoyable. Being with Steve and Cindy made it only more so.

Steve and I had been friends for at least a half dozen years. He was a stylish dresser, and fastidious in his actions. His manner made me want to be on my best behavior, and for me that was a challenge.

I mulled over the beer list, trying to remember what I had yet to sample. Finally I decided to go with a lighter wheat beer, while my companions both chose a lager. During our second round we ordered dinner. Bangers and Mash for me, even though I knew it'd sit on my stomach all night. Cindy chose a grilled sandwich and Steve the Shepherd's Pie.

While we waited for our dinner, Cindy related to us how she recently had signed up to go on a five-day bike ride through central Wisconsin. Camping was involved, and the riders were to do about sixty miles a day. The route was saturated with hills, and this time of the year the weather could be hot. I respectfully declined the invitation to join her, mumbling something about an old football injury.

Cindy just shook her head and said, "Mike." That said it all.

Cindy was a petite red head, and I was pretty sure the color was natural. Look up the term "in shape" and you would find her name next to it. I'd always pick her for my team. She was not large in stature, but certainly was in personality. The woman was the complete package, both looks and personality. I had never known her to be without a smile.

The evening had been a delight, and I hated for it to end. We got a late start at dinner, and it was now after ten by the time we called it a night and took leave by the back door. Going this route was a shortcut to the parking lot behind the Main Street stores.

The sun had long ago set and the only light out back, aside from the one over the pub door, was from a distant security light. The light shone off the glossy paint of the many cars scattered about the lot. I was unsure of what Steve was driving this evening, or where he had parked, so I let him lead the way.

Earlier, I had walked to the bar and met my dinner companions there. However, since I invited them back to my place to sample some after dinner liqueurs, I was hitching a ride with them. I saw now that Steve had parked way out in the main lot. He would walk a few extra feet to save a ding on his car door.

As we strolled toward the car, Cindy once again remonstrated me for being a wimp. I took the grief from her because she was in such good shape herself. Small and strong, without an once of body fat, Cindy had the look of an Irish beauty. Her large green eyes and ivory complexion were windows to her personality.

We had not traveled but a few feet, and I was laughing at her vivid description of me, when I caught something out of the corner of my left eye, and stopped walking. I turned my head that direction and stared into the dim light. What I thought I had seen had been nothing more than a blur, but it was enough to garner my interest.

I interrupted Cindy's retort, excused myself, and began working my way past parked cars scattered behind the back entrances of the Main Street business establishments. I assumed most belonged to pub dwellers, since stores had long ago closed for the day. Curiosity had its hold, and I was busy perusing the area for anything that appeared out of place.

Steve and Cindy now had stopped walking, and watched me, but I heard Steve ask Cindy what I was doing. I still had not seen anything out of the ordinary when I reached the one particular door I had been aiming for. I stopped, and once again scanned the area to see if anyone was about. I saw no one but my group. I could have sworn I had seen something or someone, maybe someone in particular. Now I began doubting myself.

There were only a few scattered cars nearby where I stood, and I momentarily considered looking around them. Instead, I marched to my target door. The dimly lit sign screwed onto the heavy, metal fire door said, "Adams Gallery".

Figuring the door would be locked, I hesitated. Then, thinking *what the hell, I'm already here*, I turned and pulled on the knob anyway. To my surprise, the door yielded. That meant not only was the doorknob unlocked, so was the deadbolt. That didn't seem right. I begin to wonder what I might have found. I let the door once again close the inch I had moved it. All the retail stores were supposed to be closed for business this time of night. When I studied the door, it showed no signs of forced entry. This indeed was perplexing. Perhaps someone was inside working.

Cindy interrupted my contemplation when she called out from a distance. "I thought we were going for a drink?"

I waved my hand over my head at her without looking back, never taking my eyes off the doorknob. What had I thought it was going to do, turn itself?

I shook my head, pursed my lips, and pulled the door open just enough to peer into the dark interior. Then, I released the knob, and the heavy door closed again. There must be a hydraulic closer on the door.

What struck me was the smell of smoke that wafted out at me. It was not cigarette smoke. I knew that smell. It had to be wood smoke.

It smelled like a campfire. Shit. I knew that wasn't right, but what should I do? Calling 911 seemed like the appropriate action.

"What's up?" Steve asked.

I jumped. "Shit, you scared me, Steve!" I had not heard him approach. I caught my breath and said, "I thought I saw something."

"What?"

"I'm not sure. It looked like maybe a light, or a reflection."

"From inside here?" Steve asked, pointing at the door.

I looked at Steve. Even in the near darkness his good looks came through. Strong features and a chiseled face made for a handsome appearance.

"Couldn't have been," I said. "The lights inside are off. It's darker than the ace of spades in there."

"But the door's unlocked, I saw you open it."

"Yeah. That shouldn't be, should it?"

I was trying to figure things out. Maybe with a couple of fewer beers it would have been easier.

Steve leaned in and looked at the doorknob. "No. You're right. That shouldn't be. Doorknob looks okay, though, so maybe nobody broke in. Did someone come out?"

Here I hesitated. "I'm not sure," I offered. "Something caught the corner of my eye. I was listening to Cindy . . . I'm not sure what I saw."

I wasn't exactly telling the truth, but there was a good deal of uncertainty for me as to what exactly I had seen, and I did not want to sound stupid. It was like seeing a U.F.O. You saw it, but could never tell anyone that.

"If someone had come out, you could have seen a reflection off the door from the street light," Steve suggested, as he looked up at the distant light source.

I thought briefly before answering. "Maybe, but I don't think I saw anyone. Shit, I don't know what I saw, Steve."

I looked at Steve to gauge his reaction. His handsome face was passive. Here I was lying, or at least not telling everything I knew, and

I was not quite sure why I was doing it. I usually chose not to lie, especially to good friends.

And I considered Steve a friend. He was a large, good-natured man, taller than I was and about as muscular. He played power forward on the basketball team of a private Minnesota college. Dark-haired and good-looking, Steve broke a few hearts when he and Cindy married.

"What are you guys doing?"

Cindy had arrived.

"I smelled smoke," I said. "I'm going to take a look. Got your phone, Steve?"

"No."

"I've got mine," Cindy responded.

"Good. Listen up. I smelled smoke when I cracked the door. I'll take a quick look inside, and if I see fire, you call it in."

"Maybe we should call it in anyway, just in case," Cindy argued. Concern distorted her features.

"Whatever, I'm going in," I said and I cracked the door.

I pulled it open just far enough to cast minimal light inside. If there was a fire, I did not want to fan the flame with fresh oxygen. Then I squeezed through the opening, pulled the door closed, and felt for a light switch. I found one to my right and flipped it.

Through a smoky haze, I saw I was in the back storage area of the store, about ten feet deep from the door at my back to what I supposed was the back wall of the main exhibit area. I saw a few cardboard boxes stacked on the heavy-planked wood floor, and rolls of bubble wrap on spindles attached to the wall over a bench. Tools lay scattered on the workbench. I took in all this in a nanosecond. It was not my purpose in being here.

A single door led to the store proper, but when I tried it, I found it locked. Turning, I saw another door to my right and when I approached it, I noticed smoke billowing from the small space between the bottom of the door and the floor. Obviously this was the fire source.

I rushed back the three paces to the outside door, pushed it open and hollered, "Fire."

Without waiting for a reply, I turned and let the outside door shut, once again entombing me in the confined space. I was alone. Smoke continued to rise in great puffs and with no outlet it was getting thicker. Suddenly I coughed from the smoke that had begun its insidious invasion of my lungs. In a reflex action, I put my left hand over my nose and mouth before moving forward. Then, I slowly approached the hazardous door.

I was all alone in a dangerous situation, and I was surprised that had just suddenly occurred to me. I hesitated. My right hand, which reached toward the door handle in front of me, trembled. I considered taking flight. I could claim the smoke was too thick to see anything, and it was. "Let the pros do their job," I murmured out loud.

Then, before I could make my escape, I heard the door behind me creak open. Without looking, I knew Steve had followed me inside. For some reason that renewed my courage. Now I couldn't leave.

Steve coughed.

I gingerly touched the door handle before me. Not hot. I tried to remember fire training from grade school. A cool handle probably meant there was no fire immediately on the other side. Encouraged by that information, I turned the handle and pushed the door open, revealing what appeared to be stairway leading to a basement.

I was greeted with a blast of heat and a thick cloud of black smoke. Startled, I reflexively leaned away. When I again looked down into the din, light leaped from flames somewhere just out of sight to my left. I couldn't locate a light switch, but I was able to see somewhat from the glow of flames that came from below.

Standing there, frozen with fear, I scanned the small area in my line of sight. It was a basement, yes, but the glow revealed something bundled at the foot of the stairs. It was dark in color large. I squinted in an attempt to better see. It didn't help much. The swirling smoke made identification impossible.

My brain began processing possibilities as to what the object might be when suddenly it dawned on me it was a body. Shit. If it were a pile of rags, I could get out. *Yeah, it does look like a body. What do I do now? Wait for the firefighters?*

I decided to take a closer look. Turning my head, I hollered over my shoulder at Steve, not knowing if he heard me. Then I cautiously started down the wooden stairs, hanging onto the handrail with a grip that might at any moment crush the wooden rail. This stilled the shaking in my hand, but not in my heart. The stairs seemed solid enough, but a little slippery. I moved cautiously. The smoke was horrible, and I was having difficulty breathing with my hand over my face. I paused partway down, and pulled out my handkerchief, holding that over my nose and mouth. At least it filtered some of the smoke, and let in a little air. Hell, there was damn little air. It was mostly carbon monoxide.

My throat was feeling raw, and my eyes were watering. I could feel the heat building in this small confined space. What was I thinking? I clung to the handrail on my right like my life depended on it. It did. Having it there seemed to give me some degree of comfort and courage. I needed courage. What the fuck was I doing?

At first my movement was tentative, but then I realized I had to hurry. The heat and smoke were too intense to spend any amount of time down here. To make matters worse, it now appeared that the body's pant legs had caught on fire. It was a man, a large man.

When I saw the fire, I sailed down so fast I nearly stumbled over something on the floor right at the bottom of the stairs. Whatever it was, it was metal, and when I came into contact with it, it skittered across the floor and banged into the wall. It was too smoky to see what it actually was, and I knew it wasn't a priority. Saving this man was.

The floor and the walls were concrete. I knew the steps were wood. If they caught fire, I'd be in deep shit. I had no time to waste.

Steve screamed something down to me, but I couldn't understand him. My ears were beginning to ring, and I didn't know what was causing that. I just didn't have time to analyze all this crap. My time was limited. I had to get out before I died.

I took the handkerchief and attempted to tie it around my mouth. It was too short. Shit! *What do I do now?* Maybe it was time to get out and let someone help. Fear gripped me. Not fear of dying, but fear of failure. I felt a chill. Instead of quitting, I quickly took off my shirt and tied that over my face, leaving barely enough room to see. Let me tell you that knit golf shirts do not make great smoke masks.

I could feel the heat against my bare skin, and breathing that way was nearly impossible. Every move I made got me deeper into trouble. Steve still was hollering from the top of the stairs, but I ignored him. I couldn't understand him anyway with the roar of the fire. Maybe he was rooting me on to victory. I had no idea.

I struggled to drag the body toward me a couple of feet. Shit, was this guy heavy. Now, at least, I had been able to move him away from the fire. His pant legs were on fire from the knees down, and I considered attempting to put out the fire with my hands. That didn't seem like a good idea.

Instead, I unbuckled the man's belt and pulled down the pants inside out. I used the upper part of the pants to smother most of the fire on the pant legs. I was not able to escape burning myself, however. Now the smell of burned hair mixed with all the other noxious smells. My burns hurt like hell, feeling like needles jabbing into my skin. The hair on my hands and arms was singed. My hands ached, my head was pounding, and my lungs were burning. I began to cough uncontrollably. I was on my hand and knees fighting for control.

I had to get out. I was fading fast. I didn't have much more time. I told myself to leave him, to get out. I would not, could not do it! I couldn't quit now.

When I tried to lift the body, I almost collapsed. I considered myself strong, but certainly not trained in fire rescue. A firefighter would know what to do here. I was clueless. I wasn't getting enough air. I was thinking I might pass out.

Leave, stupid. Get the hell out. Leave him. I wouldn't listen. I couldn't. I need to try again. Sitting up the victim, I pulled him up two stairs. Then I got below him and got him against my chest. While kneeling, I put my arms around him and gave him a bear hug. Now, I buried my face against him to cut off the smoke. It also cut off my oxygen, so I knew I only had a few seconds more. Finally getting the body over my shoulder, I struggled to stand. My legs were weak. It felt like I had just run a marathon.

I did not know if my subject was breathing or not, but I knew if I left him, I might as well stay here myself, because afterward I would never be able to live with myself. I had invested too much now to quit.

Maybe it had been all those football drills I went through in high school where the coach wouldn't let us quit. We learned to push through the pain, stand up against adversity. Whatever it was, something would not let me quit here.

I needed to grab the handrail with my left hand, but my hand hurt. What was that all about? I grabbed the wooden rail anyway. With all the weight on my back, I could barely walk, much less climb stairs. I had to pull myself up each step with my left arm. Each step was agony. I pushed with one leg and pulled with my arm. My legs were beginning to quiver. My face felt like it was on fire, and my chest was about to explode. Tears poured from my eyes, soaking the victim's shirt. I could see nothing. I was doing this blind.

I nearly had reached the top step when I felt extremely dizzy. My wet palm slipped on the rail. My momentum shifted. I felt myself begin to tilt backwards. I knew I was going down. This was it. I had lost.

Someone grabbed the two of us, and propelled us through the door, and out the back of the building into the cool night air.

The load was lifted from me, and I slithered to the ground. I could hear the sirens of emergency vehicles coming to the rescue, while I sat on my ass gasping for breath.

Cindy and Steve were laying the victim onto the tarmac and preparing him for artificial respiration. I saw it, but could not react, could not help. Suddenly, my head began to spin. I sank to the ground. That was the last thing I remembered from that night of terror.

Chapter Seven
A Hospital Stay

Later that night, as I lay in a hospital bed, I found out I was suffering from smoke inhalation and had been administered oxygen at the scene. Also, my hands had been immersed in a cold solution to keep the burning from going deeper into the tissue. Then I was taken to Methodist Hospital in St. Louis Park via ambulance for treatment. I remembered being awake for a time in the ambulance, because that was when I found out what had occurred.

The whole hospital thing was a nightmare. God bless those emergency room folks, but I had never seen such a screwed up mess in all my life. How they did it day after day was beyond me. Finally, about 2:00 a.m., I was moved into a room. They kept me overnight.

The next morning I learned that Steve and Cindy had followed the ambulance to Methodist, had stayed a couple of hours, but we never saw each other, so they had gone home. The next morning Steve came back.

I spent a restless night. I had oxygen administered to me for four hours. Then they determined I was okay. I was coughing a lot, so I never really slept. Plus, they kept checking on my status, so if I did doze off, their ministrations woke me. But, hey, I wasn't complaining. Yes, I guess I was.

I shared a room, but the curtain between our beds was drawn, and I had not as yet met my roommate. It was a typical hospital room, one that made me want to get home as soon as possible. I was served breakfast, but I had no appetite, and my hands hurt. I didn't care to use them for something as unnecessary as eating. Besides, my stomach was upset, and I was having difficulty breathing. I was wheezing a bit.

I was pleased when about ten o'clock Steve stuck his head in.

"You don't look too bad, Mike. How do you feel?"

"Shitty."

Steve started to laugh.

"Not funny, asshole," I snarled. "Why aren't you at work?"

Now we both laughed.

"I'm okay. Lucky I guess," I said. "The burns aren't too bad, according to what I'm told. Can you smell the burned hair?"

"No."

"They must have scrubbed me clean, but I still can smell it. I wonder if I have burned hairs up my nose?"

"Maybe up your ass. What's it smell like?" Steve asked with a grin.

"Jerk. Can't explain it. Look at my arms. I had a hair treatment," I laughed. "So what happened last night? You pulled me out, right?"

"Yup. When you went down, I looked for a fire extinguisher but didn't see one. So then I went to the stairs to see if I could help. I kept screaming at you to get out, but you were being stubborn as usual. I suggested I come down to help, but you ignored me. You always were a glory hound." Steve laughed self-consciously, but I was in no mood to join him.

"I didn't know what to do, Mike. It didn't look like there was enough room down there for both of us, and when I asked if I should come down, you didn't answer." Steve had a concerned look on his face. "The smoke was terrible. I couldn't breathe. I had to run outside for a moment to catch my breath. I got back in just as you came up the stairs. I don't know how you did it. The smoke, I mean."

"Don't sweat it," I answered. "I never heard what you were saying. My ears got all plugged up."

"You looked like you had everything under control," he said hopefully.

I started to tear up. My chest was quivering.

"You okay?" Steve asked.

My chest heaved, and I wiped my eyes with the top of my bed sheet. I tried to speak, but my voice broke. I waved my hand at Steve and got myself under control.

"I don't know what more you could have done, Steve. There wasn't enough room on the stairs for both of us and the victim. I'm just glad you were there at the end. I was all sapped out. You grabbed me, right?"

"You were struggling to make it up so I grabbed the two of you and dragged you outside. I don't want to say anything, but the guy didn't on have any pants. What was your plan there?"

Steve barely could restrain a laugh. I ignored him. My chest was too sore to start laughing again.

We both sat quietly for a while and then I asked. "Say, who was the victim?"

"I don't know. Maybe the guy who runs the store."

A wave of nausea came over me. I should have made the connection, but everything had happened so fast I never thought about it. Maybe it was Grace's husband.

Steve saw the look on my face. "You okay?" he asked.

I coughed up some mucus. I reached onto my tray and took a tissue and spit it into that. Then I said. "Yeah. I felt a little weak there, but I'm all right now. How is the guy?"

"I don't know. I haven't heard."

"Was he breathing?"

"Barely. They put him on oxygen. Took him in before you. Pretty serious, I think. Did you know he had a big gash on his head?"

"I didn't notice. I couldn't see much in that damn smoke. Do you think I did that to him while carrying him up?"

"Gosh, I don't know. Do you remember slamming him into anything?"

"No, but I was a little foggy about what was going on. I was running on battery backup."

My nose now was running and I wiped it with a tissue the best I could with a bad hand.

"Do you think they brought him here?" I asked.

Steve shrugged. "Maybe."

"So, you don't know his name?" I asked.

"No, you?"

I shook my head. I had never met Grace's husband. I had no idea. Of course this might not be her husband, but the man I carried up the stairs was larger than the one I talked with in the gallery.

"I think I almost passed out when you carried us out."

"Almost? You did, good buddy, and the two of you together as dead weight were too much. You've got to go on a diet, man."

"Maybe you need to start lifting weights."

Steve smiled.

"They gave both of you oxygen and put some little do-dad on your finger to monitor the oxygen content in your blood. You were better than the other guy. John Garaghty was a first responder. He said you were going to be okay."

"What did they do to you once they had you in here?" Steve asked.

"They told me this morning, but I don't remember it all. I guess they checked for soot in my airways. Let me think. Swollen membranes. Said my eyes were red. Are they?"

"Yup. You look like Dracula."

"I look good, huh?"

"Never did."

"Thanks. They said I'd maybe cough up some mucus; probably have a headache. Told me not to hang out with any assholes." I started laughing and was unable to stop. It hurt.

Steve just shook his head. "They tell you your brain was screwed up?"

"That's a preexisting condition," I wailed.

The nurse came in and took my vitals. She said a doctor would be in shortly to release me.

"Cute nurses must be on another floor," Steve commented.

"You come to give me a ride home?"

"It's my Christian duty to tend to the weak and infirm. Say, what about your burns?"

I looked at my hands. They were red all over with blisters popping up here and there. "Sore, but I think I can still hold a beer bottle."

"Good."

The doctor came in a short time later and advised me on the care of the burns. I was told my lungs looked all right, but to get checked out if I had any trouble breathing. I probably would be coughing up shit for a while, but that was good. I had not burned my lungs, just irritated the hell out of them.

Before we left for Excelsior, we inquired about the other victim. No one knew anything about him. He must have gone to another hospital.

The ride home gave Steve and me a chance to talk. Traffic was heaviest going east, so our journey was an easy one heading west.

"I don't think I want to go to the pub anymore," I said.

"Bad memories?"

"Maybe. What a shitty night. Say, what about you, Steve? You okay?"

"Sure. I ate a little smoke, but not like you. No worse for me than sitting around the campfire."

"Good." I felt relieved, since I felt responsible for getting him into the situation.

"Whatever possessed you to go into that building?" Steve asked, as he braked for a stoplight.

"Some hunch, I guess. The door wasn't locked. Then the smell of smoke . . ."

"I meant more like how'd you get up the nerve to go down. Fire scares the hell out of me."

I sat for a moment reflecting. "I don't really know, Steve. Once I started down, I practically fell down the stairs. I had to do something once I was down there." Again I began to tear up. "Damn it, Steve. I couldn't let the guy burn up." I again wiped my eyes, using a sleeve.

"I guess. Pretty brave," Steve said, looking out the window to his left.

I looked at Steve and said. "No, pretty stupid. You know, I was thinking, you were smart."

"What!"

"Well, if you had followed me down to help, you know."

"Yeah."

"Well, we both might have been overcome with smoke. Then who would have pulled *us* out? Close call, man. Thanks. You're the best." I almost began to cry again. My eyes teared up and my chest shuddered. My emotions were about to explode.

I caught Steve blushing when I glanced in his direction.

We got to my place and Steve asked. "Want me to come up and tuck you in?"

"Gee, thanks, but I can manage." I held my hand up in an Indian salute and said, "Thanks for everything."

I climbed out of the car and went up to my door. My hands were pretty sore and I saw I would be having trouble with little things like door keys and doorknobs, but at least I was alive.

Chapter Eight
Recovery

After Steve dropped me off at my place, and I'd let myself in, I felt a deep sense of relief at being secure in my home. With my hands as sore as they were, I even had difficulty getting in the front door.

The first thing I did was to go down to the lower level and drop a plastic bag with my soot-stained, smokey clothes on top of the washer. Then I headed into the kitchen where I opened the freezer door and stuck my hands inside. The cold air felt refreshing. After about a half minute, I withdrew my hands and closed the door.

My place had been closed up since I left the previous evening. Using an elbow, I slid open the patio door to let in a fresh lake breeze. My living room had three glass panels facing my deck and the lake, though I just opened the one, it was enough.

I then went upstairs to my bedroom.

Steve had thought far enough ahead to bring me a change of clothes, knowing mine possibly were ruined. We were about the same height, so his things fit me reasonably well, though the pants were a little long. I changed out of those togs, piling them to put into the laundry.

I had some colored gunk on my arms where the nurses had cleansed me with antiseptic wash, and I felt totally dirty from the fire experience the previous night, so I decided to take a cool shower. When water hit my hands, it hurt, so I was careful to hold them out of the spray. I found turning off the water to soap up worked best. Then I rinsed off. I must have looked like a football official signaling a touchdown the way I was forced to stand. Nevertheless, it felt so good I stayed under the water for a long time.

When I exited, I was flummoxed that I still could smell smoke and singed hair. Wondering at that, I took a little rotary tool and trimmed my nose hairs. Then I took a Q Tip and wiped the inside of my nose with petroleum jelly. It seemed to help.

My head was beginning to pound, so I took some extra strength Tylenol and drank some water. The instructions in leaving the hospital had been to drink lots of liquids, so I knew I'd better follow those instructions. It was up to me if I wanted to feel better.

Steve had offered to let me stay at his house for a couple of days, but I quickly declined. I was not in need of nursing care, and I was comfortable being alone. I preferred doing what I wanted, when I wanted.

Before Steve arrived to convey me home, I had called my office, telling Janet I was unavoidably detained and would try to get in later in the day. I had not told her about my overnight experience, since I thought that information would come better from me in person.

Right now I was feeling like shit, so I decided to lie down on my couch for a nap. Lying prone caused me to cough, though. After reflection I decided to incline myself on pillows. It had a beneficial affect. I was not sure how long I slept, but I woke to the ringing of my landline. I lay there without moving, feeling numb all over with exactly zero energy. Even lifting my eyelids was a chore. Thus, I ignored the phone, but now was awake. My hands rested on my stomach and when I moved them, they hurt. So I stopped moving them.

After a few minutes when I did get up, I poured myself a cold drink of water. It was awkward holding the glass because the skin on my hands felt taut, and it hurt to bend my fingers. I opened the freezer and again stuck my hands into the cold air for a few seconds. I thought maybe I was on to something.

Then I checked my phone messages. There was just the one. The call had been from John Brooks, my friend and a local insurance man. I decided to call him back, not knowing what he might be after.

"Brooksie, you called?"

"I wanted to see how you were, and to thank you."

Somehow John must have heard about last night, but why he was thanking me was a mystery. I said, "I'm doing okay, I guess. Thank me for what?"

"For catching the fire early on."

A light bulb came on in my head. "You insure the building?"

"Yes."

"Just a lucky break, Brooksie. I won't be able to play golf for a couple of weeks, though."

"Why?"

"Burned my hands."

"Shit, Mike, I didn't know. You okay?"

"Sure. I'll milk this for a couple of days and then collect my hero badge."

There was a moment of silence. Then, "Say, Mike, you feel up to coming uptown?"

I hesitated. "I'm supposed to take it easy, John. What do you need?"

"I'm taking an adjuster into the building at three, and thought maybe you could tell us what you know about what happened. Have you talked to anyone about it yet?"

"Anyone like who?"

"I figured the police or fire marshal might want to know what happened when you were there."

"No, I haven't talked to anyone. I just got home from the hospital a bit ago."

"For your hands?"

"That and smoke inhalation."

"Oh, god, Mike. I didn't know all that. You're sure you're okay?"

"Could be better, Brooksie, but considering everything, I'm doing just fine."

"Are you up to seeing us or should I reschedule with you?"

"Sure. Maybe, if there's a cup of coffee in it for me," I joked.

"Deal. I'll make it two. Why don't I pick you up?"

"Thanks, but I'll walk. I need the fresh air. Listen. Will you want me to go inside?"

"I guess so, maybe."

"Could you get some of those breathing masks? My lungs are a little raw. I don't want to smell that shit again if I don't have to."

"Sound idea, my man. We'll all wear them. I'll take care of it."

"Where and when?"

"Behind the store at three."

"Okay, see you then."

I looked at the clock. It was 1:45. I decided to call the office. I had wanted to tell Janet in person, but decided to confide in her now before she got the news elsewhere. I told her I would be in about 3:30.

I saw no reason to go into too much detail, so I simply said I had burned my hand and had spent the morning getting it taken care of. She got all motherly on me and said for me to take my time. I hoped she wouldn't be too upset with me when she found out the actual truth.

Then I sat down to a bowl of soup. I actually could smell the soup and there was only a small aroma left of fire smell. Hell, I was well on the road to recovery.

It was an easy walk uptown, and I enjoyed the fresh air. A breeze off the lake seemed to moderate the sun's intensity. I wore a cap, but had forgotten my sunglasses. Squinting got me by. When I arrived behind the gallery, John was waiting outside smoking a cigarette.

"I thought you gave those up," I said.

"I did for three years. Somehow they got me again."

John was twenty pounds overweight and out of shape. He spent too much time at a desk. His washed out blond hair had thinned, but he wore it long and brushed back. This helped to conceal his large ears. A bulbous nose anchored a fleshy face, while gray-green eyes contrasted to barely discernable eyebrows.

John reached out a hand to shake mine, but I demurred by holding my hands in the air.

"Sorry. Sore, huh?"

"Yup. You were able to get keys from somebody, John?"

John got a sheepish look on his face. "This is my building. Don't tell anyone. I don't want people to know I'm a real estate mogul."

I smiled. "Mum's the word."

"The adjuster's inside. Want to come in?"

"Sure."

John gave me a filter mask, and he donned one as well. I had not realized before now how much I did with my hands. Now everything I did with them hurt. It was difficult getting my fingers under the straps to get them over my head. I finally got the mask around my neck and then pulled it up over my mouth and nose.

We entered the back door into the rear storage area. I felt queasy for a moment smelling the burned and water soaked wood below. Then I began to cough. The smell triggered the response, and I momentarily wondered if I was going to be able to do this.

John had entered the gallery while I stood in the back room hacking, and remembering the previous night's adventure. He turned around and asked. "Is everything okay?"

"Yeah, I'm just getting my mask on."

I soon followed him inside.

A man I assumed was the adjuster was looking through the main store area when we entered into the back of the gallery exhibition area.

When the adjuster saw us, he said. "Of course, Mr. Brooks, we aren't the insurer of record for the contents."

"I understand," John replied, nodding.

"The tenant will be responsible for contents, while we'll take care of any smoke damage to the building's interior."

John nodded. He then said. "Mr. Smith, this is Mike Connelly. He discovered the fire, got the victim out and called the fire department. Mike, Bill Smith."

Bill put out his hand, and I raised my two into the air in self-defense.

"You're hurt."

"A little."

"Here?"

"Yes."

"Will you be putting in a claim?"

I was surprised at the question. "I hadn't thought about it," I said.

Bill gave me a quizzical look, and suggested. "Let's talk about downstairs."

Bill Smith was a small man, standing about five-foot-eight. He was thin, but wiry. His suit appeared to hang on him. He looked to be in his forties and wore his light-colored hair in a crew cut. A blanched complexion gave him a sickly look. Bushy eyebrows contrasted with his short hair.

I went over events as best I remembered them. I had to pause occasionally to catch my breath, and I sucked on a cough drop to ease my throat.

The adjuster said. "We found an extinguisher at the bottom of the stairs, just laying there. It hasn't been used. Do you remember seeing it, Mr. Connelly?"

I shook my head. It was hard breathing with the mask, and I wished I could have a cold beer. I sighed and said, "It was dark and really smoky, and I was preoccupied. I don't think so. I did trip over something, so maybe that was it. I just don't know."

Bill nodded. "That's okay. It's not important.

"The man . . ." here Bill checked his notes. ". . . Marshall Adams may have gone down with the extinguisher to put out the fire. Perhaps he was overcome by smoke, or he might have slipped and fallen on the way down. I understand he had a nasty head wound."

So it was Grace's husband. I needed to call her and see how he was doing. I had never noticed any head wound, and I kept that quiet. The first I had heard about it was from Steve. I was unsure how I could have missed it, but it had been smoky and I was a just a bit preoccupied.

"Is there a problem with the stairs?" John asked.

"Liability wise?"

"Yes."

"Not that I can see," Bill answered. "Everything seems to be to code, but that won't prevent a lawsuit if the man fell. Once the inspector assesses the cause of fire, liability may shift away from us. There appeared to be a lot of junk stashed down there."

"I know we could get sued, but I'll hope for the best," John said dejectedly.

Bill sensed John's mood and whispered. "There'll probably be a finding of arson."

"Arson?" John asked.

"Looks like it from what the fire inspector said. Not official yet, of course, but looks that way."

"Jesus," John said.

Bill went on, not missing a beat. "Probably have to replace the floor in the back area. The supports should be all right. You have those old heavy twelve-by-twelve wood beams. It would've taken a lot to burn through those. Lot more durable than steel. Steel would have melted and the whole floor would have collapsed. Contractor'll probably scrape the soot off and you'll be good to go. We'll see what he says."

"That's something encouraging," John replied.

"Let's check the second floor."

"Do you need me any more," I asked.

John looked at the adjuster, and he shook his head. We all walked out back.

"Thanks for coming, Mike."

"Glad to help. Say, what's upstairs?"

"An apartment."

"Really. I didn't realize that. Could I take a look?"

"Sure, come on up."

We walked outside and then entered an adjacent door. I had wondered where that led. I previously surmised it led into another store. We climbed up the back stairs, which led to a hallway that ran from the back to the front of the building.

"Where does this hall go?" I asked.

"There's a stairway that goes out the front of the building," John answered. "There's access to two apartments here, one on either side of the hall."

I had remembered single doors along Main Street, but never in all the years I had lived here made the connection to where they went.

John unlocked the apartment door after first knocking. I was surprised on several levels. First, at the roominess of the space and then, at how sparsely the rooms were furnished. I pulled down my mask, but still smelled smoke. It wasn't as bad as it had been downstairs, but it was there. I kept the mask on. The other two men had removed theirs.

"Doesn't anyone live here?" I asked.

"It's leased to the store tenant. They occupied it for a while until they found another residence. They chose to keep it for their occasional use. I think they come up here for lunch and such," John replied.

While the two insurance men conferred, I wandered into the front room. I pulled a tissue from my pocket and coughed into it. The deposit was not attractive. There was good lighting from the windows overlooking the Main Street, and it was being taken advantage of by someone working on a large canvas painting. They had set up an easel near the windows, and a partially painted canvas rested there.

At first I paid it little attention, but then I noticed photographs arranged next to the easel on another support. The painter was copying the photos for his painting. I figured that was smart. It kept the painter out of the weather while he worked.

Then I observed several more canvases leaning against a nearby wall. They were partially covered with a light cloth. My curiosity got the better of me, and I peeked beneath, only to receive a shock. The first painting appeared to be a reproduction of the one I had seen downstairs, the western scene painted by the dead painter, Jimenez. I could not be certain, but it appeared identical. I gingerly touched the edge so as not to hurt my fingers, and tilted the first canvas forward against my leg. The second was identical with the first, as was the third. Now I was dumbfounded.

I wondered what is going on? Something did not seem quite right. I was no expert on ethics, but this had to be walking on the edge, if not illegal. I waved to John, who is waiting for the adjuster to finish his perusal. John walked over.

"I see you brought your camera, John. Could you do me a favor?"

"Sure, Mike."

I pointed to the partially covered canvases. "Could you uncover those, set them side by side and take a couple of shots?'

"I guess. You have a reason?"

"I'm not sure, but I want a record of what I'm seeing here."

John paused momentarily as he thought through my request. Then he did as I asked, putting the paintings back as they were, fully covered when finished.

"They're all the same," John, said.

"I know, and that doesn't seem right, somehow."

"What are you going to do?"

"I don't know. Now, could you get a shot of the one by the window?"

John again complied, getting both the canvas and the photos into the shot. He played back the shots, and what I saw that he had captured seemed sufficient.

"When you have time, John, will you download those on your computer and e-mail them to me?"

"No problem. You'll let me in on what's going on?"

"Soon as I figure it out myself. It may be nothing, but I'm curious."

"Is there something wrong with them copying these paintings?" John asked.

"Not if it's just for their personal use, maybe. And maybe with copyright laws, that might even be wrong, technically. But if they were going to sell them, damn right it would be illegal. Don't say anything about this, John. We don't want something blown out of proportion until I research my law books on it."

"You got it."

"Well thanks, John. I'm going to run over to my office, now. If you need anything, give me a call."

"What about the coffee I owe you?"

"Lets make it another time, okay, I'm getting a little tired."

"Sure. I probably should stay here with Bill anyway."

"That's the ticket."

John walked me to the apartment door.

"Can you believe it might be arson?" John asked, shaking his head.

I hesitated while chewing my lower lip under the mask. "You don't think you might be suspected, John?"

John's face reflected a look of shock. "Me? Why me? Shit, I hadn't considered anything like that. Why would they consider me?"

"It's your building," I said.

"You're right there. Damn it. This could be real trouble for me."

I felt bad for bringing up the subject. "Maybe it was Adams who started the fire," I said in an attempt to defer the blame.

"Maybe," John said, in a funk now, and his mind had not grasped my alternative as a possibility.

Then John said, "Why was Adams downstairs, anyway? Was he trying to put out the fire?"

"I don't know," I answered. "Seems possible."

"Maybe he fell down the stairs with the extinguisher as he went down."

"How'd the fire get started, then?" I asked.

John sighed. "I don't know. Every time I look for a solution, it makes me look more guilty."

"Don't look at it that way. You didn't start it, did you?"

John looked at me with a horrified expression. "Of course I didn't, Mike. Why'd you say that?"

I shrugged. "Then quit looking guilty, man. It'll just bring suspicion onto you. If someone comes around asking questions, don't say too much. Remember, you don't know anything about the fire," I reminded him.

"Good thinking."

"Do you know how this inspection thing works?" I asked.

"What do you mean?"

"Okay, so they determine its arson, somehow," I said. "Does that say who did it? I mean, who started the fire?"

"No, of course not."

"So then, after it'd determined to be arson, the police try to pin it on someone, someone logical. To me that seems to be whoever would collect insurance. You would collect on the building, right?"

"Right," John said, dejectedly. "But I'll probably lose on the deal."

I nodded and then added, "And Adams, or whoever owns the business, on contents."

"Yes."

"Better lawyer up," I recommended.

"I will."

"Can I go out the front door?" I asked.

"Sure. It should just push open."

"Thanks."

On that note I left, feeling glad I was done with the mess. Done except for whom I thought I had seen leaving the building. Now I did feel queasy.

Chapter Nine
Police Beat

I left John and walked to my office. Janet was understandably upset upon seeing me enter. With her reaction, I realized I should have warned her about my nighttime adventures instead of minimizing the effect.

"Look what's happened to you." she said leaping from her desk chair. "You didn't say it was this bad." She looked frightened. "What did you do?"

I was wearing a short-sleeved shirt for comfort so she saw everything. Suddenly, I felt ill at ease. "It looks worse than it actually is," I said apologetically. I found a chair and sat. Then I explained in detail what had happened. Janet held her hands to her mouth and struggled to hold back tears. Her actions were making me feel uncomfortable. I already was exhausted, my chest ached from coughing, and my hands tingled from the skin shrinking. I couldn't minister to Janet too.

"How are you feeling, you poor man?" Janet put a hand to her eyes, and looked as if she might begin crying at any moment.

"I am a little better, I think." I walked over to her and put my less burned hand on her shoulder, squeezing lightly. It was all I could do. It hurt like hell, but she deserved it. "My headache's gotten a little better," I said, "and I don't think my lungs are making as much mucus."

Janet looked up at me, and I saw the questioning look, thus causing me to spend some time explaining the effects of smoke inhalation.

I went to the refrigerator and took out a bottle of water. "I am supposed to drink a lot of liquids. Do you think that includes beer?" It was a lame attempt at humor.

"Men," she said in an attempt to sound stern, but there was a twinkle in her eyes. That statement seemed to alter the mood and Janet managed a smile.

She looked more closely at my hands, taking me gently by the wrists. "How bad are the burns?" she asked.

"Minor," I replied with a grimace. A needle of pain had emanated from my right hand and shot into my wrist. I tried to ignore it, but it was difficult. I chewed my lip and then said, "I was lucky. There's some pain, but the nurse said I can expect to feel better any day now." Pain had lessened some, and I smiled at my witticism. "I just have to be careful not to break these blisters or they might become infected."

"That's pretty sketchy."

"Yes, I guess it is. Then I changed subjects. "Have you been able to keep things under control today?"

"I think so. You have some messages on your desk, and some signatures are needed. There's no coffee. Want some?"

I thought of how it might feel holding a hot coffee cup and demurred.

In my office, I sat in my overstuffed desk chair and flipped through the messages. None seemed important. There was one from an Officer Bill Rehms. I suspected that might be a follow-up to the fire. I stuffed his note in my shirt pocket.

It was late, and I was tired, so I decided any necessary work could wait. I signed the documents Janet needed and then begged off work and headed home. The light on my home phone was blinking, which indicated I had a message. It turned out I had three. One was from Officer Rehms, one from Steve and one from Grace. My mobile was sitting on the counter from when I had changed clothes. I decided to check that later. I was feeling fatigued and nothing seemed important, but I had to carry on. Stiff upper lip and all that as the British said.

I called Grace first. "Grace. You called. I'm glad. I so wanted to find out what happened."

"I'll call you right back," she whispered.

I was fighting off sleep and I wished I had left the call go till later. Five minutes later my phone rang.

"Hello," I answered.

"It's me."

"Where are you, Grace?"

"At the hospital."

"Which one?"

"The U. They have a good burn unit here."

"So that was your husband then at the store?"

"Yes. Thank you for getting him out of the fire, Mike. They told me who saved him, and I just couldn't believe it. What were you doing there?"

I didn't know what to say in response. My mind was flooded with the memory of our nighttime encounter together. That was a more pleasant thought than that of the fire.

The pause must have been long because she asked. "You still there, Mike?"

"Yes, Gracie, I'm here. How is he? Marshall, right?"

"Yes, Marshall. Not good, I'm afraid. So many things to deal with. You knew he was burned. Of course you did. They told me you pulled him out. You would know that."

Grace was rambling, but I didn't interrupt. If I was tired, I could only imagine what she was going through.

"He inhaled a lot of smoke, I guess. They tell me that's worse than the burns, actually. It really messed . . ." Here Grace began to quietly sob. Then she garnered some control and said, "Messed up his lungs."

I had been given the primer on smoke inhalation, so I did understand.

"Take your time Gracie. You don't have to talk about it if you don't want to."

"No, that's okay, it helps. He has a fractured skull and a concussion. That's not good either."

"He must have fallen down the stairs," I lamely offered.

"That's what the police say."

"The police?"

"Yes. They stopped in here this morning. I think they wanted to speak with Marshall . . ." Here she broke up again. ". . . but of course he can't talk."

"I'm so sorry, Gracie. Would it help if I came in?"

"Thanks, Mike. No. I have my sister here with me, and I'm going to go home soon. There isn't much I can do here. This is going to be a long fight."

I wanted to suggest I come to her house, but then I scolded myself for my over active libido.

"Call me, Gracie, when you feel like talking."

"Thanks, Mike. You're a prince."

I gritted my teeth and rolled my head carefully to loosen my neck. Then I got some ice water to drink. Once again I held my hands in the cold air of the freezer. The escaping air felt refreshing as it swept over my face and neck.

I was sick to my stomach and didn't feel like eating. Then I awoke to the fact that I might be hungry, and that may be the cause of the stomach upset. I hadn't eaten in twenty-four hours. I made two slices of toast with the idea of eating them dry. I wanted to see if I kept them down before I tried anything else. I remembered that toast was what my mother always gave me after I had been sick. I did not know if it applied here, but it couldn't hurt.

I sat with the toast and water in my lounge chair before the TV. I began watching Fox News, but awoke to a totally different cast of characters. I realized I had been asleep. I got up, used the bathroom, refreshed my drink, and cleared my lungs the best I could. There did not seem to be as much phlegm as there had been earlier that morning. God, I hoped I was getting better.

Then it was back to the chair. The Twins game was about to start, so I planned to hunker down there and relax before going to bed. When once again I woke the game was over. I turned off the tube and remained in the chair, deciding that, if I slept sitting up, I might not be as congested. It worked, and I slept reasonable well until six-thirty the next morning.

I had perspired like crazy overnight, and the thought struck me that I might have a slight fever. I did not remember discussing that issue at the hospital, but perhaps we had. I actually did not remember much of what was said. It was a good thing they sent home several sheets of instructions. I looked through those, but found nothing about fever.

Okay, let's get on with it. Don't be a pussy. This will get better just persevere, I thought.

I carefully showered, shaved and brushed my teeth. The shaving part was tough. After dressing, I ate a bowl of Cheerios. My stomach felt fine. I tried to cough up any accumulated mucus, but little came. That made me happy. Either things were improving, or my sleep choice had helped the process. My hands still tingled, but the minor sores on my arms looked and felt better. There were just a few remaining red spots there. Fortunately, I had not blistered anywhere besides my hands.

I once again used my rotary tool in my nose to eliminate any remaining hairs, and applied petroleum jelly. There was little remaining burnt smell. It actually could all be in my brain. *Yeah, what brain?*

I still felt tired, but I knew I had plenty of sleep. Maybe it would take a couple of days to fully recover. I planned to work a full day today regardless.

I decided to not call Steve until this evening, but realized I should return the cop's call.

He was not in, but returned my call a short time later. He invited himself over to my place, and I let him come. I figured I might as well get it over with. I could always start work late, and stay longer in the afternoon if my body held out.

Now, I merely had to decide what to tell the police when they showed up. I was assuming they wanted to talk about my involvement at the gallery fire.

When the officer with whom I had spoken, Bill Rehms, arrived he was not alone. He had a woman officer with him. I invited them both in. Rehms introduced the woman as Sergeant Bishop. I declined to shake hands with either of them, and they understood. When I suggested the deck, they agreed, so we went outside. It was chilly, but the early morning sun made up for it, and we were all dressed adequately.

I offered coffee all around and both accepted. I had not had coffee since returning home from the hospital, but I thought I would give it a try. I started the pot when I first talked to Rehms. When I delivered the refreshments in insulated mugs, they thanked me.

It had been a cool overnight, but now it was late enough in the morning that the sun was shining directly on us, and reflecting off the building. That gave us about ten degrees more comfort than the ambient air provided. There was little wind, and the lake was still. I wistfully wished I was out fishing.

"Mr. Connelly," Rehms began. "I just need to ask you a few questions to complete the report on the fire."

"Sure. I'll tell you what I can." My guess about the subject matter seemed to have been correct.

"You're an attorney, right?"

"Right."

"Do you want representation for this interview?"

"Why? Am I being arrested?"

"No, I just thought . . ."

I was having a little fun with the man, though I had no real idea what he was after. We were seated in wicker chairs with cushions. I was facing both officers, while facing the house. The sun was at my back, but in their eyes. It was a power play on my part.

I responded to his question. "No, you just ask your questions. I'm fine."

Officer Rehms was a powerfully built man, standing about six feet tall. His dark-brown hair was cut in a crew cut. The man had a swarthy complexion and dark eyes. He had a military look about him. I had yet to see a smile from him. He was all business.

"All right then," he began, "what can you tell me about the fire?"

"It was hot and smoky," I answered.

Rehm's face and neck began to turn red, as if he had been in the sun too long.

"I would like serious answers to my questions," he blurted out, barely controlling his anger.

I was surprised by both his demeanor and the short fuse, so I said. "I am serious. What's your problem? I was in a god-dammed fire. It was hot and smoky. Okay?"

I had raised my voice and now felt bad for doing so, but I didn't care for the man's manner. Now I began to cough. Apparently, my fiery response had triggered the coughing. I pulled tissues from my pocket, turned my head and cleared my mouth of a glob of phlegm.

"Listen, you," Rehms began. His own voice had risen.

My emotions still were unstable from my recent experience, and I was about to cut the interview short when Sergeant Bishop intervened by clearing her throat. We both turned to look at her. Then she placed a hand in front of the other officer with her palm facing him.

"Perhaps we should begin again," she suggested in a soft tone. "Bill, why don't I ask a few questions here? Please take some notes."

Rehms slunk back into the chair with a moody look on his face. I was not sure why, but I got the impression he didn't like me. I had no recollection of meeting him previously, though I may have seen him around town. I usually did not frequent joints that need a police presence. Maybe he was new to the local force. There normally was turnover in small departments like ours.

Bishop took the lead. "Mr. Connelly, you are an attorney with an office in Excelsior, correct?"

"That's correct."

"I've seen you around town," she said with a smile.

I wasn't surprised, as I did get around. *At least someone has a personality on this force*, I thought. I smiled back, while I appraised the officer.

Bishop's pleasant looking face had complimentary features, and nice bone structure, with a peaches-and-cream complexion. Her makeup was subdued, including no lip gloss on full lips. Short, black hair parted on one side and scooped forward complemented large, dark-gray eyes, which were wide set under professionally done eyebrows. She wore eye shadow and mascara. The woman was conscientious about her appearance.

She had a flat spot on the bridge of her nose, indicating it may once have been broken. A strong chin supported a wide mouth. The powerfully built woman wore single studs in nicely shaped ears. Other than a watch and a couple of rings, that was her only jewelry. I noted that her left ring finger was bare. The woman's thick waist didn't detract from a good figure. I thought I might like trying to wrestle with her.

She interrupted my review by saying. "You chaired the charity drive last year for autistic and disabled children."

"Yes. That's correct."

"Nice job there. Good cause. I gave money to that."

"Thanks. I'm sure the recipients are grateful." I could see she was trying to put the interview on a different track. My breathing was coming more naturally, now. I took a sip of my coffee. It seemed to irritate my throat, so I set it onto the table next to me and carefully unwrapped a throat lozenge. I began sucking on that.

"So, let's start with where you were that evening. That would have been Wednesday."

"When? I mean what time?" I asked.

"Earlier that night."

"I was having dinner."

"Where?" she asked. "Could you elaborate?"

"At the pub."

"The one on the corner?" she asked. "How's the food there, I've never been?"

"Good," I answered. "Nothing low calorie, though. If you like beer, they have quite a variety of good brews."

She smiled. "Do you remember when you arrived there?"

"Why?"

"She seemed surprised. "Why what?"

"Why do you want to know?" I asked.

She laughed. I'm just trying to get a picture of the evening. We know what time the 911 call came in, but little else. You might be able to help us with that. We're trying to form a picture here."

"Sure. I see," I answered, though I could not see the relevance.

"So, let's say you were at the pub for a while, and left about when?"

"I'm not trying to be evasive here, but I really have no idea. I think about ten."

"Ten. And what did you do then?"

"I walked out into the parking lot to get into a car to go to my place."

"Did you spend much time out in the parking lot after leaving the pub?"

I thought a bit. "No," I said, shaking my head. "We just started walking to the car. I don't know, maybe a couple of minutes. We were talking and walking slowly."

"Fine. Is that when you noticed the fire?"

I felt a trap. I hadn't noticed fire then, and she probably knew that. If I said yes, she would have me in a lie, or at least have a hole in my story. More people go to jail for lying than for the original crime.

I answered, "No." Then I cleared my throat. My voice was becoming raspy. This was way too much talking for me.

"No?" she said.

"That's right. I never knew there was a fire until after I entered the building."

"Well then, what made you enter the building?" she inquired.

I put my hands up in a gesture of futility. "I really don't know. Maybe a sixth sense led me to that door."

Rehms smirked and started to say something, but Bishop stilled him with her index finger held high toward his face.

"You were with companions at dinner, correct?" she asked.

"That's correct."

"Did you all leave together?"

"Yes.

"Did you see anyone exit the building where the fire was discovered, as you were walking to that car?"

I was trapped, but I had to lie. " You do mean the door where the fire was, right?"

"That's correct."

"No," I replied in as normal a voice as I could muster.

"But you went toward that building, and then entered it?"

"That's correct," I answered.

"How long were you in the building alone?" she asked.

I thought for a bit. What was she after? "Which time?" was my response.

"There was more than once?"

"Yes."

"Each time then," she said.

"Let's see. I went in to check for fire, since I'd smelled smoke when cracking open the outside door. That time maybe half a minute to a minute. I think I just checked the two doors and left. I went back out and returned inside to go downstairs, and it was about the same amount of time before my friend came in after me."

"That would be Mr. Anderson?"

"Yes."

"Fine. That helps a lot. Just trying to establish a timeline. Oh, I forgot. Did you by any chance hear anyone in the store?"

I contemplated that one. "You mean up front in the gallery?"

"Yes."

"No, I don't think so. Not as I remember anyway. I do know that door was locked."

"How'd you know that?" Rehms asked.

"I tried it."

"When you first went in?" he asked.

"Yes."

Bishop waited to see if her partner was finished, and then asked, "When you were at the bar with your friends, were you all together the entire time?"

I smelled a rat. I replied. "Mostly."

"Mostly?" she inquired.

"We were drinking beer."

"Ah, the rest room," she said.

"Yes."

"Just in case it came up, were any of you out of each others sight very long?"

My feelers were up for this one and I answered. "Not for more than a couple of minutes."

"That's all I have for questions, Mr. Connelly. Any more Bill?"

"No."

Bill closed his notebook, and I began to relax.

"Just one more thing, Mr. Connelly," Officer Bishop said. "This has nothing to do with the investigation, but I'm personally curious. "What ever possessed you to go down into that firestorm?"

I just shrugged.

"Mr. Anderson said that when the basement door was opened foul smoke rolled up the stairs and he barely could see you three feet in front of him."

I thought back to the night of the fire. "Yeah, I guess that's a fairly accurate description."

"How could you do it then?"

I reflected on that question for a minute. Then I said, "I didn't want to. I was scared to death, actually. I wanted to leave. I really,

really wanted to leave, but then Steve came in behind me, and I felt I had to go forward. I don't know why."

"We gain courage from our comrades," Bill interrupted, staring out over the water as he chewed his lower lip. He had a far away look in his eyes. Maybe he had been there before himself. "It's sort of a crowd mentality," he continued. "It allows us to do things we might not do alone." He now looked at me with an intense gaze.

Tears formed in my eyes as I recalled that night. My chest began to quiver. I had to hold it together before these two.

Bishop looked from Rehms to me. "Weren't you terrified to go down those stairs," she asked. "Anderson said there was fire present. You realize you're a hero. The city should hold a ceremony for you. I'm going to see to it the paper runs an article on you."

I pursed my lips and tried to control my emotions. "No!" I shouted. "Don't even think about something like that. I'm a cockleshell hero." I looked down at my feet. Then I whispered. "Flame was licking out from under where we stood. It would flick out like a snake's tongue and then recede. If I had been alone, I would have run. I'm no hero. I was scared to death."

Bill Rehms interrupted. "Mr. Connelly. We're all scared at one time or another. There have been times when I've been scared to death, also. I know what you went through. The person who says he's not afraid is either a fool or a liar. Real courage is being afraid yet persevering despite that fear. That's what you did. You had real courage. Yes, you are a hero, Mr. Connelly."

I looked up at Rehms with tears in my eyes. My chest heaved once again.

"What was it like after you got down those stairs?" Bishop persisted.

I bit my lip and shook my head. Then I said. "I could hardly breathe, but somehow I blotted out the fire and concentrated on the body. Once I was all the way down, all I could think about was getting out. I think getting burned on my hands and arms steeled me to continue. I wasn't about to give in after what I already had gone through."

Bill was nodding along with my recounting.

I shrugged. "That's it, I guess. I just did what I had to do."

"Magnificent effort, Mr. Connelly," Officer Bishop concluded. She stood, as did Rehms. He walked over to me and patted me on the shoulder.

"Thank you for your time, Mr. Connelly," she said. "You've been very helpful, and I hope you're feeling well again soon. I can't imagine what might have happened if you hadn't spotted that fire early."

A thought struck me suddenly and I asked. "Why didn't the sprinklers go off? I thought all the stores had to be hooked up?"

Nobody said a word. I stared at Bishop and she stared back. When she didn't answer, I said, "It was arson then, and someone disabled the sprinklers."

Officer Bishop smiled and turned to go. I opened the patio door and stepped aside to let them pass. Then I led the two officers to the front door.

"Before you leave," I said. "What's your first name?" I asked, looking at Bishop.

"Nancy," she said with a slight curl to her lip. She took out a card and handed to me. Bill Rehms did likewise.

"Nice to meet you, Nancy."

I nodded at Rehms. He gave me a smile. Then they were gone.

I went downstairs and considered making myself a drink. I thought I needed one. Then I figured it would dry me out, so I settled for water. I turned off the coffee. I didn't want more caffeine. Then I returned outside, and carrying a folding chair out onto the grass, I sat in the sun for a few minutes. I relaxed and thought about the conversation I had just held.

After a while I came to the conclusion we had two investigations occurring as one. One for arson and one for attempted murder. No other conclusion could be made for the questions I had been asked.

With the amount of smoke in Adam's lungs, it was obvious he had been exposed to the fire for a period of time before I arrived on the scene. Steve and I had not arrived too much later than when Marshall had been overcome, and once that had been established, our whereabouts for earlier in the evening had come into question.

But why us? I could think of no reason other than the police were covering all bases. I wondered if they knew about my relationship with Grace. It would not surprise me. That might put me on the top of someone's list.

Now things were beginning to make sense. Maybe with the right amount of convoluted thinking, they imagined I tried to bump off the old man to get at Grace. *I have to be careful what I say, and if they ask me about my relationship with Grace, I better not lie.* It was a good thing the three of us were in the pub together as well as in the parking lot. The police would not be able to incriminate all three of us, especially since we called it in. Or would they?

I remembered there was one more phone message to return and I addressed that now. Steve answered his cell.

"Listen Mike," he began. "I got to thinking and wanted to alert you."

"To what?"

"I had a visit from a Shorewood cop yesterday afternoon at my office."

"Who?'

"An Officer Bill Rehms."

"Yeah, he's already been here."

"Oh. Well, I guess it's too late then."

"What's too late?"

"It's just that the whole line of questioning. He wanted to know when we got to the restaurant. Wanted to know if we were all together the whole time. Then he asks how long you were inside the gallery alone. Did I see you and Adams together? Did I hear any argument? I think he was trying to say we, or you had something to do with him getting hurt."

"I see. I wondered where he was coming from in his interview with me?" I said. "Don't worry about it, Steve. The facts will prove us right. Just some over zealous cop. Maybe he's trying to make a name for himself. I'd advise you not to answer any more questions, though, without counsel."

"Gee, that sounds serious."

"No, just prudent. An attorney will put the man in his place soon enough."

I thanked Steve for his concern and rang off. Now I had to decide what I was going to do. So much already had happened today that I was exhausted, and I needed badly to go to the office.

Somehow, I would get through the day. I sucked it up and managed to put in a good day's work at the office to end the week. I knew by Monday I would feel much better.

Chapter Ten
Research

When the early morning sun's rays began glistening off the tranquil waters of Excelsior Bay, my eyes already were open. A small gap in the heavy bedroom curtains allowed me an assessment of the hour without having to turn my head to read the nearby clock.

The darkened room spoke of my mood this early Saturday morning. I as yet had made no move get up because sacking out in bed seemed the appropriate thing to do. Though I was tired, and feeling poorly from my fire experience, there were things I needed to decide. I hoped relaxing in bed might help me to think.

Since the accident, I was compelled to sleep with my arms outside the covers to protect my hands, but I unconsciously pulled them under when a cool breeze from the open window washed over my bed. Then I wakened immediately, which resulted in a restless night's sleep. I would be glad when things were back to normal.

I moved my tongue over my front teeth. My mouth was dry and my teeth needed brushing, but I ignored my personal discomfort to remain under the bed covers. I closed my eyes to better concentrate, but that only brought Grace's image to mind, plus I swore I still smelled her scent in the room. I knew I was in trouble dredging up those memories.

The foremost problem I had to resolve was my feelings for Grace. I needed to do something, because her reappearance into my life was driving me nuts. I even had questioned myself as to what I might have done had I known the victim at the bottom of the stairs was Grace's husband. Would I still have tried to save him or would I have claimed it was too hot and dangerous, and left him there to die? I knew I couldn't go on harboring those thoughts, or I would go stark raving mad. But how could I go about clearing them out of my head?

My world had been so well ordered, so comfortable before Gracie reentered it. I longed to return to that normalcy, or did I? Maybe a normalcy that included Grace? There I was chasing my tail once again.

I sighed and rubbed crust from one eye with a finger that hadn't been too seriously injured. I scolded myself to concentrate and stay on point. Where was I? Yes, there was an even bigger issue concerning Grace besides my obvious longing for her. It was no small matter how I had lied to everyone, including the police. For sure, that potentially could really immerse me into the deepest possible trouble. For only I knew that I had not told the truth of what I had seen that night, which had prompted me to approach that fateful door.

Yes, something had caught my eye, and I do in fact believe I knew what it was. I had told everyone that it had been a trick of the brain that sent me over to that door. That was not entirely true. I went there because I believed I saw someone come out of that very door, and I'm sure that someone was Grace.

My bladder was telling me it was time to move, but I ignored its pleading. I had to work this through.

So then, if it had been Grace I saw that night, why was I protecting her? Was it because I thought she had something to do with her husband's accident? Had it really been an accident? Was it even Grace I saw? I hadn't had much of a look. Why were the police asking the questions they were asking if it was an accident? No. They think it was attempted murder. Shit, I seemed to be coming up with more questions than answers.

I had tried to convince myself I held my tongue only because of an uncertain identification, but was that the truth? No, probably not. If I could not be honest with myself, I was doomed.

I had to ask myself hard questions. Could Grace have killed her husband? If she could have, she was not the person I thought she was. The person I thought I saw that dark night did have light-colored hair and had moved more like a woman than a man. But, what could I actually swear to? I never saw a face.

When I got over by that back door, I'd seen no one nearby. I never got a close look at the phantom. No, I couldn't swear it had been Grace, but I was damn worried that it might have been. Then too, was that an act she put on when I spoke with her at the hospital, when she talked so tenderly of her husband? Could she be that good of an actress? How could I believe what happened with us the night of the reunion was real, and accept as real any feelings we might have for one another if she merely was acting out her affection for her husband?

The only way to be sure of what transpired that fateful night at the gallery was to find out if Grace had an alibi for the critical time. I could not disclose what I saw until I knew for sure. I would have to just keep everything I knew to myself until I found the answers. I wondered if the police were questioning her. Surely they must have been by now.

I was guessing I had not resolved anything, but at least I now had something of a game plan. Feeling more in control of the situation, I rose and attended to my morning needs.

Later, when I was more fully awake, I decided to quietly start asking questions on my own. After much deliberation, I decided to begin with John Brooks in order to ascertain what he might know. Since pumping John would be the least intrusive way to begin, I called his office from my landline and left a message inviting him to lunch. I suggested he call me when he got the message.

Now I was feeling more energized. I quickly finished my morning ablution and tended to some home chores. Periodically, I would stop what I was doing and study my hands. The skin looked like parchment paper, almost translucent in spots. I bet it was about to shed like a snake's skin. My hands were feeling much better today, although they still were sore. My cough nearly was gone. Lying flat in bed last night had not started me off on a coughing jag, anyway. One little step at a time. I realized that the smell of burned hair was not evident this morning. The thought brought tears of relief to my eyes.

Later that morning, John returned my call, and we set a time to meet.

When we were together, I said to John. "I hope I'm not taking you away from any important work."

"Not at all. A fellow has to eat. Thanks for thinking about me."

"No problem. We don't see enough of each other."

We were in a booth facing one another at a cafe out near the highway. We could see the traffic whizzing past on Highway Seven through the large window framing our booth. After perusing the menu, we both opted for sandwiches and coffee.

"Have you had anyone in to look over the damage to your building?" I asked.

John nodded. "This morning. Hanson Builders stopped by. They said I need to replace the floor in the back area and recommended I add a support post to that main wood beam, just to make sure. Then, I need to get Gertson in to take care of the smoke."

"They do that kind of thing?"

"Yeah, that's their business. Smoke and water damage."

The waitress filled our cups and left a pot of coffee behind.

After taking a sip, I asked. "Have you heard anything about the contents?"

"Not yet. Of course Adams is in the hospital, and I haven't heard anything from the Mrs."

"I talked to her at the hospital day before yesterday," I said. "Her husband's at the U."

"I better drop in and pay my respects," John commented. "Is it hard to get there?"

"I'm not sure. I don't know if you can see him, though. I think he's in I.C.U."

"Oh. Maybe I should send flowers, then." John puzzled.

"Maybe." I said. Then I thought I should be doing something myself.

Our lunch arrived, and we dug in, waiting on any further conversation. Then I asked. "What about the assistant?"

"Huh? Oh, the gallery. I haven't seen or heard from him, and I don't have any contact information for him. My agency doesn't cover the contents, so I wasn't going to push it. Do you think I'm okay with that?"

"Sure, I suppose so. You're not responsible. Won't they have to move out their stuff for you to clean?"

I don't know," John replied, taking a bite of his sandwich. "I guess Gurtson'll tell me that when they look over the place. They could always get a storage box dropped outside the back door and store the artwork there while the interior is prepared.

"You know what's funny though?" John asked, when he had finished chewing his next bite.

"What?"

"I was in the building again this morning, as I said, with the builder. We went all over the whole place to make sure nothing else needed repair. It didn't look like any merchandise was moved from the main floor. At least not so I would notice. But upstairs, you know the stuff we photographed?"

"Yeah."

"It's all gone."

"Really?" I was surprised by the comment, and I sat reflecting. When I didn't say anything more, John added. "I was thinking maybe that's private stuff the assistant was working on, and he took it."

I considered John's statement. "That's probably what happened, but it does seem strange." I let my comment hang in the air a moment and then added, "I wonder if the Mrs. was at home the night of the fire? I mean so they could reach her about her husband."

"I understand they didn't reach her until the next morning," John answered. "She said she'd been asleep, and they don't keep the ringer on in the bedroom."

I thought about my own phone location and said. "That's probably not unusual."

Watching John for a reaction, I said, "You'd think maybe she'd notice her husband not being there."

John's eyes widened as he realized the significance. "Yes, you would think that for sure."

John appeared to be puzzling over that situation, and I did not want to force the conversation. I waited a few moments before asking. "Have you heard anything about what the police think might have happened?"

"Just scuttlebutt around town. Nothing direct. They have this new guy on the force that appears to want to make a name for himself. New on the job, you know. Keeps telling everyone who'll listen that it wasn't an accident."

"The fire or Grace's husband?"

Here John puzzled. "Both I guess."

"Why do you suppose he would he think that?" I asked.

"He's out to prove that Adams was conked on the head before he tumbled downstairs."

"Really? That would be a whole new wrinkle, at least in my thinking."

"Yup. You were there. Think that's possible?" John asked.

"I . . . I would have no idea. How would I know? Maybe the doctors could tell from the wound. I had assumed he fell down the stairs." I reflected a moment. "You know, John, I was there, but too busy. I mean, I was so engrossed in the rescue I didn't see much. Does that make any sense to you?"

John bit his lip. "Yes, I can understand what you're saying. Yes, that makes sense. The doctors might be the ones to ask."

Now we were both silent for a minute, and I began thinking about the interrogations of Steve and myself. Those actions and the questions asked of us supported what John was saying to me here and now. Now I had a real reason to keep silent about the woman I saw that night, with the cops looking to make this into an attempted murder investigation.

I decided to bring up the subject of the fire. "John, I heard a rumor the water to the building's sprinkler system had been shut off."

"The fire department told me that," he answered. "You know, Mike. I think someone was trying to burn the place down."

"It's starting to look that way, but why?" I wondered briefly if John had a reason to burn his own place?

John dispelled my fears when he said, " It really frightens me, Mike. Is someone out to get me or was it a cover for knocking off what's his name? They couldn't have given it much thought. Do you realize they could have burned the whole block?"

"Good thing I caught it early then."

"John saw my smile and retorted. "Don't make light of it, Mike. If you hadn't seen the fire and done what you did, I don't know what might have happened."

"Just lucky, John. Just lucky."

When we finished lunch and had walked back downtown, I said goodbye to John and briefly stopped at my office. There was not much to do, but at one point I leaned back in my chair, stared at the wall, and once again considered what I thought I had seen that fateful night. After much reflection, I decided that any conflict between Grace and her husband was none of my business. If the couple had a quarrel, that was between the two of them. As long as Adams recovered, I did not think any of it mattered. Keep it in the family. If something happened, and he did not recover, well that was a bridge to cross when we got there.

I decided any work at the office could keep until Monday. On my walk home, I looked at the various buildings wondering what secrets they held. I would never be able to walk through town with the same naïveté again.

Upon arriving home, I considered options for dinner. Pizza sounded good to me, but not the amount of calories involved. I decided instead on fish. I had a package of frozen walleye fillets in the freezer, and I took those out and immersed them in water. While I waited for them to thaw, I fixed a brew. *Two days is long enough to abstain. I will drink plenty of water tomorrow.*

Generally, I wasn't much of a cook, but I did learn to fry fish over the years. Later, when my meal was ready, I took it out onto the deck and enjoyed it there with a cold beer. When finished, I sat back and relaxed, while watching the boating activity in the bay. There were plenty of boats running to and from the waterside restaurants.

I lit up a cigar and relaxed. My thoughts drifted to a subject I almost had overlooked. I began wondering about the paintings that had gone missing from the upstairs apartment. There was something unethical about copying another painter's work, but I was sure that art students did it all the time. The more I thought about it, though, the more I realized an amateur did not make the copies. Those copies were really good. I was unable tell the difference from the original. Though I had to confess I didn't know that much about art.

I decided to call my buddy Paul. He'd be able to enlighten me.

He answered on the third ring.

"Paul. How goes it?"

"Mike. I'm just fixing a gin and tonic. Then I'll go out onto my patio and watch the sun go down as we talk."

"Fine. How've you been?" I asked.

"Good. You?"

"Couldn't be better."

I decided not to tell Paul about the fire. It didn't concern him, and frankly I didn't want to go through that whole ordeal again.

"There I'm set. Talk to me," Paul said.

I could hear him sliding a table closer to himself.

"Paul, I'm following up on those photos of the paintings I sent you. Do they show up very well?"

"Enough for me to see the arch isn't the same one as mine."

"Good. But can you tell anything about the quality of the painting itself?"

"Like what?"

"Like is the painting job any good?"

"Let me go in and grab those printouts I made. By the way, how's your weather there? It's a perfect night here. It was in the nineties today, but it's supposed to get into the fifties up at my elevation tonight."

Paul chatted as he searched for the copies he had printed.

"Here they are. Okay. My printer isn't the best, so I can't comment on brush strokes from these, but coloring is wonderful. Blending and shading are excellent. Very good work."

"Could they have been done by Jimenez?" I asked.

"Hmmm. Jimenez wasn't top tier as far as American masters are concerned, but he was accomplished. Yes, these could have been done by him."

"Then what would you say if I told you I thought they were copies done by someone right here in Excelsior?"

"I'd say whoever did it is a very good artist, indeed. Of course, it's one thing to copy color, its another to duplicate stroke work. I can't tell the quality of that from these e-mails."

"No, I suppose not, but that's okay. Listen. If these were copies, what would be the motive?"

There was silence while Paul reflected. Then he said, "I can only assume someone wanted to sell those copies as originals. Thinking about it a little, considering how few of his works are on the market right now, prices are high. Some collectors want to get in before probate releases the remainder of the works."

"If they were to spread these around the country, no one might know of the existence of duplicates," I said.

"That's possible." Paul answered.

"Say, do you know what this painting is of?" I asked.

"Yours? Yes. It's an arch in Arizona, unnamed I believe. As a matter of fact, people refer to it as Unnamed Arch. It's near Many Farms. That area is beautiful with fantastic rock color. I visited it a couple of years ago and just loved it. Jimenez captured it wonderfully."

"Are you still in the running to buy them?"

"You mean the rest of his works?"

"Yes."

"The contract is signed. We merely need court approval."

"Then it's fraud," I said.

"Could be. I'd be interested in following up once the works are mine. I don't want bootleg works out there competing with me."

"I can see that," I said. "I'll keep you in the loop of what I know."

"I appreciate that," Paul replied.

"Did you get a chance to look at the picture of the partially completed oil I sent?" I asked.

"Yes, I did.

"Do you know what it is?"

"I found that out. It's a work by the Spanish painter, Francisco Goya. Done about 1826. He's known as the last of the Old Masters. Considered a Romantic. This particular work was done in what is called his Black Period. They say he had this absurd fear of insanity at the time.

"The work's titled *Milkmaid of Bordeau* and it hangs in the Mureo del Prado in Spain. The interesting thing is that soon it'll be on loan to the Walker in Minneapolis. It's going on a six-city tour of the U.S."

"Boy you sure know your stuff."

"Why thank you, my good man."

I had to laugh at that. "Do you have any idea, Paul, why someone would want to copy it?"

"Maybe someone saw it, liked it, and wants a copy."

"Can they do that? I mean do you see that done?"

"You know they sell prints of many works right in the museum gift shops?"

"Yes, but this appears to be an oil copy, an exact duplicate.

"Okay then, sure it happens, but only if its done privately. There's no law I know about against owning a copied work unless someone tries to market it."

"So owning a copy probably isn't illegal, but surely if the guy who is painting it sells it, that's illegal."

"Probably. But if it's on the QT, nobody's going to know. You should know more about that than me. Do you think that gallery in your town is involved in something?"

"I do think there's a possibility something's going on, and I'm not in that field of law, but I'll research it," I advised.

"Well, stay away from whatever it is. Someday it may drag them down. Like I say, I might pursue it once my deal is done."

"Thanks for the advice, I'll be careful not to get involved. Paul, thanks for all your help. If you think of anything else, let me know."

"Sure thing, buddy. Have a great night. Bye."

"Bye."

Now I had even more to think about.

Chapter Eleven
The Scam

I let my personal concerns lie dormant on Monday, going to the office and concentrating on work I had neglected or had left for Janet. She had taken on the extra load without complaint, but I was feeling guilty. I should only expect so much. Thus, I worked straight through until one.

I skipped lunch with the idea of working continuously all day, but by one o'clock, fatigue began to set in. My good intentions had gone awry. I realized my mistake, because along with the hunger came fatigue, as well as thoughts of the whole mess with Grace, the events surrounding the fire, and the suspect paintings.

I as usual had carried my lunch, so I grabbed an apple from the refrigerator and headed for the door. I needed fresh air to wake me up. Janet already had returned from her lunch break so I felt things were covered. I devoured my apple as I crossed the parking lot. It had been an impulse that carried me unannounced to see John Brooks. When I arrived at his place, John's receptionist called to him on the intercom, and he came out of his office.

"Mike."

"Brooksie, got a minute?" I asked.

He was sans sport coat and moisture showed under his arms. It was cool in the office, which told me that earlier he had spent time out in the heat.

"Gosh, Mike I have an appointment with a client in about ten."

"I won't take that long."

John shrugged and turned toward his door. I followed into his personal office space. It was a neatly organized room, as usual. I have always been impressed by the look of it. A place for everything and everything in its place as the old saying goes, and clearly John was a proponent. The furniture was utilitarian, but serviceable. Obviously John preferred to put his money into investment property rather than into show.

I had known John for a long time and early on had formed the impression he was a fastidious guy. He always kept his hair neatly combed and had no facial hair. He tanned easily, gaining a nice color just from a couple of rounds of golf each week. Never without a coat and tie at work even if it was with a pair of khakis, he was always the professional that exuded the air he could help you with all your insurance needs. Today, I needed him and his insurance knowledge.

"Heard anything about Adams's condition?" I asked.

"Nothing new. Nobody seems to know much. I don't think he's doing too good, though. I don't know much about any of what's wrong with him, so I have no idea . . . what's a normal recovery?"

John moved around behind his desk, but remained standing. His manor was not inviting me to prolong this visit. I intended to be brief.

I watched him and then answered his question by saying, "Beats me."

"I did have that cop Rehms nosing around again," John said, reluctantly.

That statement surprised me, since it must have been a second visit. "Really. What did he want now?"

"Anything and everything I knew about anyone and everyone," John said, as he finally sat in his chair. Placing his elbows on the desk blotter, he picked up a pencil and started playing with it. "I had met him briefly at the store that first time, but this time he came here."

"You're getting to be best buddies, huh?" I took the chair in front of him and asked, "What did you tell him?"

"I did a Sergeant Schultz on him."

My face must have asked the question, because he answered. "I know nothing, nothing."

Then I remembered *Hogan's Heroes*, and we both laughed.

"Listen," I said. "I won't keep you, and I'd like you to keep this very quiet. I don't want to get anyone into trouble if I'm barking up the wrong tree here."

John looked bewildered, but shook his head allowing me to continue. I leaned forward and lowered my voice a bit. "Here's the thing. You and I saw where someone was copying that large oil upstairs above the gallery, right?"

"Right," John replied hesitantly, nodding.

"So, let's say that the painting, when completed, was going to be involved in some sort of a scam."

I had placed my hands on the edge of his desk. Now I removed them and sat back in the chair, feeling relief at voicing my concern.

"A scam? What kind of a scam?" John asked.

I chewed my lip. The first statement had been easy. The hard part was defining my fear. "I'm not sure, John. I need help figuring that out. That's where you come in. Can you find out if there's been any pattern of art heists or fire losses or some such thing of expensive art works?"

John looked at me and furrowed his brow. "I get it. You're trying to see if copies of paintings could somehow be involved in false insurance claims."

"That's right."

"Are you thinking of just local, then?"

"No, nationwide would make more sense."

"I guess you're right. Yes, that would make more sense." John's eyebrows pinched and he looked concerned. "I'm not sure how something like that would work," he said, "but I guess it's worth looking into." He was thinking now. "I can ask the underwriters for a list of losses for expensive art, for what? Let's say the past five years?"

"I guess. Whatever you think would be a representative sample."

"Yes. I think five years would do. Do you think I should limit it to paintings?" John asked.

"As apposed to what?"

"Other forms of art, like sculpture or . . . I don't know, other stuff."

"I think so, at least as far as our initial inquiry is concerned," I said. "I don't want to get too far a field here. All we know about right now is copied paintings. Let's stick with that."

John seemed excited now. "I think I can accomplish that. Yeah, I should be able to do that. This could be fun."

I smiled at John's enthusiasm. "Good. Is it any kind problem for you?"

"No, not at all. What are you thinking precisely?"

"I'm not certain, unless you find something to point us in a certain direction."

"I think I understand," John said. "I'll get on it soon as I have the time."

"Thanks buddy."

I knew John was busy so I shook his hand and said goodbye. I left somewhat relieved, since I was not sure I was doing the right thing, but John's agreement to help told me my idea was not that far out in left field.

Returning to the office, I mulled over the idea of calling Grace. I had spoken with her only once since the fire, and that avoidance was making me feel guilty. Since I had no good reason to prolong it further, I put in a call to her at her home. The way I figured it, if she was at the hospital, I wouldn't be bothering her. I got the service and left a message. I really wanted to check on her old man. I hoped he was getting better for a couple of reasons. I didn't want my rescue effort to have been for naught, and well . . . the guilt of that night for us together . . . well enough of that.

It had been a beautiful summer day, although hot, and the evening looked to be a winner.

Being a Monday, there were not a lot of people just hanging out around town enjoying the weather. Just us locals, so I decided to take advantage of the conditions and spend time out of doors. I forsook a large dinner for cheese, crackers, and a jar of pickled herring, while sitting on my deck. Of course I had to have something to drink to keep my fluids up, and scotch seemed to do the trick.

I liked to drink my scotch on the rocks. I never could drink it without ice like they did in Europe, but I didn't like to dilute it with water either. Drinking it this way caused me to sip it. It was better for me that way. I drank less.

When I was at work, I wore a suit. When I was at home, I wore any old grubs I had, as long as they were clean. Tonight I had on an old pair of jeans cut off short and a tee.

I was still out watching the boats cavort on the Bay when Grace called me back. It was about eight, and I was no longer feeling any pain when I grabbed the phone. I was excited to hear her voice. Right then she could have talked me into anything.

She sounded tired when she said. "I see you called earlier."

"Yes," I replied hesitantly. I wasn't sure how this conversation would go. "I really didn't want to bother you, Grace. I know you've had a lot on your plate, but nobody I've talked with seems to know how your husband's doing. I was just wondering."

"Thanks for asking. He's coming along slowly. His burns are healing, and his lungs are getting better slowly."

"Is he conscious?"

"Yes, but groggy. He initially had suffered from bleeding on the brain, so they cracked open his skull to relieve the pressure. That seems to have done the trick, and he's improving. I'm hoping he can move out of intensive care soon."

"That's good news, Gracie. Are you getting any sleep?"

"Some. With wanting to spend time at the hospital and trying to control the children, it's been a battle."

"What's up with the kids?"

"I think they're acting out because of this. They're worried sick and don't know what to do to help, so . . . you know kids."

"Yeah," I said, though I didn't know kids.

"Can he be seen? I mean, could I get in to see him?"

"He's still in ICU, only family, but I could probably get you in. Why?"

"I don't know. I feel connected somehow."

"Oh, look, Mike, I'm sorry I haven't called you before now. I wanted to thank you for saving Marshall, but . . . but after the way I acted at your place, I was too ashamed to call. I'm really, really sorry."

She started to cry, and I wanted to hold her in my arms and make it better.

"Look, Gracie, stop it. You didn't cause this to happen, and I'm more at fault for that night than you. You worrying yourself to death isn't going to make anything any better for you or Marshall."

She sniffled. "I'm sorry, Mike. This is why I didn't want to call you. I was afraid I wouldn't hold it together and look at me."

I wished I could look at her just now, but instead said, "Well, calm yourself now, and tell me if there's anything I can do to help with the kids."

"Gee, thanks, Mike, but I don't think so. They'll be all right and my sister's helping me out. Neighbors have been great, and the church too. I've got so much food here I could open a deli."

I could imagine her smile after that statement. Her voice seemed to show it. Grace seemed to be in better control of her emotions, so I asked, "Weren't the kids at home the night of the accident?"

"Yes, why?"

"Just that I had heard that no one could reach you to tell you what had happened at the store."

"Oh, you mean earlier in the evening. They weren't home then. Andy was working at his busing job at Fletchers and didn't get home until after eleven. Allie was on a date, and she was home about midnight. Someone had called to let me know, and the service had picked it up. Nobody checked for messages."

"You either?"

"No."

"I wanted to press her on where she was that night, but I was afraid of the answer. Instead I asked. "Have you heard what started the fire?"

"No. No one's spoken with me about it."

"That seems strange. They know it was your husband's business, don't they?"

"Yes. A policeman stopped by the hospital and was asking me questions, so they know that."

"What did the police want?"

"Oh, just who owned the store, and who was working that night, and where I was, where the kids were. Did I know you?"

"What?" I exclaimed.

"What?" she repeated.

"He asked if you knew me?" I mumbled.

"Yes."

"Why do suppose he asked that?"

"Probably because you were hurt. Thought maybe I hadn't known, I guess. I don't know. Maybe wanted me to be able to thank you."

"Had you known?"

"Of course, right away, well right away the next morning. Oh, Mike, I'm so sorry you got involved and got hurt."

"Don't worry about it, honey. I'm perfectly all right. You worry about you and your family."

I decided to let Grace think that that had been the reason for the cop's visit, but now I was worried. He seemed to be pursuing this thing with a vengeance. I wondered what he knew.

"Listen, Grace. When you think the time is right, let me know, and I'll go in and say hi."

"Thanks, Mike." And we said good-bye.

I sat and mused, wondering what would happen next.

Chapter Twelve
Art Fraud

It was a dreary Tuesday afternoon when I received a call from John Brooks at my office. He let me know he had some results from his inquiry into the art theft question, and wanted to know if we could meet after work some night to discuss them. The implication was clear this project was taking up more of his time than he had planned, and he wanted to move it to after hours. For a moment, I regretted pushing him into this.

I couldn't blame him for wanting to meet with me after work, since I already had imposed on him for what, in the end, could turn out to be a complete waste of time. I was free the coming evening, and he said he had a small window, so we set the time. We agreed to meet at my place at six.

It was raining pretty hard when it was time for me to go home, and I had not come to work prepared, so Janet, once again coming to my rescue, drove me the two blocks to my place. I thanked her and rushed inside, getting only moderately wet. Disgusted with myself for my poor planning, I changed clothes, abandoning my suit and tie for slacks and a clean, but old, sweatshirt.

Then I turned off the air conditioner and cranked open several windows just enough to obtain some fresh air without letting in the rain. I also slid my patio door open about a foot, but placed a bath towel in front of the door to collect any moisture that might blow in. The humidity was high, but the rain had cooled things off to a comfortable temperature. I would take fresh air any day of the week over air conditioning.

Once back downstairs, I turned on all the living room and kitchen lights to overcome the dank and moody atmosphere created by conditions outside. I was a sun lover, and today's conditions might have put me in a foul mood, but for the anticipation of what John perhaps had obtained. I felt surprisingly cheery.

I had fixed myself a drink and was rustling together some snacks when the doorbell rang. Glancing at the kitchen clock, I noted it was a couple of minutes before six. I hustled up the stairs, not wanting to see John waiting long in the rain. When I opened the door, John was standing under a protective umbrella. I motioned him inside, and unburdened him of his raincoat, hanging it in the front closet along with his umbrella.

"Should I leave my shoes here?" John asked.

I scratched my head and said. "No, that's okay, John. You can't hurt my floors."

The wood floors in the living room and kitchen had a polyurethane finish, and I did not think a little dampness would hurt them. I brought John down into the living room where I had left the hors d'oeuvres.

"Brooksie, help yourself. Want to get rid of that jacket?"

Fresh air was wafting into the room from the open door. John looked that way and then shrugged.

"Thanks, Mike." He pulled off his sport coat and laid it over the back of the couch. Then he unbuttoned his shirtsleeves, rolling them up.

"These look good, Mike," he said reaching for a snack. "Thanks. I won't be getting any dinner tonight."

"Why's that?"

"I've got a meeting with a potential new client at seven," he said, as he seated himself in front of the food tray.

"Want a drink?" I asked.

"Just water, thanks. I don't want to smell of alcohol."

While I got the water, John had opened his case and laid some papers out on the coffee table adjacent to the food.

"I think maybe I've got what you're looking for," he said.

"That's great."

I sat next to him and glanced over at the first sheet, wondering what he had.

He picked up one sheet and said. "First let me explain what I did."

"Shoot."

"In this age of computers, I thought it would be easy to compile a list of insurance losses for works of art. However, I missed two things. First, there would have to be a program written on the computers for the companies that I represent to do the search and there isn't. Second, the whole art area is such a gamble that most primary insurers hedge their bets by laying off some of the risk."

"You mean by reinsuring?"

"Exactly," John said, as he shoved a cheese-covered cracker into his mouth.

"So that was a dead end, then?" I asked.

John wiped his fingers on a napkin as he swallowed. Then he continued, "Initially, yes, but then I had a go at the reinsurer. There I caught a break. Lloyds is the principal reinsurer to cover art. They are very good at it and know the risks well. They even have a department dedicated to the area, and they're right on top of any losses. They know more than the police do about art loss."

"Sounds impressive," I said, taking a sip of my drink. I rattled the ice and looked at the refreshing amber.

"It is," John continued. "I talked to a Julie Harris, who works at the New York Lloyds branch, and she told me she had been doing this work for nine years. She was very knowledgeable and helpful. So now we get to this paper." John held up a single sheet and waved it.

"I printed out everything Julie sent me," John instructed, "but used my discretion to X out those items I didn't deem relevant."

I nodded.

John turned the paper sideways and pointed to a five-line section that had a large red X in front of it. "See here, this first one I

X'ed out. Family in Naples, Florida. Adult kids came to visit, left the house and didn't arm the security system. Boom, three paintings vanish while they are gone to lunch. Six months later the paintings were recovered when the perps tried to fence them. Turns out the culprits were a couple of lawn service guys who wanted to make a quick buck. They had no clue what they were doing and got caught as soon as they came up for air. Art was recovered. It had been a crime of opportunity, just a bunch of One Time Charlies.

"Those kinds of things I left out, but you can look them over if you want."

"I appreciate you going through them," I said. "So no insurance was paid on the Naples thing?" I was trying to interpret what was obviously abbreviated wording on the printout.

"Nope. Claim got filed, but was being reviewed when the perps got caught.

"Okay then," John continued. "Say, these little rolls are good. What are they?"

"Cheese tortillas. Freezer to microwave in a minute and a half. Go easy though, lots of calories."

"Yuck, saboteur." John gave me a disgusted look and then continued. "As I was going to say, there are five instances on these printouts where expensive paintings were stolen and then later were ransomed back to the owner."

"Five? That seems like a lot," I ventured.

"Maybe, but these were over a span of six years, and that's throughout the whole country, so maybe it's not a lot. I don't know," John offered.

"Is that legal?" I asked.

"No, but sometimes these art aficionados are plenty attached to their treasures. They want them back. Paying money to retrieve them is quicker than waiting for the police."

I stood up and walked over to the glass patio doors that overlooked the lake. Rain pelted the glass, and I slid the door closed some. I stood looking while seeing nothing, as I reflected on the news John had brought. Then I turned and looked at him, asking, "Why is insurance involved? Did they pay out on the claim?"

"No," he replied, "but a claim was put in when the theft first happened. Then when a ransom was paid, the owner who had paid the ransom said nothing about ransom to either the police or insurance company. They simply said they had recovered their work and dropped their claim. But there was a file on the theft, even without an insurance payout."

"Could they have collected insurance on the ransom payout?" I asked.

"You mean to recover their money?"

"Yes."

"No. The company doesn't pay on that kind of claim. It's an exclusion on all valuable items policies. You either lose the painting and collect or retrieve it and don't collect. You can't have it both ways."

"But I thought you'd want to see these claims, anyway, because there's a pattern here," John said. "I didn't see it, but the Harris gal saw it and pointed it out to me. She just hadn't been able to know what to make of it, other than straight theft for ransom. The company hasn't pursued it because there was no loss for them in any of the cases.

"I thought I might talk this over with you, Mike, before I say anything about my suspicions to anyone else." Here John stood and paced back and forth, his hands behind his back. He looked serious.

"What?" I asked, intrigued.

"In light of the partial copying of the artwork we saw upstairs over the gallery, I'm inclined to this thought. In the case of the ransoms, what if the painting that was returned wasn't the original?"

I looked at John and realized this was something I had not considered. "Hey, you might just have something there, John. Do you suppose anyone authenticates the paintings when they're returned?"

"I don't know for sure. Since an insurance payout wasn't involved . . . Well, let me put it this way. Yes, the insurance company would have if there had been a loss payout, so they didn't. From what I could determine in these cases, no one did. Who would? The owner? Why would he ever think it wasn't his painting he was getting back?"

John was getting excited and was talking with his hands.

"So, everyone just assumed they got back their original art works?" I asked.

"Yes, looks that way. And you know, Mike, for all we know they did."

"But maybe they didn't," I suggested, now warming to the idea myself.

"That's what I'm thinking. See, sometimes there are marks on the backs of canvases that would distinguish it, or maybe the owner marked it someway. He gets it back, sees his mark and is satisfied. It's easy enough for the forger to duplicate those marks. The owners aren't art experts themselves. I'm sure real experts wouldn't have had the scam attempted on them.

"Again, if we hadn't seen the copy . . ." John mused.

"I agree." I nodded.

All of a sudden a gust of wind blew heavy rain onto my front windows. "I wonder if it's hailing?" I asked no one in particular. I absently took another sip of my scotch.

John didn't reply.

"What kind of money are we talking about here, John?"

"The ransom amounts were each in the area of two hundred grand. Another pattern."

"What were the paintings worth?" I asked.

"That's always difficult to tell until one is sold You know how art pricing works, but the best I can figure in talking to Julie is that in each case the item was valued at over one million."

"One mil each? Wow! That's a lot of hay," I offered. I stood thinking. "So it costs a few bucks to come up with a copy. They make two hundred K on the ransom and then sell the original painting to someone else for a big killing on the black market."

"That's the way I'm seeing it," John said. "Even if they get half the going price for the original, they still make just south of a million on each job, John said.

"I'm thinking just the opposite," I said.

"What?"

"I'm thinking the price would be over the market value. If the buyer wants the painting bad enough to have it stolen, he's going to pay whatever it takes to get it," I said.

John thought, rubbing his tongue on the inside of his cheek. "Maybe you're right, but in either case, there's a lot of money involved."

"Yes there is," I reflected. "And they'd have the intervening time after the theft until the return is made to copy the work."

"That's right. They wouldn't have to copy it from a picture, either," John answered. "They'd have the real thing."

"Yup, that's the reason for the delay in the ransom request."

"That's the way I figured it, Mike."

"But why would it work?" I asked. "Who would want to buy a painting no one but themselves could see?"

John jumped on that statement. "Oh, when I asked around, I was told there are a lot of collectors who would do it. They would keep the work in their private vault, and still be able to see it every day. That's all they cared about, knowing they had what no one else could have."

"You think?"

"Yes. That's what I'm told," John replied.

"We're talking big money here, then."

"You said it. Big money."

"So this could be all organized?" I said.

"Yes, no doubt," John said, obviously thinking. "This could be very big business. Could I get myself more water?"

"Here, let me," I said on my way to the kitchen.

When I returned with the water, I asked, "Pretty common knowledge on the ransoms that were paid, then?'

"What do you mean?" John asked.

"Well, for instance, the two hundred grand. Everyone knows about that?"

"No, the thing is that was pretty hush, hush. The company found out about it only on the third recovery. Prior to that, the owners simply said they recovered their paintings and made no mention of a payout."

"But the company found out?"

"Yes, on the third deal, and then they bird dogged it once it came to light. Twisted a few arms, got people talking and found out it had taken place on the previous two."

"That's it then."

John smiled. "No, there's more."

"More?"

"Yes." John picked up another sheet of paper and showed it to me. "There have been three instances in the last four years where claims have been paid for fire losses. Well, there have been a ton of fire losses, but three instances with million-plus-dollar art losses."

"So those fire losses actually were paid out?" I asked.

"Yes. Definite losses. Checked and studied and confirmed losses."

I didn't see the connection, and John waited for me to say something. I could see it on his face.

"What?" I asked.

"Don't you see?" John said. "This confirms what you suspected all along. That's what got this whole thing started. It's just the opposite of the fraud in the stolen paintings we just discussed. Here it's the owner who wants to collect the insurance, but doesn't want to lose the painting."

Suddenly it made sense to me. I had gotten so involved with the other scenario I had forgotten my original idea.

"Oh, I see. He gets a phony duplicate painting, and burns that phony one."

"Yup. Pays a fee for the phony, burns that one and hides his original. Collects the insurance, and splits with the crooks," John said.

My heart was pounding I was so excited. "So what do we do?" I asked.

"I don't know. We think we're right, but we have no proof. Do we turn in Adams and let the police follow up?"

Suddenly, this no longer was just a cerebral exercise. This could tear Grace's life apart. She could go to jail. Was I prepared for that?

"Let's think about this," I said. "If we go off half cocked, we might blow the whole thing."

"You're right, Mike. But we have to tell the insurance people of our suspicions."

"I know that, John, but let's make sure we get it right. All we have right now are those photos you took. The insurance company has all the information we do, and up to now they've been satisfied. Another day or two won't make any difference. Let's talk tomorrow, and then you can be a hero with the company." I needed time to think.

John gave me a queer look and then said, "Right. Look at the time. I've got to get to my meeting."

John stood, and then his expression changed. "Wait a minute, I just thought of something."

I stared at him and waited, while he organized his thoughts.

"If we're right, and the ransomed paintings are phonies like we think they are, then the insurance company is covering a worthless painting for millions of dollars in coverage."

I thought a minute and said, "You're right."

"Then, they have to be alerted to the possibility."

I mulled this over and replied, "Yup. Better tell the insurance company what we suspect, and let's hold off on contacting the police about the local angle until we think this through."

"Deal," John said.

He grabbed his sport jacket and put it on. As he was climbing the steps to the front door, he turned over his shoulder and said, "One more thing. I'm not sure it's relevant, but it's a strange one."

"What?" I asked, as I followed him up the stairs.

"There was an art theft at the Metropole in Chicago. It was discovered last year, and there was a large payout. A Rubens was found to be a phony."

"How the hell could that happen?" I asked.

John was putting on his coat. "Well, they know it was real when they bought it some time ago, but they were taking it down to clean it when they discovered it to be a fake. Somehow, someone had replaced the original with a fake."

"Wow. That would take some doing," I said.

"Yes. No amateurs there. I'll get back to you, Mike, once I've talked to the insurance company."

"Thanks."

I watched John dart across the street in the rain. His umbrella bounced as he hopped over a large puddle. Then it collapsed and disappeared into the car. The wind had eased, and the rain was a steady drizzle. This was exactly what we needed, but it was doing nothing for my mood.

As I tripped my way back downstairs, I realized that I now had a problem with going to the police.

Chapter Thirteen
Self-Analysis

After John Brooks left my place for his meeting, I bussed the snacks and dishes into the kitchen. After putting away the perishables, I considered another drink, but passed on that idea to return to my living room.

My head was spinning with the complexity of information John had passed along earlier. I certainly had a lot to consider, and for that I needed time. I was not one who made snap decisions. My best results came after I had chewed on an idea for a while. The difficulty of this situation would demand nothing less

I looked out at the soft, steady rain and decided to check the towel I had placed on the wood floor in front of the open patio door. It was damp so I decided to change it out. Earlier when it had been blowing harder, some rain had found its way through the screen and onto the floor even though the door was open only six inches. I wiped the floor dry and then tossed the damp towel on top of the dryer. With the storm passing, the moisture was more manageable. I slid the door open a few more inches to admit the smell of fresh ozone-laden air.

To the east the sky was the color of plum jam. Beneath the dark sky, cool rain was attacking warmer lake water, which caused mist to rise and merge with the falling precipitation. Mired in my surroundings I was feeling depressed, for even with all the lights on, my environment seemed gloomy. The rain had lessened now, but condensation on the outside of the windows from cooler inside air meeting the higher outside humidity diminished what little outside light there remained, all of which added to the sense of disquiet creeping over me.

I sat in a chair facing the lake, and softly rubbed my temples. It was all I could do to not injure my already sore fingers. My head was spinning with competing thoughts as I tried to deal with the abundance of new information conveyed to me by John. I realized I was losing control of the situation, for John was about to release previously secure information to the insurance company. Soon he would be pushing to involve the police. I wondered if I was ready for that.

I sighed and looked up through bleary eyes. Soon it would be sunset, and I no longer could blame the rain for the darkness in this room. It now was a question of whether the darkness came from the room or from within me? Maybe if I redecorated with lighter colors? Shit, maybe I should get a life and quit living in some dream world, as I had done the past few days.

I was physically and mentally fatigued, and tired of the dismal weather. I stood and moved away from the outdoor view, choosing to sit in a chair with my back to the window. As I glanced about the space, I admitted my error. It was not the rain or the decorating that had me down, it was my involvement with Grace that had done it. Was the saying the first step toward salvation is admitting to your situation? It worked here. I had done this to myself.

My collaboration with John, in what had begun as a relatively minor engagement, had inexplicably morphed into what was likely to become a major incident. I only had wanted to get an explanation for the thrice repeated copying of the Jimenez work found upstairs above the gallery. Somehow everything quickly had spiraled well beyond that point and totally out of my personal control.

The only part of the information I had managed to contain was the subject of the paintings being done here in Excelsior. I was beginning to understand now that very soon with the exposure resulting from John's inquiries, those local activities would now need to come to light.

My intended purpose in all of my actions had been to protect Grace. I had acted without even knowing if she had been involved in any way, shape or form. I slowly comprehended now that maybe I had better find the answer to that question and do it quickly. Meanwhile,

I needed to think through the level of my involvement in the whole mess and consider any potential liability on my part, since I had not been exactly forthright with information only I knew.

As I was working through this mental process, I noted also that the police might consider me to perhaps be involved in the injury to Marshall Adams. Since I knew that was not true, they would have to discount corroborating witness statements from both Steve and Cindy. I did not see that happening, so I believed I was okay on that point at least.

Then too there was the issue of the copied paintings found upstairs over the store. In order to cause any action against me for not reporting those, the police would have to bring a like action against both the building owner and the insurance adjuster. They both had seen the paintings at the same time as I had, and we all can claim we had no notion whatsoever that anything was wrong with what we had seen. I could say that as soon as I suspected something, I reported it. There was no way for the police to know when I first suspected something. That realization made me feel better.

Finally, and perhaps the most damaging knowledge for me, was that of having seen someone leaving the building just before I discovered the fire. Time certainly had played tricks with my memory. The more I had thought about the incident, the less convinced I was of what I actually had seen.

I felt I had seen someone. I do know that, and it certainly was not Harvey the Rabbit. Can I say the person emerged from the art store door? No, in all honesty I couldn't swear to that either. I had assumed they emerged from there because they suddenly appeared into my field of vision at about that location. But that could be because I had not been looking in that direction earlier, so they could have walked to that point from somewhere nearby before they caught my view. No, I could not swear to that point.

Okay then, what had that person looked like? Blondish was all I could comment on. That and the fact that they had not appeared to be tall. But they could have been stooped over trying to remain hidden as they wove between the cars. Then how tall would they have been?

I just did not know the answer. Build? No, too dark to determine that specifically. Clothes? I could not recall since I had not been interested enough until after the fact, when the fire and rescue had been accomplished. Add to that that I had been out of it until the next morning, and I did not know what I remembered. Perhaps I dreamed the whole thing?

Man or woman? I think woman. Why though I really could not say. More of a gut feeling I guess. I visualize an image moving more like a woman then a man. *Would that be valid testimony? I think not. Am I right to keep it quiet? I think so, at least for now.*

So with all the uncertainty why did I think it had been Gracie I saw? I could not recollect that the thought entered my mind at the time. The idea must have returned to me the next day upon further reflection. Why then? Medication induced recall? No, that's stupid. Maybe I was making an association of Gracie with her husband's accident. Perhaps. Subconsciously, did I think she wanted to do him harm, or had it been wishful thinking on my part to believe that idea because I wanted Gracie to become mine?

What exactly were my feelings for her? Did I really have any feelings for her? Damn right I did, but just what were they? There cannot be any future for us, at least not as long as she was married.

What about her husband? I think he was expected to recover. Would she divorce him? She had kids. Did I want kids?

Was Gracie the type of person to sneak around behind her husband's back? She did at least one night. Would I want her to continue? Yes, I would!

I cannot believe I was thinking that way.

Was I willing to throw everything away that I had worked for all these years for a lost love?

I sat thinking about that whole subject for a good long time and just chased my tail around and around.

Coming to a resolution on this subject matter was going to be very difficult.

Chapter Fourteen
Walker Alert

The hour had gotten quite late during my musings. I wanted to make a phone call, but wondered about the time. Since I was calling the Mountain Time Zone, I had an hour's grace. I took a chance.

Paul Johnson finally answered. "You sure stay up late," he said.

"You knew it was me?"

"I have caller I.D."

"To answer your question, I'm up late because I got involved in something, and I wanted your help."

"Is everything all right?"

"No," I answered. "Am I interrupting anything on your end?"

"No. I was just watching the ten o'clock news."

"Want to call me back?"

"No, go ahead. What's the problem?" Paul inquired. "If we get cut off, I'll call you back. There's a storm here on my end. Sometimes it wrecks havoc with the cell.

"No problem. Remember the Goya work you put me onto?"

"The pictures you sent me, yes."

"That whole thing may be a bigger deal than I initially had suspected." I walked from the kitchen where I had picked up the phone and settled into the living room. As I passed the patio door, I looked out at an inky night.

"You told me that the painting is going to be exhibited at the Walker in Minneapolis soon, right?"

"That's right."

"Is that common knowledge?" I asked.

"The Walker's running ads. It's their big fall promotion."

"No secret then."

"Hardly. What about it?" Paul inquired.

"Since I last talked to you, I've learned a lot about the world of art fraud. In fact, my contact in the insurance field is about to blow the lid on a major high end insurance scam for works of art."

"What's that all about?"

I went on to explain to Paul what we had learned about the art lefts and fire losses.

"This is more than speculation, then?" he asked.

"Pretty sure. We'll know shortly."

"What's that got to do with the Goya?"

"I wanted to give you background on what's going on in the shady underworld. We also found out that the Metropole Museum in Chicago recently found out a Rubens had been stolen from their gallery and replaced with a fake."

"I heard about that," Paul said.

"They knew the painting was the real thing when hung, but when they took it down to clean it, they found it was a fake."

"Actually," Paul interrupted. "There was a two-week period between when it was removed from display and when it went to the restoration department. Authorities feel that is when the exchange took place."

"I didn't know that. Do they know how it happened?" I asked.

"The suspicion is the copy was shipped in under a fake shipping order as some expected painting. Then someone on the inside hid the fake and later made the exchange. Since no one had published when the painting would be taken down for cleaning, the copy could have been inside the museum for weeks."

"So, you think the robbery was recent?"

"There's no way to say for sure, but that's the most likely explanation. It would've been a lot more difficult to exchange the two while the Rubens hung in the gallery."

"Makes sense."

"How does this tie in with the Goya?" Paul asked.

"I think the crooks are planning the same thing at the Walker."

"Making an exchange when the painting arrives. Hmmm . . . Do it while they're still crated up. Might just be possible."

"Could you alert the Walker?" I asked.

"Why don't you?"

"They'll listen to you before listening to me," I said.

"Maybe. I'll tell them to be on the lookout."

"Thanks, Paul."

We signed off for the night.

Now all I had to do was deal with Grace.

Chapter Fifteen
Taking the Plunge

When Wednesday morning dawned, I woke feeling more refreshed than I had in days. I showered, shaved, and got dressed with renewed energy. Going downstairs, I made myself a sack lunch for work—kippered snack sandwich on heavily buttered whole wheat bread, along with fruit. Then I poured myself a cup of freshly brewed coffee. It really hit the spot. I was well organized for a change.

Reflecting on my night, I realized I had slept better than I recently had, and I woke this morning with little of the accumulated overnight mucus I suffered from earlier in my recovery. Perhaps my lungs were getting back to normal. It was probably no secret why I was sleeping better if I didn't have to wake up numerous times coughing to clear my lungs.

My hands also felt pretty good. Although I still tried to shield them from the direct shower spray, when they did get hit, they barely hurt. The raw looking redness had pretty much disappeared, with only a few remaining crimson spots resembling cold sores. The elasticity of my skin also seems to have improved. Gripping things like a doorknob no longer was a problem.

The only troubling aspect of my night was the nightmare that woke me at about 2:00 a.m. Normally I might not remember dreams, but this one was so vivid I had lain awake for long minutes rehashing it.

Then, being awake, I thought I was hungry. I went down and made myself a sandwich. All I had in the fridge were some cooked brats, so I had one with spicy mustard. You can imagine how well I slept after that. It did give me plenty of time to rehash the dream, though.

The gist of the dream was that I had not tried to save Grace's husband, but rather had tried to kill him at the store. When I'd failed, I tried again at the hospital. It seemed so real I wondered if I was fey and was somehow predicting the future. Did I truly want him dead?

While I made myself a bowl of instant oatmeal, I thought about how I might ameliorate this whole awkward subject of Grace and myself. After considering a handful of options, I criticized myself for not manning up before now. Clinching my jaw I decided to take the initiative.

Before I lost my nerve, I called Grace on her cell. I didn't care if I was bothering her, I needed resolution. When she answered, I went right into my spiel. I was so nervous I think my voice broke.

"Listen Grace, I'm sorry to bother you, but I had to discuss something. You busy?"

"I'm making the kids their breakfast and then driving into the hospital to see Marshall. What's up with you this morning?"

"Is he still in I.C.U?"

"They're thinking of moving him today. The doctors will make a decision today."

"Doctors, like plural?"

"Yes, there's one for the concussion and brain stuff, and one for the burns."

"I see. Is Marshall awake?" I inquired.

"Kinda, sort of. He's been in a coma. Maybe you didn't know that."

That revelation surprised me. "No, I hadn't heard," I said scratching my head.

"Yes," she replied, "but then when he started to come around from that, they sedated him. He had swelling on the brain for a few days, and they wanted to keep him quiet."

"That makes sense," I offered, even though I had nary a clue on any of the medical stuff.

"He was groggy yesterday, but managed a few words. They didn't make much sense, but he was talking. I tell you, Mike, I was so happy I cried."

I began to tear up at her story. "That's great, Gracie. Maybe I could stop in after lunch and see him. I won't stay long. I know he needs his rest."

Did I want to see Marshall, or Grace?

She answered. "That'd be great, Mike. I haven't told Marshall yet you were the one who saved him, but maybe today. Heck, he probably doesn't even know what happened to him. He needs to meet you."

"So after lunch, maybe?"

"That should be fine. You carry your cell with you?"

"Yes."

"Give me your number. I'll call later and tell you where we are. Might save you some time."

"That'll be great."

I gave her my number. She repeated it while writing it down.

"Listen, I have to ask you something. Okay?"

"Sure," she replied.

I was really nervous now, and I began pacing back and forth in the living room. It's a good thing I was in my stocking feet or I would have made a terrible racket. "Now don't take it the wrong way," I squawked.

"Mike, you sound serious. Is this about us?"

"No, no. It's about officer Rehms. The local cop."

"That's the guy I spoke to," Grace said.

"Yes. I spoke to him, also. He's been going around talking to anyone and everyone trying to make a case for someone deliberately attacking your husband. That might be true, but I think he knows about our past."

"Of course he does. I told him."

"You did? Why?" I asked, startled.

"Why not? He asked if I knew you, and I told him we were sweethearts many years ago."

"No wonder he's been trying to pin this whole thing on me. That fact alone gives me a good motive to want Marshall out of the way. Shit!" I suddenly felt lightheaded.

"I don't believe it," Grace said, softly.

"What? You don't believe I want Marshall out of the way, or that our past gives me a motive that the cops want to pursue?" I was irritated, and it was showing in my voice. There was a pause, and I think Grace was thinking about how to answer. Now I regretted losing my cool.

Finally, she said. "Neither."

"Neither? Why not?"

"I don't know, it just seems silly for either."

"It's not though, sweetie. Not to the cops. They—at least Rehms—is dead serious about trying to pin this thing on someone, anyone."

"I hadn't thought."

"What did you tell him?" I asked.

"Just that we dated in high school."

"Did you tell him about last week?"

"Of course not. I'm not stupid. I didn't want that to come out in light of everything that's happened. You think I'm an idiot?" Her voiced had risen and taken on a scornful tone.

Sensing I had caused a problem, I said, "Gee, I'm sorry, Gracie. This whole thing has me bonkers. The cops have pressed me pretty hard. Of course you're not stupid. I'm the one who hasn't figured this whole thing out."

"I didn't know you were in trouble, Mike. I thought you were the hero of this story. Don't you have an alibi? I heard you were out with friends, and they helped with the rescue. How could you be involved?"

"Fortunately, yes. Rehms has been trying to find holes in my story, even though there aren't any to find."

Then I summoned the courage to mention the real reason for my call. "What about you, Grace?"

"What about me?"

"It's just that the cops'll go after anyone. Can you account for your evening to keep them happy and off your back?"

"I told them that when they came to the hospital."

I interrupted her. "They?"

"Yes, there were two of them, that Rehms guy and a woman. She didn't say much, and I don't remember her name."

"Bishop."

"Huh?"

"I think her name's Bishop."

"That's right, I remember now. I told them I had been out to dinner in Waconia with a couple of girlfriends. The girls dropped me off at home at about ten-thirty. I don't think I have anything to worry about, though I'm told they did call my girlfriends to ask about the timing. I didn't think much about it at the time, but I wondered about that."

"So you weren't anywhere near the gallery on that night?"

"Heavens no. I was dead tired when I got home. I didn't even stay awake to hear the kids come in. I very seldom wait up for them. Why are you asking?"

"I just was worried about you. I know how these bulldogs can be when they smell blood. I'm just glad you can prove you're in the clear."

I paused to see if I wanted to relate anything else. Then I said, "I'm heading to the office in a bit. I have my cell. Give me a ring when it's convenient. I'll try to make it in. You think he might be awake today?"

"I think maybe so, but how lucid I'm not sure."

"Well, thanks, Gracie. I'll talk to you later."

We hung up, and I poured myself another cup of java. I was so excited my hands were shaking. I was relieved about finding out Grace had an alibi, and I felt so good I couldn't begin to describe my feelings. That put her in the clear. I shook my head and then slammed my fist onto the counter. I admonished myself for not finding it out earlier. Why hadn't I? Because I was so certain she *had* been at the gallery.

I put myself through hell for nothing. I couldn't believe how stupid I'd been.

If not Grace, then who? That wasn't for me to worry about or discover, and I decided I could put myself in the clear by telling what I knew to the police. Now, I just had to figure a way to explain to them how I just happened to remember the fact one week after the event.

Chapter Sixteen
Amended Story

Overnight the hot July weather moderated with the aid of a strong northwest breeze. Humidity levels also were lower than in the past week. Stepping outside, I noticed the difference right away. A cloudless morning sky was robin's-egg blue and glistened in its clarity. Later, as the sun rose higher, the temperature would climb, yet for my early morning walk to work, it had remained chilly.

Living and working in Excelsior made me wonder why I owned a car at all. I used it so little I have often surmised I could ditch it and get by with a taxi when I really needed to get somewhere. I was glad I did not drive more, though. I hated to think what my waistline might look like if I didn't walk as much as I did.

Once at the office and settled into my routine, I phoned the Southshore Public Safety office, asking for Officer Rehms. He was on patrol, but I was told he'd return my call shortly. I asked for him instead of Officer Bishop because I knew he likely would give me the most grief, and if I got my story past him, I felt I'd be in the clear. The last thing I needed was a charge of obstructing a police investigation.

It was not long before Rehms called me back. In response to his question, I told him I wanted to discuss the fire event with him, because I believed I could shed new light on what had taken place that fateful night. I wetted his appetite sufficiently, because he agreed to meet me at my office at about ten-thirty.

By the time Officer Rehms arrived, the temperature had warmed perceptively, and I suggested we drive to the Commons. I knew Janet was curious and I did not want to cause her any undue alarm by meeting at the office. I had told her it was merely a consultation to follow up on the fire rescue.

We parked his squad and walked out onto the grass of the park. Few people were about. We could talk freely. The officer checked in with his office, and we abandoned his car for a bench near the lake, facing the sun.

Notebook ready, Rehms asked. "Okay, what's so important?"

I heard the edge to his voice, and I knew I had my work cut out for me if I was to win him over. I had to be careful.

"I want to maybe clear some things up." I turned my head toward him as I spoke. "We didn't get off on a very good footing when we first talked. And you have to appreciate I wasn't feeling too well at the time."

Rehms did not say anything in response, he merely stared at me with a grim expression.

I didn't back down. "Okay, here's the thing," I said. "When I said that the fire was hot and smoky, that was the truth. Imagine for a minute, if you will, being trapped in a hole with a smoky fire about to burn you, and then think what your emotions might be like."

"Do we need to go there?" he asked. "We've been over all that already."

"Yes, I know, but I believe we do," I responded tersely. "I think the background is important for you to understand my story. You know, the context in which everything happened, but you need to understand things from the perspective of how I felt after the fact. That greatly influenced me and my view of things. This way is important to me."

Officer Rehms shrugged and gave me a stern look, but said nothing more. When he didn't argue, I continued. "So then once I had escaped that trauma, I passed out and was sent to the hospital. By the time I actually had a chance to reflect on what had taken place that night, it already was the next day. A person can mix things up or forget things in that amount of time, especially as traumatized as I was."

"I'm not sure what you're getting at. Let's cut to the chase," Rehms interrupted. "You went through a lot, but why are we here?"

It was clear he was impatient, but I was just as determined to do this my way. I had put a lot of thought into my presentation, and I knew my story had to be properly sold.

"I'm getting there," I scolded, "but this is important. You're going to want to know all this later so I figured I'd start with it. Sorta keep it in sequence so it's more easily understood from my point of view."

He sighed disgustedly, "All right. Go ahead."

I shifted slightly on the bench so I was turned toward the officer. "The bottom line is I've had a tough time of it since the fire. Nearly dying and rescuing someone who may yet die has done nothing for my mental stability. I haven't exactly been thinking very clearly since the fire, and quite frankly, I've avoided thinking about it whenever possible."

I was laying it on pretty thick, but that is what I had planned to do. "My headaches are just now subsiding, my lungs feel like someone reached down my throat and tried to pull them out, and I haven't slept well nights. To top that off I've been confused about what actually took place that night."

Rehms now looked interested for the first time. "Go on. Confused about what?"

"I've been having nightmares." Here I paused because a speedboat was passing by close to shore, its motor shaking the environment, and I did not want to shout. My throat probably could not handle it, anyway. When the noise had abated, I said. "As I was saying, I've been having restless dreams about the fire, wondering if I could have done something different, or if I should have gotten involved at all."

"So? The bottom line is you did do it."

I nodded, not wanting to be sidetracked. "Well, last night I had an entirely different dream. It helped me remember what took place in the parking lot before the fire. The three of us had left the pub like I had previously related to you. We were out in the parking lot when I turned and saw a figure up near the buildings."

Rehms looked up from his notebook. From the look on his face, I realized I had him.

"Thing is, I couldn't identify who the person was. It was dark back there against the blackened structures, and I was standing maybe a hundred feet away. Then too, the person wasn't posing for a picture, if you get my drift. They were moving and moving pretty quickly."

I paused to collect my thoughts and make sure I was not leaving anything out.

Rehms was eager now. "Go on," he admonished.

"There isn't a lot more to tell. When I saw the person, they were near the back door of the gallery. Then they quickly moved behind parked cars and out of sight."

"Were there many cars?"

"Not that many, but they were scattered here and there, and you know there isn't a lot of security lighting back there."

"I noticed that. Do you have a description of the person?"

"Not much of one. Light hair, maybe blond, but in that light . . ." I shrugged.

"Short, long?" he asked.

"Oh, I see. Short, but like a woman's haircut. You know, neck length. Not short like yours."

"What else?" Rehms asked.

"Not much. As I think about it, they were dressed in something like jeans, and maybe a dark shirt. Walked sort of bent over, like they were trying to be invisible."

Rehms had an incredulous look on his face.

"But I had the impression it was a woman," I added quickly.

"How can you say that?" he said scratching his head.

"A woman walks differently than a man. You get used to seeing that over the years. You just know." I shrugged.

Rehms nodded in agreement.

"The thing is, I don't know for sure the person came out of the gallery door. It could have been the restaurant behind us for all I know and merely had been walking to their car along the buildings. I just happened to see them at the back of the gallery."

"But you saw them there and what? That's what led you to go there?"

"Yes. As I told you before, I saw something that led me to that door. At the time I wasn't concentrating on what it was. I merely was intrigued, and I think that's what led me to investigate. If I'd had a little more to drink, maybe I'd have ignored the whole thing. I wish I had."

"But you didn't think about a person then?'

"I must have been blocking it out mentally speaking, because I didn't remember what it had been. Now I know. Now I remember."

"So, perhaps you saw a blondish woman coming out of the building and then drift away. You never saw her again when you were approaching or got close to the building?"

"She'd disappeared by then. She could've ducked down behind a car, but after I pulled on that door and smelled smoke, I forgot about her. I wasn't really looking for her, it was the door that intrigued me."

"Why the door?"

"It had a sign that said Adams Gallery. I had just visited it earlier in the week, and I was intrigued as to what had led me there. Without thinking I just reached out and tried the door. When it opened, well . . ."

Rehms did not immediately respond. He sat thinking. "This could be the person who started the fire," he finally said.

"That's what I was thinking. I want you to know I've given this a lot of thought. I didn't want to go off half-cocked. I see two scenarios. First, the fire is accidental, and Adams happens upon it and goes down to the basement to put it out. Maybe he becomes overcome with smoke as he tries to leave. He collapses on the stairs, falls and hits his head. That would account for all his injuries.

"I had postulated the same thing," Rehms said.

"Okay. Then second, someone tries to do him in and starts the fire to cover the murder. Since the Fire Marshall says the fire was deliberate, I lean toward number two."

Rehms didn't comment on my analysis, but he didn't have to. Number two it was.

"Of course, this merely could be the result of your dream," he stated.

"Yes, but I don't think so. It's too vivid. I think it's recovered memory now that I'm getting better."

"But you can't identify the person?"

"No, I don't think so. Not unless I saw them in similar circumstances."

"Okay, we'll get on it. I'll get this typed up and e-mail it over to you to read over. If I get it right, I'll formalize it, and you can sign the statement."

"Does this mean it was attempted murder?"

He hesitated, but then said. "Sure looks that way."

"I hate to get involved, but I suppose you have to look into the Adams guy now and see who had it in for him."

"That's the normal avenue," he answered.

We got up and walked across the grass to where we had parked. We weren't hugging one another, but the previous animosity seemed to have evaporated.

My revelation could bring a load of crap down on Marshall, but I figured Grace was out of it. That was my main concern. I did not give a shit about her husband, and now I was concealing nothing. There could be no blowback onto me in the future no matter where this ended up.

Rehms dropped me off at my office. One more thing had been accomplished. Now I needed to ask Grace about the paintings and see if she had any knowledge of what was taking place above the gallery.

Chapter Seventeen
A Bump in the Road

The weather was sunny, a complement to my mood. Things were beginning to fall into place, and my life was beginning to return to normal. Now, I merely had to clear my head about the mysterious paintings, and sort things in my mind about my relationship with Grace.

It was close to eleven-thirty when I received the call from Grace that I had hoped for.

"Grace, thanks for calling. Is everything on track?"

"Concerning Marshall, no. There's been a delay."

I thought about my work schedule and realized I could go to the hospital later than I had planned. "You mean as far as moving him?"

"That's right. They're not going to move him today."

I was disappointed at that information since I had counted on seeing Marshall, as well as Grace. There were things I wanted to discuss with her.

"Oh," was all I could manage.

"You see, the doctor wants to do a scan today to make sure there's no more bleeding on the brain. If that turns out all right, he can be moved."

"He's coming along okay then?"

"Pretty much. He's rousing out of his induced coma now that they stopped those drugs—"

"Wait a minute," I interrupted. "What's this about a coma? I didn't know about that."

"You knew he had a head injury. I thought I told you about the coma."

"You probably did, but I didn't remember. I guess I wasn't tracking too well. I knew he cut his head. I remember that. And you said something about relieving pressure. I guess I just zoned out on that one thing, he had so much wrong with him." I was rambling and stopped talking.

"I guess maybe I never mentioned it," Grace answered.

"No, no, that's okay. You've had a lot on your mind. Do you have time to explain?"

"Sure. See, Marshall had a fractured skull and the scalp laceration, but it turns out he also had a hematoma . . . bleeding on the brain. They had to open him up to relieve the pressure and stop the bleeding. They're pretty sure that's okay now, but just want to make sure."

"I'm sorry. I didn't know it was that bad. I was more concerned with the burns. How are they?"

"Coming along as expected is what I'm told. His feet are okay since he was wearing shoes. His ankles are the worst. He was wearing those damned synthetic socks he liked, and those melted onto his skin."

"What!"

"I guess synthetics don't really burn, they sort of melt. Then too, there's not much loose skin on one's ankles so that'll be a problem. He may need some grafting. His legs are healing nicely. He has you to thank for that. One of the nurses told me if the fire had burned a few more seconds it would have been really bad."

"It's hard to say he's lucky, but I guess he is," I offered.

"Well, in this case, that's true. And the broken wrist is minor compared to the rest."

I didn't even bother to comment that I'd known nothing of a broken wrist. Instead, I said, "Maybe I still could come in and see him."

"Not today, Mike. They'll be running tests and who knows at what time. I've got the kids here with me. We figured since he was coming around, they'd say hi. I'm not sure he realized we were there. Maybe he was and just couldn't acknowledge us. Anyway, I'm going to leave shortly and take the kids home."

"I bet this whole thing has been hard on them."

"That's for sure, but you know teenagers, they're resilient."

There was a pause in the conversation, and then I said, "Listen Grace, I wanted to talk to you about a couple of things. They concern the gallery, and then the insurance guy wants to talk to you also. I had told him not to bug you, but can you call him this afternoon?'

"Sure, Mike. Give me his number."

I did.

"If you have time. Then give me a jingle. It shouldn't take long."

"I'll call, Mike, when I can. Now I'd better run."

"Just one more thing, Grace. I really would like to come in and see Marshall when I can. I don't know, it's funny, but since I rescued him and all, I need some closure. I need to see he's all right. I don't know if you can understand that?"

"No, I can't, but that's okay, Mike. You can come in. Probably tomorrow."

"Thanks, Grace. Talk to you later."

I hung up and sighed. Marshall had a lot more problems than I had known. But he was coming along, so that was good. I needed to find out what Grace knew about this Ray Singer that no one could seem to find and see if she could shed light on those damn paintings.

Chapter Eighteen
Face to Face

I walked home to eat lunch, just to get out of the office, and to kill some time. I carried my lunch bag with me. Now that I knew I might be talking to Grace later, I was like a little kid at Christmas—the waiting was too much.

Wearing my suit coat on the walk also had been too much. The wind had switched to the southwest, and the sun beat down onto my back, the coat trapping the radiated heat. I squirmed a little to move my shirt against my skin to gain some relief. Then I yielded convention to comfort and took my coat off, carrying it over my shoulder.

The light breeze against my damp shirt felt a lot better. As I neared the lake, I saw very few ripples to disturb the water's surface. Later, as the day heated up, I knew that was likely to change. The weather service was predicting rain for this evening, possibly thunderstorms if the atmosphere got charged enough. That usually brought plenty of wind along with the moisture.

While still at the office, I had called John Brooks to tell him to expect a call from Grace. I related to him my concern for her and understanding, he promised he'd go easy on her. We had agreed I'd ask Grace about the paintings and John would confine his questions to things relating to his getting the building back into operational shape.

As it turned out, Grace appeared to be in the clear as far as her husband's injuries were concerned, and if she also was clear on the duplicated paintings, I decided it is my duty to inform the police of the whole situation. They then could decide if they wanted to pursue it. Maybe it was not even a matter for the locals. Maybe the F.B.I. would get involved.

Those thoughts got me home, where I kicked around for a bit, not feeling especially hungry. Finally, I opened a beer and ate my sandwich. I sat out on the deck and enjoyed the lazy summer day. My mind was active, however, with thoughts of where Grace and I were headed once her husband had recovered. Those thoughts occupied me on my walk back to the office. So engrossed was I that one obvious visitor to town asked me if I was lost. I must have looked the part.

Once back at the office, I dug right in to my workload, stopping periodically to check the time. The wall clock became my focus, and it seemed to have stopped, as it moved ever so slowly over that long afternoon. Finally, at about three o'clock, Grace called my cell.

I saw her number on the face and eagerly answered. "Grace."

"Hi, Mike. Listen, I'm coming over to Excelsior to meet with a John Brooks from the insurance company at the store at about five. Could I stop in at your office say about four-thirty, instead of doing whatever over the phone?"

"Yes, that'd work fine." I was ecstatic at the change of plans.

"Is that enough time?" Grace inquired.

"Plenty."

"Okay, I'll see you then. Oh, wait. I need to copy some stuff for John. Could I make a couple of copies at your place?"

"Sure, no problem."

"Thanks, or I guess I could do it at the library. I don't want to impose," she said.

"Not a problem, Grace. Bring it in."

"I don't need anything for our visit, do I?"

"Nothing but your pretty face."

"Bye, Mike."

"Bye, Grace."

The afternoon continued to drag, but four-thirty finally came. Shortly thereafter, Grace entered the office, and I went out to greet her. I barely recognized her. Although her hair was combed, it lacked that special something beautiful women take care to do just right. Looking at her, I noted the fatigue in her eyes, which appeared lifeless and dull. There was no smile, and her face was drawn and pale. Grace seemed somehow diminished.

I stepped forward and gave her a hug, not holding too long or too hard. Then, I tried to put up a pleasant façade, although I was troubled by what I observed. I couldn't believe such a drastic change could take place with a person in such a short time.

I quickly composed myself and said, "Hi, Grace, thanks for taking the time to stop in."

"That's okay, Mike. I need a break from reality."

So now I was a break from reality.

I introduced Grace to Janet and then said. "Come into my office." I showed her the way. "Won't you sit," I said, managing to keep my voice even.

Grace was looking over my small office, which housed a desk, credenza, visitor chairs, and a series of file cabinets.

I motioned Grace to a chair near the glass partition and I took the one adjacent and facing her. Our knees nearly touched. I leaned slightly forward.

Grace placed some papers on the small table in front of us.

"Is that what you need copied?" I inquired.

"Yes."

"How many copies?"

"Just one."

"Let me get that started." I walked the papers to the outer office and asked Janet to copy them.

When I had seated myself, I asked. "How are the kids doing? You have a boy and a girl, right?"

"Yes. Tyler's the oldest. He's sixteen. Lauren is fifteen. Well, almost."

"Are they handling this thing with their father okay?"

"It's hard, Mike. They're at an awkward age, and Marshall isn't their natural father. We've been married only two years."

Grace was looking down at her hands while she spoke. Her fingers were busy touching the other hand for something to do. Obviously this conversation was disquieting to her, and she was nervous.

I was surprised, and confused at the two-year marriage. I tried to fathom where the children had come from. "I don't understand," I confessed. "You were married previously?"

Grace began her explanation in a monotone. "I went to North Carolina University on the swim scholarship, but left after one year. I met Todd during his last year, while still a freshman. He was graduating. I left school so we could get married.

"Todd had an engineering degree and went to work for an oil company. We moved around a lot, but stayed mostly in the south, places like Texas and Louisiana. I had the two children, and we were living in Houston when Todd was killed in an off-shore well blowout in the Gulf. It was a very bad time for me, and I cried on Marshall's shoulder. Marshall was a friend of Todd's. I glommed onto him for security, and we eventually got married."

"So there's that whole stepfather, teen thing going on?'

"Right. Marshall isn't a touchy, feely kind of guy with the kids, and I think that's working okay, because they'd resent him trying to take their father's place. But, you see, that complicates things here with his injury and all.

"This brush with death has really affected them. They now are once again reliving losing their dad and are feeling a little guilty for not having accepted their stepdad," she related.

Grace stopped and there was silence.

Then, I said, "Makes sense. You seem to have it analyzed pretty well. Would you like something to drink? Water, or coffee?"

"Water would be nice."

I stood and went into the outer office where I retrieved a glass of water for Grace and a cup of coffee for myself. I brought back her paperwork as well.

After returning, I said, "I'm real sorry about your first husband, and now to have this happen . . . you should have asked for some help."

"My sister's here, and I can't impose on anyone else. Besides, there's nothing anyone can do that isn't being done."

"Maybe we could help with the gallery," I offered.

"Yes, I don't know what is going to happen there. Ray seems to have disappeared. I guess I'll have to dig through the records and see what's what."

"You haven't been involved in the running of the business, then? I mean on a day-to-day basis?"

"No, not in the least. I have no clue as to how anything is set up. I'll have to find that out."

"I can help you go through things if you want."

"Thanks, Mike. Let's see how Marshall's feeling tomorrow, and maybe he can give us a head start. Then you may have to. I don't even know what to look for."

"That makes sense. We'll start with Marshall," I said. "Say, on a related note, I saw a painting in the gallery by a painter named Jimenez, a southwestern landscape. Are you familiar with that one?"

Grace shook her head.

"The reason I asked is that upstairs in the apartment there were three exact copies of it. The insurance people and I were trying to figure out why."

Grace's expression had not changed. She either was a very good actress or knew nothing about the copies.

"So, do you have any idea about those?" I continued.

She shook her head. "No, nothing. Why do you ask?"

I hesitated and then decided to jump right in. "The word on the street is that there's some forging going on of artwork. Before I alert the police on this as a possible link, I wanted to talk to you first."

"I see. No, I can't help you. There must be an innocent explanation for it. We can ask Marshall. See if he knows."

"That seems fair. Maybe I can stop in at the hospital tomorrow and see how he's feeling."

"Sure. I'll let you know when he's moved, and if he's awake."

"Fine, that'll work. Probably morning?"

"Probably," Grace answered.

Then I switched gears. "Does Marshall paint?"

"Some, why?"

"I wondered how he got into this business."

"Oh. He was an art student in school. Tried his hand at painting, oils, water colors whatever, but never excelled. Finally, he decided he had to work for a living and make painting a hobby. He got work in galleries. That's what he was doing when Todd and I met him."

"Working in a gallery."

"Yes."

"So how'd you guys end up in Excelsior?"

"Funny deal. Marshall was approached by someone who wanted to open a place here. He was hired to manage the business, and given an opportunity to gain an equity piece in the business. I grew up here, so it seemed like an opportunity of a lifetime."

"Yes, amazing how that worked out. Do you know much about that Singer fellow who was working there?"

"Marshall hired him. Apparently, he came highly recommended."

"Do you know if he paints?" I asked.

Grace shook her head. "I'd have no idea. Why are you asking?"

I hesitated, and then said. "Someone painted those copies and also was in the process of copying an old master that soon will go on display at the Walker in Minneapolis. I'm trying to figure out who did it."

"Are you accusing Marshall?"

"I'm not accusing anyone. I'll have to turn the info over to the cops before the insurance company does to keep my skirts clean. Then I'm out of it. I was just curious as to who did the work."

Grace thought. "Was it good work?"

"Superior from what I'm told."

"Then it wouldn't be Marshall. He was just good enough to attract attention, but not good enough to get anywhere. Even copying something, he'd fail."

That news, if true, was a relief. "Then maybe it was the Singer guy?" I offered.

"Maybe."

Grace looked at her watch. I'd better get over there."

"Can I walk you?"

"Not necessary, Mike. I'll drive."

"Okay. What should we do about tomorrow?"

"Why don't you plan on coming in? I'll call you in the morning about nineish and give you directions. They're digging up Washington Avenue for the light rail, and it's a mess. I'll tell you where to park and stuff. Okay?'

"Sounds good. Thanks, Grace."

"No, thank you, Mike."

I walked her to the door. When she had gotten into her car, Janet asked. "That the girlfriend?"

I gave her a dirty look, but answered, "Yes."

Then I sat in my office and dissected the whole gallery deal. Things were beginning to fall into place. Someone approached Marshall with an offer he could not refuse, found out where Grace was from and opened a store there to clinch the deal. The store was a front for an art scam. That might be putting it simply, but I'd lay odds that was what had happened. Now that things were going bad on the deal, I wondered what would happen next?

Chapter Nineteen
A Surprise

I didn't have long to wait to have my question answered. It wasn't ten minutes after Grace had left before my cell rang.

"Mike, can you come over here. Everything's gone."

"Is that you, Grace?"

"Yes."

"You're where, at the store?"

"Right. Everything's been moved out. What does it mean, Mike?"

"I don't know, Grace. I'll pop over."

I hurried across the parking lot, and through the alley. While I hustled, my mind played a series of scenarios of what could have happened, none of which made sense. Then I jogged between cars to get across the street over to the gallery.

The building's front door was closed, but unlocked, and I walked right in. Immediately I was slapped in the face with the pungent odor of wet charcoal, that residual smell of fire still present, and the smell kindled a memory for me that shook me momentarily. Scenes from that fateful night overwhelmed my conscious self, and then just as quickly departed, leaving me standing just inside the open door, shaken.

I still felt hot under the collar and reached for the wall for support. Removing a handkerchief, I wiped my brow. If there had been a nearby chair, I may have sat. Then just as quickly, I felt better and the moment had passed.

Thankfully, no one had been there to see my moment of weakness, and I quickly had recovered, looking about the abandoned interior. The area was empty of all objets d'art. Backdrops and display pedestals were present, but that was it. The place had a whole different look with the primary objects removed. It made me appreciate what the world might be like absent art.

A bell over the door had tinkled upon my entry, which must have alerted John and Grace, because they appeared from the rear office. Grace didn't look any better than she had previously in my office, and John, as well, seemed on edge.

"Everything is gone, then?" I asked, as I swung my arm in an exaggerated arc around the room.

"Everything of value," John replied.

Grace was holding onto John's arm and looked small.

Any sign of forced entry?" I asked.

"None that we've seen so far," John answered. "There's only the two doors."

I turned toward Grace and asked. "Grace, do you have any idea who owns the art work that was displayed here?"

She looked at me with a blank look, and then as waking from a dream, raised her head slightly and shook it.

"What are you thinking?" John said.

"If these works were owned by someone and merely consigned to the store, might that person or persons have picked them up for cleaning or safekeeping or whatever?"

No one immediately replied.

Then John said. "Why not? Seems like a logical explanation to me. I wonder, though, how they got in?" He scratched his head.

I thought about the possibilities as I strolled about the front of the store, fingering a nail here and a wire there. Then, I asked. "Grace, what's the relationship with this Singer fellow? Might he have a key?"

"I certainly would think so, after all he did open and close the store. He'd have had to, right?"

"Seems so," I said. "Unless someone has robbed the place, the art has been removed for safekeeping. Just to make sure, Grace, I think you should report it to the police. Also when you talk to them, ask them who they have listed as contacts in case of emergency. They might have Ray's phone number."

Grace gave me a forlorn look. What I was saying seemed to go right over her head. I looked at John. "Listen John, You own the building and have an interest in what's going on here. Why don't you take the burden off Grace and make the call. I think they'll listen to you.

"In the meantime, Grace, why don't you go home and rest? John and I'll see if we can find anything in the paperwork here that'll help."

I sneezed just then from the odor in the room and took out a handkerchief and rubbed it back and forth across my nose.

"Would you do that for me?" Grace asked. "I don't think I could do anything at this point. I'm at the end of my rope."

Grace looked like she was about to cry. I put my arm around her shoulders. "Where's your car?"

"Out front."

I walked her through the front door and released my grip when we reached the sidewalk.

Grace looked up at me. "Thanks, Mike."

Her eyes filled with tears. I took my index finger and wiped one swipe under each eye. Despite how ragged she looked and all the turmoil about us right now, I still felt a sexual longing for her at this very moment. I ignored it. "Get some rest and don't forget to call me in the morning. I want to come in and see Marshall."

"Okay."

I turned and walked back into the store.

"You have your keys, John?"

"Yup."

"Lock the front door. I don't want curiosity seekers coming in."

John complied.

Then we set about rummaging through the office, looking for anything of value. The computer was a no go, because we didn't know the password, and it hadn't been conveniently left for us in many of the places I carelessly kept mine.

While we were searching through papers, I updated John on my recent activities. "So, I'm going to tell the police about the paintings we found upstairs, and what you and I feel is their significance."

"Might that get Grace and her husband into trouble?" he asked.

"Might affect him, but it can't be helped. I don't see how Grace can be involved. If I don't tell the police and they find out later that we knew, it could be construed as we were withholding evidence. What I intend to say is that you found out about the fraud shortly after we saw the paintings and that's when we decided there may be a link. Thus, it's our duty to say something."

"Sounds good. I'll confirm that story if asked."

"You probably will be. Just keep it simple. Remember, there was nothing to know until Lloyds told us their information. Before that they were just paintings."

"True."

We went through every desk drawer and every file drawer. "There's nothing here, John."

"Looks to me like the place has been cleaned out," he moaned.

"I think so too. No paper trail. Why? This might just confirm our suspicions about a link to the fraud, because if it was only a matter of moving the art for safekeeping, why the secrecy and housecleaning?"

"I don't like to speculate, Mike, but it might just say something else."

"What?"

"Let's just suppose Marshall's fall wasn't an accident." John paused and looked at me.

"Go on," I said.

"Maybe someone was trying to get rid of him?"

I was startled by his accusation, and said. "But why?"

"He knows too much," John answered.

I relayed my recent thoughts. "I've been thinking along the lines that someone set Marshall up in business as a front for this fraud we've uncovered," I said. "If someone wants Marshall out of the way, it may be because he's not involved in the illegal stuff that's been happening, and now they're getting rid of him as a loose end."

"I see where that logic fits," John answered. "If you're correct with your assumptions about the Goya, the Minneapolis operation will be complete when the painting at the Walker's stolen. Then they move on to the next job. No need to be here."

I rubbed my chin as I thought about what John inferred. "So, what you're saying is they don't need this place anymore, and when Marshall didn't die, they decided to cut bait and scram."

"I think so," John answered. Then he pointed to the two back rooms, which had not been disturbed. "Why didn't they take the prints and local works?"

"Maybe it's not worth enough and can't be sold elsewhere."

"Makes sense," John said. "So, I'll follow up with the cops. What are you going to do?"

"Tomorrow, I'll try to see Marshall in the hospital. If he's conscious, I'll see if he can shed some light on all of this."

"You think he might confess?"

"With what he's been through, maybe yes."

"Okay then, Mike. Let's touch base after you see Marshall, and maybe I'll know something from the police."

"Night, buddy."

"Bye."

John let me out of the store, and I went home. I thought that maybe I was close to seeing the light at the end of the tunnel.

Chapter Twenty

A Hospital Trip

I spent a restless night dreaming of circumstances related to the past few days' activities. It seemed like the hundredth time I had rehashed those events, but there was nothing I could do to purge the thoughts from my overworked mind.

When I awakened at 4:00 a.m. to use the bathroom, I was up and knew it was pointless to try to go back to sleep. I was too agitated. Today was going to be a big day for me, and I eagerly anticipated it.

Still dark, only the glow of a single streetlight glowed outside my front window. I walked to the door, pulled open the blinds, and gazed outside at the early morning quiet. A solitary car, its headlights splitting the night, rolled slowly down the block. I momentarily stood there wondering where that poor soul was headed this early in the day. Could that be why I was awake? I doubted it.

I carefully rotated my neck and worked my jaw, listening to the crack of the joint. I wasn't feeling rested, and after going back to the bathroom and looking in the mirror, my image confirmed the fact. My eyelids were heavy, my jaw slack, and I felt limp all over, devoid of energy. But I decided to stay up. After slapping my face with cold water, I went down to start some coffee, making a full pot. There was barely enough grounds for that. I needed a run to the store. Most mornings I held off having that first cup until after I reached the office. Today was different. Today I needed it. I knew I would be wired before six.

After my second cup, I returned upstairs to the bathroom to brush my teeth, shower and shave. I had the time so I trimmed my mustache. Checking out my work, I saw no gray hairs yet, though a few were creeping into my sideburns. *Maybe I will touch those up sometime.* My hazel eyes seemed more alive now than they had earlier when I first crawled out of the sack. I checked my nails and decided they could use a trim. I postulated I wasn't that bad looking for a guy beginning to go to seed. I needed to work on that.

Then, having completed all this, I had nothing further to do but wait around for Grace's call. That would not come anytime soon. I didn't expect to hear from her before nine. I briefly considered driving to town early to await her call there, but saw little point. Traffic would be tough the earlier I went. Besides, Marshall would need to be moved to his new room before I could visit. Grace had made that point clear.

I normally paid all my bills with auto pay, but I still had some filing to catch up on, so I worked on that awhile. Then I turned on the TV to catch the early morning news, followed by the baseball scores from last night. Subsequently, I listened to a reporter as he enumerated the hopes and dreams of the Vikings, as they prepared for preseason camp. Expectations were always highest at this time of year. I was not paying close attention.

By then, the coffee had combined with my anticipation of coming events to make me jittery. There was no denying today was going to be a big day. I had hashed over my relationship with Grace so many times in the past few days all my thoughts were in a jumble. Maybe today would bring me some clarity and closure.

I didn't deny my feelings for the woman, but obviously I was conflicted about those feelings due to her marriage status. That was as clear-cut as it was going to get. The situation with Marshall had me confounded. I didn't know the guy and yet felt some sort of kinship with the man. Was that because he was married to Grace, or because I had saved his life? Was I now responsible for him as some cultures believed?

Regardless of the cause, I had this overriding need to see him and make a connection. I needed to talk to him, see who he was, what he was about. Today would be the day for that. I just hope I wasn't let down when it was over. I had anticipated this for so long perhaps nothing could live up to the expectation.

Then I had a new thought. Since I'd been too weak-willed to solve the issue of Grace and me by decisively cutting her out of my life, perhaps I was looking to Marshall to do it for me. Maybe meeting him would terminate my longing for Grace. Shit, was I that weak? I was drowning. I expected a severely injured man to throw me a lifeline? Life sure can throw a guy curve balls just when things were going well. I never dreamed things could be this difficult. The summer had begun with such promise.

Finally, when the call came from Grace, I nearly had worn myself out with anxiety. I eagerly answered her call. "Grace, how are you this morning?"

"Tired, but functioning. I think we finally are seeing some progress. How are you, Mike?"

"Thrilled to be coming in to see you and Marshall."

"About that, Mike. I'm not sure what you're after, but maybe it's not a good idea."

"Why not," I moaned. I suddenly felt like I had when I was young and my mother had said no to me. *Why not, Mom?*

Grace continued. "The thing is, Mike, Marshall isn't all that alert. He may not even know you're there."

"Doesn't matter, Grace. To be totally selfish about this, it's more for me to be there and see him than it is for him. I have to see him, Grace, even though I have nothing to offer him. This is for me. I need to touch him, need to see that he's all right. I have to know my sacrifice isn't in vain. I don't know if you can understand what I'm saying here, but this really is important to me, Grace. It's something I have to do."

There was a pause where Grace said nothing. I was bereft of ideas. My emotions were spent. I waited. "But do you need to do it today?" she whined.

"Why not? I'm not sick. I won't contaminate him. I think I have this coming to me, Grace, after what I've done and what I've suffered."

I hated to play the victim card, but I was willing to do so to get what I wanted. I couldn't let myself be disappointed again after so much expectation. What was this woman's problem. Hadn't she seen what I'd gone through for them? She owed me.

Grace paused, as if thinking out her next response. "I guess you do have this coming to you, Mike. Sure, come on in. I just didn't want you to be disappointed, is all. Can you come now?"

"It works for me if it's all right on your end." My smile could have lit up the whole of Excelsior.

"I think it's okay. Marshall will be moved by the time you get here. The nurses are getting him ready now. The doctors have seen him and approved the move. The worst thing is you wait a couple of minutes. Okay?"

"Okay, no problem."

"Do you know where to go?" she asked.

"No."

"There's lots of construction by the hospital, on Washington Avenue. The light rail line."

"I remember."

"I'll give you the best place to go."

Grace told me the best ramp to use and a second one if that one was full. It sounded like a bit of a walk, but I was hail and hearty. Then she said she didn't know the new room number, so she instructed me to call her when I got at the hospital, and she would let me where to go.

I considered what to wear downtown. A suit wasn't necessary, but shorts might not be appropriate. I decided on khaki slacks with brown loafers. I chose a pinstriped button-down shirt, but declined to wear a tie.

An hour later, I had parked my car in a distant ramp, and was walking up Washington Avenue toward the hospital. What had been a peaceful day in Excelsior when I'd left home had now been replaced by the racket of road construction. Loud noise was cascading from several locations, and I wondered how anyone in the adjacent buildings could suffer the noise. I took out my cell when I was a little away from the loudest racket and dialed Grace.

"You here?" she asked.

"On Washington."

"I can tell from the noise," she responded. "Go in the main door on the cul du sac. Then take the west elevators. Room 462, Mike, west wing. Where are you now?"

"Getting closer."

"Okay, see you soon."

After negotiating the labyrinth that was the hospital, I found room 462. The door was closed so I knocked lightly and pushed it open. I had a short entryway that contained a two-door closet. The room I faced was about twelve feet square. It was painted a soft off-white, and a single fixture on the wall over the bed reflected light upward. The bed was perpendicular to me, with the patient's head to my left. Grace sat in a chair on the opposite side of the bed, holding her husband's hand.

A man that I would never have recognized, even had I known him, lay motionless. His head was wrapped in white bandages down to his dark eyebrows. Wisps of sideburns crept below the bandage. It looked like he was wearing a turban. Below that, his eyes were closed. His skin tone was insipid. He wore the typical hospital gownl. A sheet was tucked under his chin. Marshall's arms lay at his sides on top if the blankets. On one wrist, he wore an identification bracelet. On the near side of the bed, a metal pole with branched antlers stood guard, motionless like a Beefeater at the Tower. Multiple tubes ran from bags hung on the branches to the back of the patient's right hand. A plaster cast wrapped the left wrist.

A tent rose from the bottom of the bed above the man's feet. I assumed that was to keep sheets from rubbing against the unhealed burns.

I was glad the burns were hidden from view, since I needed no reminder of that fateful night's injuries. I looked down at the back of my hands and remembered the pain, which for me was almost gone. Marshall's pain had to be much greater. I shivered, and then the moment passed.

Grace, watching me, held a finger to her lips. She wore a blue dress with a scooped collar. A white sweater was over that and I could understand why. It seemed chilly in here. Pale blue studs adorned her ears and a silver choker necklace surrounded her neck. She looked better today. Maybe it was the expectation that Marshall's ordeal was coming to a close.

Grace squeezed her husband's hand and then released it as she stood and looked down on her mate. Then she touched her fingers of the left hand to her lips and touched Marshall's lips with the tips of her fingers. It was as if she was saying goodbye. He never moved.

Grace motioned me to follow. Together we walked out into the hallway.

Standing outside the door, Grace sighed, and asked. "Any trouble getting here, Mike?"

"A little. Not too much. Tell me what's going on."

"Like what?"

"I don't know. Does he just lie there?"

She laughed. "What did you expect, a vaudeville routine?"

I blushed. "I meant . . ."

"I know what you meant. I'm just being silly. I don't get a chance to do that much lately."

I nodded.

Then she said. "See, that's what I tried to tell you. He's not very active. They moved him, and that was really stressful, tired him a lot. So he'll probably sleep for a while. Maybe if we take a break and come back, he'll be more alert."

"Is he talking much? I mean when he's awake?"

"No, but he understands and tries, he's just too weak still."

"There's not a problem with his brain?"

"No." She hesitated. "No, I don't think so. Just really weak."

I reflected a moment. "He must be getting better, though, since they decided to move him."

"Yes. Let's go down the hall to the lounge and talk. I don't feel like standing here."

"Sure, Grace."

We walked past the nursing station and a little further down the hall toward the lounge. Just before we reached our destination, Grace said, "Oops. Forgot my purse. Get me a cup of coffee, will you? I'll be back in a jiffy."

By the time I had poured two coffees, Grace was returning down the hallway. There we sat each with a cup of weak brew. The room was not large, about ten-foot square, and it had only six chairs. But it did have a bank of three windows and we chose two chairs in front of those. We sat next to one another and sipped.

I asked. "How are the burns coming along?"

"I told you about the ankles, right?"

"Yes."

"Other than that, really good."

"The broken wrist is minor, I suppose."

"Compared to everything else, yes," she answered.

Looking out the window, I noted that it was beginning to cloud over, being somewhat darker than when I had walked to the hospital. I turned back and studied Grace's face. She had taken the time to fix her makeup and hair, which I considered a good sign. She was dealing with life. Despite that, she didn't smile and her shoulders sagged. For her the ordeal wasn't quite over.

I asked. "What about his head, then?"

"The bleeding stopped. That's very good news. They took out the drain yesterday. They'll fix his scalp next week. He may be home soon."

"That is good news," I answered, and I meant it.

Grace didn't talk. We sat quietly. I wondered what it would mean with Marshall home and Grace ministering to him. That probably would cut it for us. Maybe that was for the best.

Chapter Twenty-One
Unexpected Trauma

I was anxious to get back into the room with Marshall, yet I knew I couldn't rush Grace. She understood the process much better than I did and didn't want us in there yet. If Marshall was tired from his move, he'd need time, but I really wanted to speak with him. Just sitting there looking at him wasn't going to get me anywhere. I sighed. I'd just have to wait. I had waited this long. I could wait a little longer.

I had to admit, though, I was enjoying time alone with Grace, so I was conflicted. The effect of our night in the sack was being minimized each passing day, and I had seen damn little of her since that night. Yes, I could sit here for quite some time.

Looking for something to say, I asked, "Have you had a chance to talk to John Brooks since yesterday?"

She stared at her cup and said, "Not yet."

"He and I have discussed your situation. I see some things you need to do right away, as soon as Marshall's alert. You might want to make a decision on reopening or giving up the lease."

"Maybe next week. Will that be okay?"

"Sure, that's plenty good."

We chatted a few more minutes. Then I said, "I need to use the little boys room."

"Down the corridor and to the right."

Hospitals always are busy places. Someone was always going somewhere on a mission. It was so common, one seldom noticed anyone. They all just blended in. A few minutes later, I exited the men's room and was disoriented. Had I come from the left or the right?

As I looked up and down, trying to get my bearings, I noticed a woman dressed in jeans and a sweatshirt. She had short, dirty-blonde hair and looked eerily familiar. She was walking away from me, but my eyes were drawn to her. It was a walk I had seen before. I knew that for sure. I followed.

The woman's pace was brisk, which blended in with everyone else. Upon reaching a room that appeared her destination, she didn't hesitate but pushed the door open and strode right on in. I hesitated a few feet from the door, then noticed the room number. It was 462. Was my mind playing tricks or was that Marshall's room?

What the hell was this? Curiosity overtook me, and I walked to the door. Cocking my head to one side so my ear was near the door, I listened. I could hear nothing. That in itself wasn't strange. We had left Marshall asleep.

The woman hadn't been dressed like medical personnel. I had seen this person before, but where? Then it hit me, and I panicked. My heart began to race, and my breathing quickened.

I looked around for help, but no one was nearby. Tentatively, I pushed at the door, and it slowly responded. A rustling came from within, but I couldn't yet see anything. I chose to enter further, and when I peeked around the corner, I was horrified.

The mystery woman had a pillow and was holding it in the air above the bed. It took a moment for this to register, since it was so unexpected. She was so intent at what she was about, she had not heard my entry. She lowered the pillow to the side of the bed.

I shook off my inertia and sprang forward without thinking. The unidentified woman was on the near side of the bed next to the I.V. pole. It took me only three quick steps to reach her.

She turned. I blocked her exit. Without formulating a plan, I reached out my right hand and took a handful of her short hair. Stepping back with my right foot, I wrenched her away from the bed with a hard pull. My arm had the motion of a golf back swing, and the woman came sailing past me. I released my hold and she slid along the floor only to crash into the wall near the foot of the bed.

The woman was not that heavy, and my action was effortless. On the way past me, her foot had caught the I.V. pole and that came hurtling to the floor after her, striking me in the leg. If our activities were unnoticed up until now, we soon would have an audience.

What had happened so far had come so easy, that I had become overconfident. I was about to say something to the intruder when her quick recovery shut me up. I expected my victim to lie where she fell, but she was far tougher than that. She quickly jumped to her feet and howled at me. It startled me momentarily, and I was not ready for her next move.

She lashed out at me with her left foot, catching me in the right ribcage. I gave out a yelp of pain and my hand went to my ribs. I stumbled sideways and tripped over the fallen I.V. pole, nearly tumbling to the floor.

That was when my assailant took advantage. She moved in close with catlike quickness. Grabbing my shirtfront, she kneed me in the groin in one quick motion. I had tried to turn aside, but she was so fast, I did not know what had happened. I doubled over in pain.

As I attempted to right myself, she shot a forearm to my chin so hard it nearly took my head off. That's when I knew I was in way over my head, but it was too late now to quit. I nearly was done, but realized I was in a fight for my life. I had no background for this other than sports training. When we had wanted to quit then, coach had called us pussies. That motivated us then, and it helped me now.

I was not about to go easily to this waif of a woman. I did what any fighter in trouble does. I clinched. I had a weight and height advantage so when she attacked, I managed to parry her blow and grab her in a bear hug. Her arms were still free and she began to pummel me on the side of the head. I squeezed with everything I had even as my vision blurred. The blows softened, and I saw some hope.

Just then I heard. "Mike, what are you doing? Stop it."

It could only be Grace. She grabbed at my right arm and began pulling, while screaming, and crying. "Mike, what are you doing?" she screamed again.

Grace pulled so hard on my arm that my grip loosened. Just then, my attacker took advantage and laid a vicious head butt to the front of my head. I staggered backward and released my grip. As I hit the wall, my quarry wiggled free, just before I slithered down the wall and to the floor.

My brain was not functioning, and everything seemed foggy. Suddenly, I became terrified. My mind cleared enough to realize that Grace was unprotected in the room with this maniac. I couldn't get off the canvass. My heart was racing, I was gasping for breath and I felt like I had just been knocked down for the count. I managed to turn my head to look toward the door just as the woman turned the corner to flee.

"Safe," I murmured.

My adversary took but one step to leave before running into a nurse who had rushed into the room to investigate the turmoil. The nurse took a forearm to the chest and went sliding into the room and across the floor on her butt.

The mystery woman had exited in a flash, but no sooner had she disappeared, then several hospital staff members began rushing in. When the first of the relief help arrived, the nurse who had been manhandled groaned as she tried to stand. The staff member went to her aid, asking her what had happened.

"Marshall," I gasped.

A man, dressed in blue, whom I had not seen enter the room came over to me and stooped down. "Are you hurt?"

I wanted to laugh. He should be able to see that. Who was he, the local plumber?

"Marshall," I croaked before coughing hard.

Tears filled my eyes, and I groaned in pain from my ribs. I pulled my knees up to my chest and that felt better.

"Marshall, your name is Marshall?" the man inquired.

"No, that's my husband," Grace interjected, as she knelt beside me.

I recognized her voice, but couldn't see her. The sound was coming in my left ear. My eyes were glazed, and I felt very tired. The room was fading into a deep gray. Just a small pinpoint of light remained before me.

I heard the exchange.

"This is your husband?"

"No, the man in bed is."

"Then, who is this?"

"A friend."

"Do you know what happened to him?" the man asked.

I couldn't hang on any longer. "Marshall . . . breathing." The words came with difficulty.

And then it was dark.

Chapter Twenty-Two
Another Hospital Stay

I woke from a troubling dream without remembering what it had been about. Squeezing my eyes shut, I concentrated, but to no avail. I'd lost it. That was okay. What did I care? It couldn't have been that important.

I lay there with eyes wide open, seeing nothing but hazy gray. Far-off muted sound reached my ears, but I was unable to discern the source. My senses were awake now, and I smelled something foreign. I knew the smell, but it didn't belong in my bedroom. It was antiseptic. My stomach turned. I did not remember my bedroom smelling like that.

My brain seemed to be moving in slow motion. As a result, I wasn't processing properly. Then my eyes opened wide with surprise, as fear and shock simultaneously took hold. Where the hell was I?

I could feel moisture collect on my skin and heat radiate from my face. Fear did that. I needed to get control, analyze the situation. I let my eyes wander and concluded it must have been night since the room was dark, though not totally devoid of light. Brainpower at work.

When I tried turning my head to scan the room, pain radiated from the left side of my face. I quickly returned back to a neutral position and remained motionless. After willing the pain to regress, my head still hurt. So much for willpower. *Shit, what had happened to me? Why the pain?* Nothing was making sense.

I reached for my face with my right hand, but my arm barely would move. It felt as though it was strapped down. That wasn't good when you were claustrophobic. My heart began racing from panic. The blood pounded in my temples, and that hurt too. Tears formed in my eyes either from pain or fear, I wasn't sure which. I had to get my mind under control if I was going to control the pain. Where was I? Nothing made sense.

Be cool. Concentrate on finding where you are. I had the feeling I was safe, although this certainly wasn't my room in Excelsior, I could tell that much. For one thing, the walls were much too close to my bed. Even in this light I could see that. This was a smaller room. Hospital room? Maybe. That might explain things. I could begin to make out mottled shapes. Yet, I did not dare move my head again to explore further or my headache would attack. I learned that lesson well. Maybe I was not as dumb as I looked.

My throat felt dry. When I tried to swallow, it made me cough. That simple action hurt like hell both in my ribs and my head. Tears begin to form in earnest now, moistening my eyes. It'd be easy for me to feel sorry for myself, but I believed I had bigger worries.

Out of the corner of my left eye I could see a lighted panel of some kind, apparently on a stand. A monitor maybe? That seemed to be appropriate for a hospital room if that was where I was. My vision appeared to be blurry. I closed my left eye and looked with my right. That seemed okay. When I did the opposite side, it was blurry. *What the shit?* When I tried to raise my left arm to wipe at my eye, my ribs hurt. Christ, what had I done now? Out of my right eye I followed the tubes protruding from my hand, but was unable see where they went. I was determined not to move my head to find out.

I tried to take a deep breath. I couldn't do that either. I appeared to be wrapped in something. *Why does my side hurt when I breathe?*

The fog in my head cleared slightly. My memory began to return. Sore ribs. *Shit yes, I really took a pounding from that little shit. Now I remember.* I needed to take some self-defense training. I had been beaten by the proverbial ninety-eight-pound weakling. I clearly had underestimated my foe but surely never expected a confrontation in a hospital room.

Where was I then? I didn't remember driving anywhere, so I must still be at the U. I was in a hospital room at the U. Why? Am I hurt that bad? I didn't remember what happened after the fight. Could I have blacked out? I seem to be making a habit of that.

What was this? I moved my right hand as far as the restraint allowed. There was a tube in the back of my hand held in place by tape. A small tube led off from there to I didn't know where. That was right. I remembered now. I'd already seen that. My mind was going.

I.V. They have a god damned I.V. in me. How bad was I hurt? I remembered taking blows to the head. I wondered if I had a concussion? That was what Marshall had. Two peas in a pod. I wondered how he was doing? I began to laugh. It hurt, and I stopped.

Marshall probably went home, and here I was stuck in the hospital. I would never see him.

God, my head hurts. Headache, nothing worse. Maybe I should get up for some aspirin. Wait, I wasn't at home, I wouldn't be able to do that. No, I didn't think that was possible. *I will just lie here quietly.*

I began feeling weaker and extremely tired. My eyelids were heavy. Sleep, that was what I needed. *Yes, sleep.*

When I woke again, there was more daylight in the room. I could see objects with more clarity. There also was a nurse hovering over me. I had smelled her before opening my eyes. Was that what woke me? A lovely fragrance lingered over me.

"Who are you?" I asked, with a raspy voice.

"I'm a floor nurse, honey."

Honey, that's a laugh. "Could I get something to drink?"

"In a minute. First, I'm going to get your vitals."

I had my blood pressure, pulse, and temperature recorded. Then she removed my restraints and emptied my urine bag. Damn, another catheter.

"I'll get you some ice," the nurse said.

Can I get something for this headache? It feels like the top of my head's going to blow off."

The nurse checked the chart. "No, problem, the medication's been authorized."

It seemed a long time before she returned. I watched her enter the room. The woman had a round face, nicely proportioned. She was short, and overweight. I had often wondered with all the time on their feet, how could that happen? Pressure, I guess. *Causes them to eat too much.*

She had with her what I needed, a plastic cup with ice and a water pitcher. Handing me two pills she said, "These are Vicodin. They should take care of your headache."

I was provided a third of a cup of water with the pill. I greedily swallowed the medication.

"Don't drink too fast. We don't want it to come right back up," she admonished.

I didn't say anything to that.

Then I decided to ask, "Where am I?"

The nurse looked at me with an inquiring expression. "Why, in the University Hospital."

"What happened to me?"

She shook her head. "You should ask your doctor that."

Hell, I didn't even have a doctor. I just keep getting hauled off to this place or that place. I was meeting all kinds of doctors. What was she keeping from me?

"Someone from admissions will be up here shortly to file your paperwork," the nurse instructed.

"Fine." *My insurance company is going to love me.*

The nurse was about to leave. "Say, what day is this?"

"Monday."

Great, I'd be missing more work. Janet would kill me. At the moment I didn't care, I felt so crappy. Then I remembered Marshall. I wondered how he was doing. Maybe I could talk to him today. I wonder if our rooms were close?

The doctor, or resident doctor or whomever finally showed up. He looked like he was in high school.

"Well doc, how'm I doing?"

He looked at my chart without committing himself. Then he took out a flashlight and spent some time looking into my eyes, one at a time. Maybe he was searching for a brain. Good luck there.

"Mr. Connelly, you've suffered from a blackout caused by head trauma. It doesn't look like a concussion, but we have to be careful about that. Sometimes these things develop slowly. We'll have to keep an eye on you. Let us know if the headaches get worse, or if you have any dizzy spells. We'll give you a list of symptoms to watch out for when we discharge you."

Then he looked down at the chart. "It's a near thing with your left eye, though. Is your vision blurry in that eye?"

I closed my right eye and looked exclusively through the left. Nothing had changed. "Yes," I replied.

"We have to be careful we don't get bleeding in that eye, or you could loose your sight."

He went on to explain about blood pooling and a lot of medical mumbo jumbo. The result was that now I was worried. I started asking questions. I got answers but didn't feel much better about it. I'd have been better off not knowing. I may not even remember any of it.

"How long am I going to be in here?"

"I see no reason to keep you. You'll have to monitor that eye. Do you have an eye doctor?" ·

"No."

"I'll write you out an order to see a group associated with our hospital. Or you can see one of your own choosing."

"Thanks. When can I leave?"

"Just as soon as the paperwork gets done, maybe an hour or so. You'll need someone to pick you up."

"Sure, no problem."

"I suppose you'd like that catheter out now?" he asked.

"That'd be great."

I had thought he would do it, but instead a nurse showed up to do the dirty work. She embarrassed me by pulling down the sheets before putting on gloves.

"We just need to deflate the balloon on the inside and then it will come right out," she said. "You won't feel a thing," she lied.

She'd fibbed a little, but it wasn't that bad. Then, she removed the I.V. I felt whole again.

Shortly thereafter, someone came in with a food tray. Breakfast. I was not the least bit hungry, but I ate it anyway. I thought maybe that would settle my stomach. At least I hoped to keep it down.

While I waited for the breakfast tray to be removed, and for someone to process my paperwork, I had another visitor. At first glance this man did not appear to be a doctor. He was wearing a colorful sport jacket and a narrow dark tie. The two seemed at odds with one another. He carried with him a small bag, like a camera bag.

"Mr. Connelly?" the man said with a smile.

"Yes."

"I'm Bob Miller with the Minneapolis police."

Bob was a slight man, about six feet tall. He looked wiry, and because of my recent experience, I knew not to underestimate him. His oval face pinched in at the bottom, emphasizing his chin and small mouth. Sunken cheeks hinted at a recent weight loss. Dark hair emphasized his pale skin tone and was cut short except on top where it was sticking up ragged. It was groomed that way. He looked like maybe he had been ill.

He pulled out credentials and waved them in front of me. I grabbed his wrist and looked closely at them.

"Bad eye," I said. "Takes me a while to focus."

"You look like you took quite a beating."

"You should have seen the other guy," I retorted.

He laughed. His smile was pleasant, and his dark eyes shone with amusement. I liked his smile. I could use more of that right now.

"Mind if I sit down," he said as he pulled over a chair.

"No, go ahead, but move closer to the bottom of the bed. It hurts to move my head."

He complied.

I was unable to see him well, so I motored the bed into more of a sitting position. It helped.

"Mr. Connelly, I need to go over the events in room 462 yesterday. Do you feel up to it?"

Room 462, that was Marshall's room. I could remember some things. "I can manage," I said. I took another sip of water.

"Good. We would like to get a description of the person with whom you had the altercation."

"Didn't you get that from the others?"

"Yes, but from what I understand, those people were more transitory to the scene. Their views were, let's say, conflicting."

"Oh."

I couldn't imagine how that could be, but I'd give it my best.

Miller pulled out a tape recorder, started it and placed it on my service table.

"Just describe the person the best you can."

"Okay."

I raised my bed a little more so I was almost sitting up. It surprised me that my headache did not go off. The pills must be effective. I'd need to get some of that to take home.

"Let's see. It was a woman."

Miller nodded.

"She stood about five-six, built solid, thick waist. Not large breasts. Knows some level of martial arts. Tried them out on me."

Miller smiled, but motioned me to continue.

"She had dirty-colored blonde hair, cut pretty short, just below the ear." I motioned the height with my hands. "Kind of a ragged cut, you know sticking out all over."

Miller nodded.

"Wore contacts, probably colored."

"Why do you say that?" he asked.

"The color was too blue to be real. You know how contacts give off that little reflection?"

He pursed his lips and nodded. "Okay. Go on."

"Let's see. Oval to round face, long, thin nose, full lips. That's about all I can remember. Does that sound like what the others said?"

"You are much more thorough than what I had received from the other witnesses," he said, as he turned off his recorder.

"Mrs. Adams saw her. Her description must be similar to mine," I said.

"Not so much. However, she must have been under a lot of stress, so that probably explains it."

"Isn't there surveillance?'

"Yes."

"Can't you get her on that?"

"Once we know what we're looking for. That's where you come in. Now we can scan the discs and find the right person."

Then I remembered how I had entered the room. "Say, what was she doing there with Marshall?"

The detective hesitated and finally said, "Committing murder!"

Chapter Twenty-Three
Understanding the Facts

"Murder? Who?" Then it dawned on me. "You mean Marshall? Marshall's dead?" I exclaimed, incredulous. I couldn't believe it.

"You didn't know?" Miller asked.

"No."

My head was spinning, and I felt as though I might throw up. How could this have happened? No, this was just another one of my fantastic nightmares. What would happen to Grace?

"But I rescued him from the fire. He was getting better. What happened?" I pleaded.

Miller sat back down. "You really don't know? You were there."

I could see disbelief on his face. But then how could he have known the sequence of events that occurred during that short time frame in the hospital room. There only were three of us present, the victim, the murderer and myself, and now one of those was dead. Was I next?

Officer Miller waited patently, saying nothing. So I said, "I blacked out after the fight. We had the altercation, and I blacked out. I never even looked at Marshall. I didn't know."

I slouched back onto the pillows. Everything I had done, everything I had suffered had been for naught. He had died anyway. Maybe the Bedouin had it right. "So it be written, so it be done."

My breathing was coming fast and heavy. Miller let me quiet down and then said, "Perhaps you'd better tell me what happened in there. Take your time. This obviously is a shock."

"Could you pour me some water?" I asked.

While I drank, he took out his recorder and turned it back on.

Where to begin? I decided to begin all the way back at the fire. I went through all that had happened with the fire, the suspected art misdealing, and my hope to talk to Marshall about everything.

I explained my reason for being at the hospital that morning. I did not know if he could understand my motives or needs, but I really did not care at this point. Everything had turned to shit.

"Tell me about what happened in the room," Miller instructed.

"Remember the person I told you I saw coming out of the gallery?"

Miller nodded.

"Okay, after exiting the men's room, I saw a woman walking down the corridor. I thought she looked familiar, but I couldn't place her. For some unexplained reason I followed her, and was surprised when she entered Marshall's room, number 462. I think it had been something in the way she looked, or in the way she moved that reminded me of the person I had seen that night in Excelsior. At any rate, it was a subconscious recognition and subsequent urge that propelled me to follow her. I didn't consciously think about it."

I paused here and thought about that particular action. It was the same exact reaction that had caused me to act the night of the fire, and I got myself into trouble both times.

I took another sip of water. I really felt dehydrated, but did not want to drink too quickly.

Recovering somewhat I said, "She could have been anyone— a doctor, a friend, hospital staff, anyone." Here I again halted my story as I mentally formed a picture of what had happened next. Then I continued, "I paused before the door, hesitating a few precious seconds before entering the room, because I felt really foolish for doing what I was doing. Grace didn't want me bothering Marshall, and here I was about to enter the room on a whim. In fact, I nearly left at this point to go back to the lounge."

I paused again a moment and reflected on my feelings from yesterday morning. That seemed like so long ago. Miller watched me but said nothing. I took in a deep breath and my chest shuddered on the exhale. My emotions seemed about ready to run amuck. I took another drink and set down the glass. Bob Miller refilled it for me.

Then I began anew. "Where was I? Yes. When I did go in I did it slowly, and as I got past that little hallway and approached the bottom of the bed, the gal was standing over the bed, holding a pillow. Now that I think about it, I think she might have been turning to leave. But in the heat of the moment I reacted because I thought she was smothering Marshall. She hadn't heard me come in, and seemed surprised to see me."

I looked directly at Miller. "That's when she must have done it. I mean she must already have been done when I came in. It had to have been done real quick because I hadn't been that far behind her. If only I hadn't hesitated at the door."

"What do you mean?" Miller inquired.

"I mean if I had got in quicker, she wouldn't have had time to smother him."

Miller did not answer me. He said, "So, what happened then?"

I thought a little bit, wanting to get things right. It had happened so fast, I didn't have time to think about it then. "I think the woman made like she was going to shove past me, and for some reason I moved in front of her. That's what started the altercation. I'm trying to remember, but everything happened so fast . . . it's hard."

"Take your time."

"Okay. Like I said, we had the tussle."

"Which she apparently won?"

"Yes, by technical knockout. We struggled, and I never expected a fight. She acted like she was fighting for her life. When that realization hit me, I kicked it up a notch and fought for mine."

"But she got the upper hand."

"Well yes. Grace, Mrs. Adams, came in and thought . . . I don't know what she thought. She was screaming at me, and when she pulled on my arm, I lost my grip on the woman. I think that's where it ended. I really don't remember much after that."

"She grabbed your arm. To try to make you let go?"

"I guess. She probably thought I was hurting the woman."

"I see," Miller mused.

"What happened then?" I asked. "I mean after I blacked out."

"From what I've been able to piece together, after she got past you, the woman in question knocked down a nurse who had entered the room, and then pushed past other personnel responding to the racket, as she headed down the hallway. The nurse who was knocked down gave a vaguely similar description of the subject as yours, less the detail. Mrs. Adams must have been hysterical because her description was out in left field."

I thought back. "Yes, I remember she was acting quite strange. Screaming at me and all," I relayed.

"Anything else?" Miller asked.

"Not that I can think of."

Then I asked, "What exactly did happen to Marshall? You said something about murder. I didn't see anything like that, unless it happened after I was unconscious."

"I can't go into the details of the how just now. We'll need to investigate further. You say the woman you fought with was holding a pillow when you entered the room?"

I closed my eyes and tried to remember what I had seen. "Yes, that's right. I do remember that," I responded, nodding my head.

Moving my head started up my headache, so I put one hand to each temple and held it for a moment. Then I rested my head back onto the pillow and removed my hands. Officer Miller watched me.

"You okay to continue?"

"I'm good," I groaned.

"Well, it appears the victim was suffocated. There will be an autopsy for sure."

"And they couldn't revive him?" I asked.

"Apparently not," he answered.

"Will you be able to identify her?'

"The assailant? Hopefully. We have your description now, and we'll use the surveillance cameras to try and get a match. Hopefully we'll get something, if she's in the system."

After a few more questions, the police officer left. He had taken down all my particulars so that he or someone else could reach me later. Much later, I hoped.

Now all I wanted to do was get out of this place and back home. I had tried to do a good deed and where had that gotten me? I have had nothing but trouble since meeting Grace at the street dance. My luck had to change for the better now.

Chapter Twenty-Four
Back Home Again

Once my paperwork had been completed, and I was formally discharged from the hospital, I received the standard hospital advisory to not drive myself but to obtain a ride home. I chose to ignore that guidance since I had my car in a nearby ramp, and I was not about to abandon it there. I assured the sincere looking caregiver looking out for me that my ride was all arranged.

The young woman was more than perplexed when upon arriving outside I pushed myself out of the wheelchair and began walking down the street instead of climbing into a nearby automobile. I didn't care, and I never looked back. I was not about to impose on friends once again so soon after my last mishap. Besides, I knew I could handle this, maybe.

It was the walk to the parking ramp that woke me to the degree of my current disability and presented the most difficulty of the homeward journey. I still was feeling somewhat unsteady as I navigated along Washington Avenue, causing me to occasionally reach out to a lamppost or signpost for support. I took that as an indication I wasn't yet quite back to normal. I always had a knack for understatement.

While I waited at a light to cross a side street, I chuckled at my introspection. Back to normal. I wondered what that meant and if it would ever happen? After all I had been through recently, I had my doubts. Maybe this was the new normal. How could I tell?

Suddenly I had a flash of insight and checked my pants pocket to make sure I had my car key. Then I double-checked for my wallet.

I thought for a minute I might have lost those. Did I check in the hospital before leaving? I didn't remember. Boy, I was losing it. Perhaps I was not quite recovered yet. I felt damned tired. I probably should have gotten a ride. Well, too late now.

My gaze moved upward past the nearby buildings. Gray clouds mottled an overcast sky this morning and did nothing to shake me out of a disconsolate mood. What I needed was something to shake me up, but I was uncertain what that would be. Here was another one in a long list of items for my shrink. I tried to shake off my lethargy with the realization I needed to get home, get into my routine, and get some rest. That would fix me up.

Crossing the street, I worried that my car might have been towed since I wasn't aware of the parking ramp rules and restrictions. Was overnight parking even allowed? I'd soon find that out. I climbed the stairs to my garage level with fearful anticipation. Fortunately, the car was still parked where I'd left it. My only penalty was a huge parking fee. There was no discount for all night parking. I paid the hourly rate.

Once I was on the road, I took my time, wanting to make it home without incident. I encountered the most traffic while still was in the city. After exiting downtown, traffic in my direction moved along more easily.

Since my sortie into town yesterday morning, the weather had taken a turn for the worse. That realization caused me to laugh once again, since the current weather certainly was a reflection of my melancholy. I turned on the radio to check the forecast, as rain seemed imminent. While I fiddled with the dial, a rising wind buffeted my car, forcing me to grip the wheel tightly with my one hand. The car wove along in its lane as if it was losing its way. I quickly looked behind me for a police presence. None. I had to be more careful. I was not in the best of shape.

Alongside the highway right-of-way, tree limbs bent and swayed from a northwest gale. Rain spat against the glass hard enough to have been crystallized, though it was only water. My thought was that Lake Minnetonka must be churning from this torrent. Glancing at my dashboard, I read the car thermometer at sixty-seven degrees. I recollected it had felt chilly on my walk to the ramp, but at the time I had thought it was my current health condition. Apparently not.

Driving over the humpbacked bridge into Excelsior gave me a feeling of comfort and relief. My hometown looked good. This was the second time in two weeks I had returned from the hospital in less than stellar condition.

Sitting at the stop sign at the bottom of the hill, I watched the street gutter direct a swollen stream tumbling across the intersection. Good, this will raise the lake level.

My head was hurting now, along with the rest of my body. The drive apparently had been more than I should have endured. This was too much activity, too soon. That was why they told me to take it easy. *I see that now.* Why had I not listened? *I never listen.* It had been difficult to see clearly with the one good eye. I should not even be driving, since I had pretty much lost my depth perception. Oh, well, I was almost there. I just had to make one more block. I comprehended that perhaps I was getting too old for this. Now I understood the nurse's admonition to let myself be driven. Next time I'd listen. Next time?

After parking in my downstairs garage stall, I climbed the stairs to my place. The steps seemed steeper than they had in the past, while I pulled myself along with the handrail. When I entered my abode, it smelled musty. Little wonder. With the air conditioning set on eighty and the outside temperature in the sixties, there had been no fresh air coming inside for almost a day. The first thing I did was to slide the patio door wide open. The wind was coming from the other side of the building, but there was enough of a breeze to allow some fresh air to meander inside.

I remained standing before the open door with my shoulder against the doorjamb while looking out over the bay. Whitecaps skittered here and there tossing their spray at one another like a game of catch. A single boat bounced slowly from wave top to wave top sending a cascade of water along its hull. Rough ride out there today. It would not be a day for an outside lunch at the restaurants.

The boats being moored at our dock were faring better being at the lee shore. I should walk out to the dock and check my boat but did not have the energy. Maybe later, maybe not. After I had rested a minute, at least. Then I planned to go upstairs and open an upwind window. That would create a wind tunnel effect, and freshen the whole place quickly. Afterwards, I would go down and check the dock.

What do I want to do now? Entering the kitchen, I opened the refrigerator and perused my food stock. There was not a lot in there to chose from. I thought that maybe I should order a pizza? Pizza and beer. That sounded good. Were they open yet?

I looked at my watch and saw that it was close enough to lunch for them to be there. I picked up the phone and dialed the number from memory. I was told my order should be there in twenty-five minutes. That beat cooking. I removed a coupon from a kitchen drawer and then checked my wallet to see if I had the cash. I did, so that was taken care of. I plopped a twenty on top of the coupon.

There were only two cold beers in the refrigerator, so I went to the pantry and grabbed a six-pack, which I placed into the cold interior. Then I pulled out one of the cold ones. After popping the top, I took a long draught. Man did that taste good. Nothing like that first sip to get the full flavor before the taste buds got blunted. I stood in the kitchen and finished the first can. I had better go slower or soon I would be drinking warm beer.

With that thought in mind, I went back to the refrigerator and removed two cans from their cardboard holder. Then I placed them in the freezer. Those should be ready when I need them, I reasoned.

I was dead tired now, hardly able to keep my eyes open, but I did not want to go to bed. Not at this time of the day. I briefly wondered about going to work. I decided to make that decision after lunch. Besides, I had too much to do, plus I had food on the way. Maybe it was the pain medication doing this to me. My thoughts were all muddled. Had I driven home like this?

I decided I had better cut back on the pain stuff unless I was really hurting. Then I decided it might be a good idea to read the label. "Don't take with alcohol." Well, it sure was a little late for that. Better stick with the beer and stay off the pills. I threw the bottle into a kitchen junk drawer.

I had called Janet from the hospital before I left, and asked her to come over this afternoon with anything I needed to sign. I had not been sure at that time if I would feel well enough to go into the office, and I believe I made the right decision. Though I was not looking forward to her recriminations and mothering, I had to keep operations going. I was lucky to have her working for me. I'd better tell her that.

When I had called, Janet acted like she was beginning to expect me to get beat up once a week. What does that tell me about her expectations for me?

The message light on my landline was blinking and I figured I had better check my calls. There was a message from John Brooks and also one from Grace. I was curious about the one from John because he couldn't have known about my latest troubles. His message merely asked me to call, without giving any hint of what he wanted. Maybe it was about the insurance fraud.

I ignored the message from Grace, which had said she wanted to talk. I felt so lousy and my head was so mixed up, I decided I didn't need any more drama just now. I figured that perhaps was all I'd get from her. Besides, I couldn't think of anything we really needed to hash out. I had to recover before any discussion about our future took place.

I grabbed a second beer and called John while sitting on my deck looking out over Excelsior Bay. There's a remote for the doorbell located there so I was not particularly concerned about missing my meal. The rain had stopped for now, and I was somewhat protected from the wind, but an occasional gust whipped around the building and across the deck. It was a cold wind, and I felt uncomfortable, but I was too lazy to move. When the wind made it difficult for me to hear on my phone, I decided to move back inside. I was warmer.

After the usual small talk, I informed John of my most recent ordeal and what had happened to his former tenant.

"Wow. I can hardly believe what's been going on. It doesn't look like they'll be reopening the gallery any time soon," John speculated.

"No. That's an interesting line of thought though, John. Did someone sign a lease?"

"Yup, for one year with an option for two more."

I thought for a few seconds. "How did they sign? As an individual or a corporation?"

"I'll have to check. That was way last fall. I don't remember. Why?" John asked.

"I was just thinking that to protect yourself, you should give them, meaning whomever signed, a formal eviction notice, though I think the fire gives them an out if they choose to exercise it. Are they current on their rent?"

"Through the end of the month, they are."

"Okay, Mike. Thanks."

"Heard anything new on the suspected art fraud?" I asked.

"I haven't checked lately, but it's been a while now, so maybe I'll hear soon. I'm kind of curious myself about what's happening with that." John paused and then continued. "Say, Mike, I hope I'm not off base here, but that first time with Marshall . . . that actually might have been attempted murder, then?"

I sighed as I thought back to the night of the fire. My thoughts were jumbled concerning the details. "I haven't had time to think about it, John," I answered. "It does seem logical though, doesn't it? I mean it would have to be proven, but in light of the repeat try yesterday, it sure looks like it could have been, doesn't it? Besides, that's what the cops were trying to push all along, weren't they?"

I was actually shocked to hear myself admit to the possibility. The concept was too troubling to comprehend.

"They were," John replied. "Do you think we have anything to worry about?" John asked with a level of concern in his voice.

That brought me back to the moment. I answered. "You mean you and me? Like us being suspects in the murder?"

"No. I mean with everything that's been going on, might someone be out to get us, as well?"

My foggy brain jerked to alert, and I reflected for a moment. "God, I hope not. I couldn't take much more physical abuse. We'll have to think about that. I'm not sure, John. Can you see any direct connection to us?"

"I don't know for sure. I don't think so, Mike, but I am the landlord, and you did rescue Marshall from the fire."

"True. But, John, you're not involved in any of their business ventures, nor am I. All I did was rescue him from the fire. Yes I screwed up someone's plans, but if they're crazy enough to be after me for that . . ."

"I guess not," John said. " I hope you're right. I have a family."

I considered John's statement a moment. His circumstances certainly were different from mine. I said, "Again, I don't see any connection, John. Marshall apparently was the target. I don't know the why of that, but even though I thought the first time could have been an accident, the second certainly wasn't."

There was a pause and then John said, "You said he was killed right in the hospital room?"

"Yes."

"With everyone around and everything?"

"I guess. I must have walked in just after she did it." I was sitting in a comfortable chair looking out the door. My eyelids were drooping.

"How? I mean was it messy?" John asked.

I coaxed my brain into motion, and explained what exactly I thought had happened.

"Right then," John answered. "Nobody's safe anywhere, are they?"

I sighed. "It . . . it doesn't look that way."

"Hey, thanks, buddy. Hope you're feeling better. Talk to you soon. Wait! One more thing. Is there anything I can do for you? Do you need groceries or anything? Are you going to be laid up for a while?"

"Thanks, John, but I'm good, though I really appreciate your offer. But before you go, John, let me ask you what led you to believe that the first attempt on Marshall was murder or attempted murder to be more precise? I mean before the second attempt at the hospital."

After a short pause, he answered. "You know, I think it was what the cop said when he was asking all his questions, and then the determination of arson by the fire marshal. It didn't make sense to me that a fire started by itself, and then Adams tried to put it out and fell almost to his death.

"To me that seemed too contrived. Then when it was determined the fire was set intentionally . . . well you see what I mean?"

"I think so," I answered.

"Someone started it on purpose. I mean, I didn't see Marshall starting it and then trying to put it out. It made more sense to me that somebody conked him on the head and then started the fire to cover it.

"The fire guys told me you had to have gotten in there almost immediately after the fire started, or it would have gone torch city. I think that's why Rehms suspected you for a bit until your friend Steve backed you up with your story. Hell, you must have been in there not more than ten, fifteen minutes tops after the fire started. Otherwise Adams was toast."

John was rambling a bit, but I saw his point. I mused, "Very well put, John. I really hadn't thought about it that exact way. I think you're right, though. They tried once that night and when that failed, they tried again. The big questions are why, and of course who?"

"To keep him quiet maybe?" John answered.

"How do you come up with that?" I asked.

"I just thought of this. It all comes down to the timeline. You said no one could see him in Intensive Care, right?"

"Correct. Just his wife and family. Plus you said he was unconscious the whole time prior to being moved, right?"

"Right."

"Okay. So the very first day he's out in the general ward, and able to speak from what you told me, they nail him. Couldn't wait. They were trying to keep him quiet. It's too much of a coincidence to be anything other than that."

I thought about what John was saying. "There's logic in that," I answered. "But, again why, and how did they know he was being moved, and how did they know he'd been unconscious up until that time?" I stopped to catch my breath.

"I don't know, Mike. It's got to be involved with this art stuff we uncovered," John answered. "I'm not sure how or why, but I think that's the connection." John paused, and I waited to see if he had any other ideas. Then he said, "I think what clinches it is the fact that right after Adams gets conked and the fire's started, the paintings disappear."

"But why wouldn't they take the paintings first?" I asked. "They didn't disappear for a couple of days."

That seemed to stump John.

I continued. "I mean, if the fire had burned as intended, they might have lost those counterfeits. That doesn't make sense."

"No, I guess not," John, answered thoughtfully.

Neither of us said anything for a bit. We both must have been thinking. Then I said, "Let's see if we can figure out that connection."

"Maybe I'll learn something from the insurance company that'll help us," John, said.

"Maybe. Okay, thanks then, John."

"Take care of yourself, Mike."

When I disconnected, I thought about everything John had said. It appeared that while I had been thinking totally about how everything was affecting Grace, John has been operating in the real world dealing with real facts. I'd better get my head on straight and do the same.

I got distracted by the arrival of my meal, a family-size meat lover's pizza. I thought about eating outside, but demurred. I got myself a fresh beer from the freezer and put its mate in the refrigerator. This one would have to be my last.

I had always found it amazing how much pizza I could eat in one sitting, usually the whole thing. Today it was barely half. I was not sure where my appetite had gone.

It had cooled off in the house now with windows open on two sides, and I felt chilled. I realized I needed a sweatshirt. The wind had switched more to the north, and it was blowing right down the lakeshore and across my deck. When I went up to my room, I also closed those upstairs windows.

When I settled back into a comfort zone, my thoughts returned to what John had related. I had to agree with everything he had said. I did feel relief, however, that now Grace would, one way or another be extracted from the gallery business. I hoped there had been a corporation and that she was not legally involved with that. Then it would be a lot cleaner for her to cut ties with the business. If she was an officer, even a blind one, she would still be immune personally for any liability, but involved nevertheless, and she did not need that hassle right now. Of course, I was assuming she wouldn't want to run the place. Maybe I was wrong.

Never try to clear your head, because all that does is encourage random thoughts. That was happening to me now. Flashbacks to events over the last couple of weeks kept popping up uninvited. *Thanks a lot, John.* Now did I have to worry about being a target? I had seen the murderer, hadn't I?

The phone rang to cut my train of thought, and the caller I.D. indicated it was Grace. I still didn't want to talk to her. I just didn't need the drama. I let it go to voicemail. I knew she probably was hurting and had had a tough time of it lately, but so had I. I didn't want her hanging on me for support, looking to me for salvation. I wondered if perhaps that said something about my true feelings for her? Maybe when I didn't feel so shitty I'd look at things differently. I had to sort this shit out and get back to the real world like John. Now that I wasn't worried about Grace having been involved the night of the murder attempt, I could move forward with a different emphasis.

Grace's call reminded me once again of the fight at the hospital. I was bothered by the recollection because there was something about the hospital room scene that hadn't seemed right in my head. I sat on my overstuffed chair and went through the event from the time when I had arrived at the hospital to when I apparently had blacked out. Nothing came to me that eased my sense of disquiet.

What was it I was missing? Oh, well, it couldn't be that important, could it? If it were, that Minneapolis cop would be all over it. I'd better realize I was an attorney at law not a god-damned detective. Give me a break.

Eating and drinking, combined with everything else, had made me even sleepier. The comfortable chair cast the deciding vote. Though I resisted, I still fell asleep. I must have slept about an hour, and I felt terrible when I awakened, half awake and half asleep.

After lying still for a bit, I stood, teetering slightly before stumbling into the kitchen with a feeling of being drunk. Hardly on two beers I would think. Maybe it had been three. I was numb all over, and my mouth felt like cotton. I hadn't been drinking enough water, so I drank down one full glass and poured another with a couple of ice cubes. They told me at the hospital to drink lots of water, or was that the last time? Anyway, it sounded like good advice.

Shaking my shoulders, I tried to energize myself. Then I moved my jaw about trying to get rid of the lethargic feeling. That hurt. I had to remember I needed to take it easy. I also then remembered my ribs and realized I had forgotten to ask how long I needed to keep this wrap thing on. I'd look in my paperwork. Maybe that said what to do.

My thoughts went to my eye. Blocking my right eye with my hand and looking across the room, I could barely discern objects. A warm glow enveloped me as I wondered if I was going blind. I rushed into the bathroom and looked at my eye in the mirror. I carefully pulled the lids apart with my fingers. Blood did not appear to be pooling. They did say it would take a couple of days for the eye to clear up. I wondered if ice would help. *Check the paperwork, dummy.*

While I drank more water, I speculated if Janet was coming over. I never asked for sure, just said she could if she needed anything signed. I realized I needed to do something to occupy my mind so I got on line and deleted about thirty e-mails that were nothing more than advertisements. There also were two messages from Grace. The first merely stated she'd tried to reach me. The second was troubling, in that she communicated her desire for us to get through these tough times together. Now she was scaring me. I wasn't ready for that kind of commitment just now. She had two kids!

Janet did make it over a few minutes later, and I dealt with my paperwork. This time she didn't try to hold in her emotions when she saw me. She really cried. It was not just an eye moistening; she actually sobbed and had to hide her face in her hands. I found myself taking her in my arms and giving her a light hug. It hurt me, but she needed it.

I had not thought I looked that bad. So much for a judicious self-appraisal. Maybe it was just the thought of this happening twice that shook her up. I was forced to go through the entire story of what happened at the hospital, even though it was getting boring, but I figured it was the least I could do for her. Relating what had happened seemed to make her feel better.

Janet then told me my tale of the eventual murder of Adams confirmed the rumors that had been going around town concerning the fire. Was I the only one who was in the dark on that thing? Apparently so.

After Janet left, I decided to just lie around for a bit and relax. There was an afternoon ballgame on the tube, so I watched that. Later that evening after finishing the remainder of my pizza, I decided to hit the hay early. I wanted to go into the office the next day and needed no excuse to miss any more time. I was in bed by seven. I thought I heard my doorbell, but it could have been a dream. At any rate, I got a good night's sleep.

Chapter Twenty-Five
A Dead End

As planned, I went in to the office the next morning still feeling somewhat unsteady on my feet, but extremely anxious over the time I recently had lost. For a moment I had considered driving but then ended up walking. I had all the time in the world, and today I felt steadier than I had the previous morning in Minneapolis. I had needed no help from a single light pole.

I was a creature of habit, and lately my routine had been blasted too much apart. I craved normalcy. Thus, this morning was a pleasure to settle into my routine in normal surroundings. One disquieting note was Janet's alert that Grace had tried to reach me several times on the previous day. I considered locking the front door, but dismissed the idea as foolish.

It was a little after ten o'clock and I was getting into a groove when I received a phone call from police officer Bill Rehms asking me to come over to the Adams Gallery. He was close mouthed about the reason, but insisted I needed to come at once. I was put out by his demanding demeanor, and told him I wasn't ambulatory and would need a ride. I was being a jerk but did not particularly care. I could not see why I had to be at everyone's beck and call.

I had briefly thought about not going at all, but after taking into consideration that the reason for my attendance was unknown, I could hardly decline and still maintain my reputation as a solid upstanding citizen. *Yeah, right.*

Only five minutes later Officer Rehms picked me up and drove me around to the back of the gallery building. His manner was friendly, and he seemed to have no problem with offering escort service. Quite the contrary, he seemed to welcome the opportunity to pump me on the Adams murder. I answered his questions as briefly as I could, at least the ones I had answers to. His questions delayed our entry into the building by a good five minutes.

Rehms seemed generally concerned about my health, and when he heard I had been pounded on by that slip of a woman, I had expected him to laugh. Instead he shook his head and told me that it was always the smaller ones to look out for. He said that they were generally quick and could surprise a person. I could not disagree with anything he said.

When we exited the cruiser, Rehms guided me to the back door. At first I meant to rebuke him. I was not a cripple, but I let him feel he was being helpful. I still didn't know the purpose of my being here. Perhaps it was to meet with John and go over the art fraud mess. Rehms need not have kept it a secret.

When the officer had passed through the back door into the gallery, I stood before the opening while holding the door to one side. I was once again overwhelmed by the smell of burned wood. It amazed me that the fire smell was still present, as I would have thought that by now it might have disappeared. But no, I guessed until they cleaned the place, the obnoxious odor would remain.

My lungs by now had cleared from the effects of the fire, and I considered my breathing normal, so that was one less concern for me in being exposed to this environment. Clothing was another matter, however. I may have to clean my suit after I was finished here today. It was difficult getting rid of that wet, burnt wood aroma. I could not just air it out. That would only accomplish so much. It looked like a dry cleaning job was on the horizon. I wished I had known about this visit, I would have dressed differently.

Now as I stood there, I perceived another aroma I was unable to readily identify. It wasn't something I remembered from previous visits. It was more pungent and a little foul smelling. It carried the odor of dirty diapers. Before I could inquire about it, Rehms hustled me forward into the rear part of the gallery space.

The space was crowded with people, mostly with their backs to me. Gathering my wits, I looked around the tiny cramped area. There were several people, none of whom I recognized. Then I saw John Brooks. I looked at him for enlightenment, but got nothing in return. His face was pale, and he seemed to be in shock. He neither looked at me, nor did he speak.

Bill Rehms took me by the elbow, saying. "I wonder if you might be able to help us identify this person?"

Two men stepped aside, and that was when I first saw the mummy lying on the floor. There obviously was a body under the sheet, and my first reaction was to say no to Rehms's request. I was feeling so poorly from my latest adventure I didn't know how I might react when that sheet was pulled back. I did not need another jolt.

"Bill, look, I'm not sure I'm up to this. I don't feel too well."

"I understand, Mike, really I do. But it'll just take a moment. I really appreciate this. It's important."

The "Mike" did it for me. Bill wanted a favor. I took a step forward and bent at the waist to get a closer look. That's when another officer pulled the sheet partially off to reveal the head of the deceased. I recognized her immediately. It was my adversary from the hospital room fight. I was now at a loss for words, and began to feel lightheaded.

I stood erect and, looking down, stared at the remains. The person I remembered from the hospital encounter had a darker skin tone. Now she was pale and bloodless, and her skin had a waxy sheen. No one had closed her eyelids and I noticed the eyes were dark, though lifeless. The woman in the hospital room had blue eyes, but I had suspected they were contacts. This confirmed it.

I began to turn away. "What happened," I managed to choke out.

I received no response to my question. Instead I was asked, "Do you know this person, Mr. Connelly?"

I shook my head. "No, but I've seen her before. I don't know who she is though."

"No name, then?"

"No, but it might be the person I saw leaving this area the night of the fire."

"I wondered," Rehms said. "She seemed to fit the vague description you gave me previously. Any idea what she was doing here?"

I didn't respond. I couldn't.

"Mr. Connelly?"

"Huh?"

"Any idea what she might have been doing here?"

"None. Look, I've got to sit down."

I walked over to a wooden box near the main store entrance, upended it, and sat. I was feeling faint. I spread my knees and lowered my head between them, trying to regain some equilibrium. My brain was spinning, trying to explain what I had just seen. It held no answer for me. Rehms walked over and looked down at me, touching me on the shoulder.

With my sleeve I wiped my forehead, which had begun to bead sweat, though it was not warm in here. I thought I was tough, but obviously not tough enough.

"You okay?" Rehms asked.

"No, but things'll get better. They have to. Listen, I suggest you contact the Minneapolis P.D. and coordinate with them. I believe this is the woman seen leaving Marshall Adams's hospital room just before he was found dead. She may be a suspect on that. Maybe they've been able to identify her."

I contemplated for a moment retrieving the hospital scene from my memory bank. "Also check for bruising on her torso. I gave her a pretty good bear hug during our altercation. I don't know, it might show up." I chewed my lip for a moment and then looked back at the inert form. "But I think this is the same person."

"Do you know who's in charge in Minneapolis?" Rehms asks.

I shook my head. "Can I go now?"

"Okay, but there may be more questions later."

"Fine, later's better. I've got plenty of questions of my own.

"Brooksie, can you leave?" I shouted out over the conversation that had started up.

He murmured something to the young cop next to him. Then he walked over to me.

"Help me back to the office, will you?"

I stood and wobbled toward the front door. "Got your keys, John?"

"Yeah."

"Good, this way's shorter. I don't want to go all around the block."

I had asked John to accompany me rather than ride with Rehms so as to have a chance to talk with him.

"You know where to find me," I told Rehms over my shoulder.

I hoped I could make it back to the office by walking. If I thought I had been shaky on the walk to work this morning, now I was really unsteady. I was not used to seeing dead bodies except in the mortuary.

I really needed to work, now more than ever, but it was becoming doubtful I would last the day.

John and I jaywalked across the street. There was little traffic at this time of the day for me to stall. We made the street crossing fine. Then we cut down the mid block alley.

"What happened, John?" I asked, my voice sounding hollow.

"I don't know."

"Did you find her?" I asked.

"Me and the carpenter. I opened up for him, and there she was right in the middle of the floor."

I slithered between two parked cars and into the parking lot. "Do you know how she died?"

"I didn't look, but I heard the doc say there is a bullet wound in the back of her head," John replied.

"I don't understand," I said. "Here I'm thinking she's the bad guy. She looked to be the one who started the fire and left Marshall to die. She appeared to be the one at the hospital who finally did kill Marshall. Who killed her, and why? Her death wasn't an accident."

"I'm really freaked now, Mike. I'm thinking of taking my family and leaving town for a while."

I stopped walking and faced John. He was scared. I could see it in his eyes.

"Do what you have to do for your family, John."

My approval seemed to make him feel better.

We slowly walked toward my office a few paces and then John said. "We had talked about someone silencing Adams, right?"

I stopped. "That's your theory, and it seems logical."

"Okay, take it a step further and silence the silencer," John said.

I ran that thought around in my head. "But that would mean there's someone else involved."

"Probably," John said. "Whoever is masterminding this whole deal is covering their backside. Maybe this gal wanted more money, or maybe the head guy just didn't want any witnesses."

Even though what John had said made sense, I replied, "You've been reading too many mystery stories, John."

John flashed a look of anger. "Okay, then you come up with an answer."

I put my hands up in a defensive gesture. "Hey, good buddy, sorry. You're probably right. I sure don't have any ideas, though it's usually about the money, isn't it?"

We stood facing one another with John thinking. "Outside of inter family murder, money is a big motive, I suppose. Here I wonder if it all traces back to our breaking the forgery setup? Someone might be trying to clean up the mess."

I considered his statement.

"Yes. That makes sense. Unless we can find a really strong money motive, that idea of yours would be the logical reason, John. I'm glad I don't have to follow it up," I said.

"Me too. We do know though, that the fire wasn't done for profit," John said, "because I own the building. The renters stood to gain nothing from the fire itself. Therefore, I believe my other theory gains credence from that. They, whomever they are, wanted to shut up Adams. Now you have to figure out why."

"Me?"

John smiled. "Do I have to do all the heavy lifting?"

We parted, and I went back to the office. I had to catch up on a lot of work. I also had to explain to Janet what was going on. That would be the hard part.

Chapter Twenty-Six
Continuing Investigation

I entered the office, and Janet looked up from her computer. "What's going on?" she asked, "You look pale."

I poured a cup of coffee and sat in a chair next to her desk. Then I proceeded to tell her about the body. I had thought I knew a lot about what was going on with this affair, but I could only answer about half her questions. I decided I wouldn't make a very good cop.

"So you don't know who she is?" Janet asked.

I shook my head. "No."

"Why'd the police want you to identify her, then?"

"They thought I might have seen her before."

"Oh." She looked up suddenly. "Had you?"

"Yes." I took a sip of my coffee and looked at Janet's computer screen.

"But you think she started the fire over at the gallery that night?" she said.

"I think so."

"I wonder what she was doing there now?"

I wondered the same thing but had no answer.

I was back at my desk and hard at work when I received an unexpected phone call from a Sergeant Alan Tilden of the Minneapolis P.D.

He began, "Mr. Connelly. I'm investigating the death of Mr. Adams at the University Hospital. I would like to ask you a few questions."

"Sure, go ahead."

"I'd prefer to meet with you and do it in person if I can."

"Well, I'm not up to traveling just yet," I responded.

"That's all right, Mr. Connelly, I can drive out there to your place."

"Oh, sure."

"Say about one-thirty?"

I quickly checked my calendar. "Fine. Do you need directions?"

"No, I have G.P.S."

I laughed at that and gave him directions to my office.

"See you at one-thirty, then," and I hung up. I wondered how he had located me? I guess it was no secret where I lived or worked. Anyone could be found if you looked hard enough.

I knew I was not yet up to my normal noon walk, so I would be in the office regardless of when the officer arrived. I already had forgotten his name. I should have written it down.

It seemed as though my life was going to be filled with police investigations continuously now. I just got done with one, and another from another jurisdiction hit me up. I would have to think about getting away from here for a while. Why could John and I not have left well enough alone? We were in over our heads.

I had no endurance yet, so I was fortifying myself with coffee, lots of coffee. By the time the Minneapolis officer arrived, I was feeling jittery.

Our offices are set up so that I was able to close my office for privacy, and I welcomed the man into my office and closed the door.

"Would you like coffee? Is it Mr. or Sergeant, or what?"

"How about Alan?"

Now I remembered. Tilden, that was the name.

"Okay, Alan. Then call me Mike."

"Good. Forget the coffee. I'm not a big coffee drinker, Mike."

"Mind if I have some?" I asked.

"No, go ahead."

"Thanks. I'm using it as a crutch to get through the day. Otherwise I think I'd need a nap right about now."

"Tired huh?"

I smiled. "A little."

I motioned Alan to a comfortable chair next to my desk, and after pouring my coffee, I pulled my desk chair to the corner of my desk facing my visitor and sat.

Alan was a good looking middle-aged man. His six-foot frame carried about two hundred pounds, and it appeared to be mostly muscle. Dark hair, cut short, matched a well-trimmed mustache over a generous mouth. The man's oval face sported a Roman nose and a strong chin. Hazel eyes caught my attention when Alan looked at me. The man appeared to enjoy the out of doors, because his tan rivaled mine.

Alan wore gray slacks, a white shirt and tie, and a blue blazer. Gray socks and black loafers covered his feet. He was a dapper dresser.

"You look like you had a rough time of it," Alan said, as he made a point of scanning my face.

"It's from the altercation at the hospital.

Alan nodded. "How are you feeling now?"

"Still a little unsteady on my feet. My face looks worse than it feels actually. My cheeks feel a little puffy, especially under my one eye. I think my eye is going to be all right, though. The blurriness has started to diminish. I'm keeping my fingers crossed. The doctor was worried about pooling blood, but I think I'm okay there." I didn't mention my ribs, since I really wanted to curtail this discussion on my health.

Alan nodded. "That's good to hear. As I mentioned over the phone, Mike, I'm following up on the Adams death."

I took a sip of coffee and listened.

"Do you mind if I record our conversation?" he asked.

I thought for a few seconds and then said. "Okay." I would need to watch what I said.

"Good," Alan said, as he took out a mini recorder and set it on the desk between us.

"I know you talked to one of our people when you were in the hospital, but I want to give you a chance to speak when you're not under the influence of drugs or feeling as poorly as you must have felt then."

"I appreciate that," I replied. "I really don't remember what I said in there."

"Have you been having blackouts?"

"No, not since I came home, but I was pretty loopy in there."

"Good, we're all set then. Let's begin."

Alan recited standard information into the recorder such as time and date and my name and then began the questioning.

"Mike, you were at the University Hospital on Sunday morning, July twenty-eighth, correct?"

"That's correct," I responded.

"Do you remember what time you arrived?"

I hesitated as I thought. "Son of a gun. I've lost it," I said out loud.

"What do you mean?"

"I can't remember for sure. Maybe about ten-thirty. I'm just drawing a blank on that."

"Are you having trouble remembering any other things since your trauma?"

"I don't know. I haven't tried anything much since coming home. Let's go on and maybe it'll come back to me."

"All right. Why did you go there?"

I suddenly realized that this interview was going to be problematic. How do I answer a question I have no answer to? I decided to keep it simple. I explained the fire to Alan, my rescue of Adams, and a perceived need to see how the recovery was progressing. That seemed to satisfy Alan.

"How well do you know Marshall Adams?"

"I never met him before the rescue, and I've never spoken to him since. I guess that's part of the need to meet and talk to him."

"I understand."

I expected him to ask me about my relationship with Grace, but he didn't, and I was not going to volunteer anything.

"Mike, tell me about your arrival at the hospital. Did you go right to the room?"

"Yes."

"Who was there?"

I decided to play it cool. "The patient was there, of course. He was asleep. Mrs. Adams was there also. She said her husband had just been moved from I.C.U. and was very tired.

She suggested we leave the room for a few minutes to let him sleep and then return a bit later. She was very protective. She thought there might be a chance for him to talk to me once he rested."

"You wanted to talk to him, not just see him?"

"Right."

"Why?" he asked.

I shrugged. "I can't explain. I just felt I needed to."

"Okay. What happened next?"

"We left."

"You and Mrs. Adams?"

"Yes."

"Where did you go?"

"To the visitors lounge down the hall."

"You walked together?" he asked.

"Yes." I took a sip of coffee, and coughed. I was wondering where we were headed with this interview. I could not anticipate what might be coming next.

"How long were you there?"

"In the lounge?"

"Yes."

"Oh, golly, maybe about ten minutes."

"Together the whole time?"

I thought for a minute. What should I say here? I need to tell the truth. There are more people in jail for lying than for the actual transgression being investigated. I did not want to lose my law license.

"There was a brief moment when we left the room, when we were separated."

"Explain."

"We began walking to the lounge and Mrs. Adams realized she had forgotten her purse. So she went back into the room for it and caught up with me in the lounge."

"You didn't wait for her in the hall?'

"No," I answered.

"Why not?'

That was a good question. Could I remember why not?

"Let me think. Gosh, I'm not sure. Maybe she said to go ahead. No, I'm not positive of that. Stuff like that is so automatic I don't remember."

"So, you come out of the patient's room and begin walking down the hall toward the lounge. Mrs. Adams stops you and says she needs to retrieve her purse. She then may have encouraged you to go ahead and said she would catch up."

"I think she must have done that, because otherwise it would be impolite for me not to wait, or to go back with her and wait. I probably thought she wanted a moment alone with her husband so I went ahead of her."

"That may have been it," Alan seconded. "You still feeling all right?"

"Just fine."

"Did you feel a little abandoned sitting in the lounge all that time alone?"

"It really wasn't all that long."

"How long would you say it was?"

I reflected for a few moments. "I would guess one, two minutes tops. Not enough to make me think about it. I just stood around looking out the window, and tried not to disturb the others there."

"And then you were together for about another ten?"

"Yes."

I was creating an alibi for myself without thinking about it. I never was in the room alone with Marshall. I wondered if I was a suspect? Is that the reason for the questions?

Alan continued. "Good. What happened next after Mrs. Adams came into the lounge?"

"We sat and chatted. She thanked me for pulling him, that is her husband, out of the fire. Stuff like that."

I saw no need to reveal any of our personal relationship or conversation. Not if he didn't specifically ask.

"Then what?" Alan asked.

"Let's see. I needed to use the bathroom."

"After about ten minutes in the lounge."

"About, yes."

"Go on."

"I came out of the bathroom and found myself disoriented. I didn't remember if I had come from the right or the left. You know how those halls all look alike. So, I stood there for a couple of seconds getting my bearings."

"And."

A woman came walking by me like she was on a mission. You know, walking fast. At first I thought she was staff, but then noticed how she was dressed."

"And how was that?"

"Jeans and a sweatshirt."

"Handbag?"

"Golly. Hmmm. No I don't think so. I don't remember one."

"Okay, go on."

"When I looked at her back, as she walked away, it rang a bell. She looked familiar. I didn't realize it at that moment, but subconsciously she reminded me of the person I saw stealing away from the fire scene in Excelsior."

Alan looked bewildered. "What fire scene?"

I sighed. "There was this fire . . ." I told him the story as briefly as I could. I'd told it so many times, I'd got a condensed version.

"Okay. I'm not sure if that's relevant to my investigation, but go on with your story."

"I followed the mystery woman, though I was about ten or fifteen feet behind. I had to hustle to keep up because she was truckin'. She walked right up to a room and pushed open the door. When I got there myself, I realized it was Adams's room."

"What happened next?"

"I hesitated at the door, wondering if I should go in."

"How long did you hesitate?"

"Just a couple of seconds. Maybe ten."

"What next?"

"I pushed open the door and walked in. You know what the room looks like?"

"Yes."

"I got to the foot of the bed and saw the woman holding a pillow."

"How was she holding it?"

"Like this." I held a hand to each side of my chest.

"Which way was she facing?"

I thought for a couple of seconds. "She was half turned toward me like she was facing the bed."

"She wasn't bent over Adams?"

"No. Her positioning and body language led me to believe she was leaving."

"Leaving the room?"

"Or the bedside."

"Why do you say that?"

"Because she turned completely toward me and dropped the pillow on the bed. Then, she took a couple of steps toward me and tried to push past me."

"And you didn't step aside?" Alan asked.

"No."

"Why not. That would have been the polite thing to do."

"I don't know. I didn't think about it. I just reacted. Something inside me said this wasn't right."

"Okay, then what?"

"As she went past, shoving me in the ribs with an elbow, I reached out and grabbed her hair, pulling her toward the foot of the bed. She stumbled over the I.V. pole and it tumbled to the floor."

I paused, thinking.

"I know we fought then, but I don't remember exactly what happened. I guess I blacked out sometime during the fight."

Alan looked at me. "This is important, Mike. How long do you think the woman was in the room alone?"

"Alone? Let's see. I was at most about fifteen feet behind her in the hallway. That's what, about five paces? Five paces are maybe four or five seconds in time. A couple of seconds at the door and then another couple before I was there with her. What's that, about eight, nine seconds? Maybe fifteen seconds. Twenty tops."

"That doesn't give the woman much time in there. Did you see her holding a can of any kind?"

"Can? No, just the pillow," I replied.

"Did it look like she was about to or had tried to smother the victim?" Alan asked.

"That's what my thought had been," I said to the officer.

"Then or later?"

I reflected momentarily, trying to remember. My memory was hazy. I said. "I think subconsciously I was thinking about it at the time, but consciously after I thought about it later."

"When was that?"

"You mean, when was later?" I asked.

"Yes."

"After I was at home," I said.

"The next day?"

"Yes. The next afternoon."

"But no can?" Alan inquired.

"What kind of can?"

"Like a spray can, deodorant or small rust-o-leum type spray can."

"No. No can. Why?" I asked.

"Because Marshall Adams didn't die as a result of someone smothering him with a pillow. He died when someone sprayed foam insulation into his airways and mouth."

My shock must have been apparent, and I did not know what to say. I had never seen anything like that the short time I had been in Marshall's room. I was dumbfounded.

"They couldn't revive him?" I asked.

"They tried, but he'd been out too long, and the emergency trach didn't work because the goop had gone down too far in his airway. He was D.O.A.

"Man," I said as I slouched in my chair feeling totally overwhelmed. I realized it had to have happened earlier than when I returned to the room to find the interloper.

Alan continued his interrogation. We went over the same ground again, and I was growing fatigued.

"Look, Alan. I've answered everything, and told you everything I know. I don't know any more. Let's call it a day. If you need anything else, give me a call, and we can go over it again when I'm not so tired. I don't even know what I'm saying anymore."

He grimaced and then reached over and turned off the recorder. He thanked me, and put away his paraphernalia. We both stood. I walked him to the door. We shook hands and the officer left.

I looked at Janet, and she looked at me.

"You're getting to be on a first name basis with a lot of cops," she said.

I laughed half-heartedly and returned to my office, leaving the door ajar. I looked at my coffee cup and then went to the bathroom. I had plenty to think about for the afternoon.

Chapter Twenty-Seven
Grace

The clock struck five, and I considered asking Janet for a ride home, though, by doing that I would have been admitting to my current frailty. Instead, I remained after her at work, and then dragged my sorry bones toward home. I was looking forward to a good stiff drink and a relaxing night of watching the Twins wail on the Yankees. Okay, so I was not totally back to reality.

When I turned the corner by the liquor store, I saw someone sitting on my front stoop. I hoped I was wrong, but I didn't think so. She was looking down at her feet as I approached. When I pivoted to climb my stairs she saw me.

"Mike, gee you work late. I've been here ever so long."

"Grace, honey, why didn't you call?"

"I've tried for two days, but couldn't reach you."

"Sorry, I'm not feeling so good and haven't been doing much but sleeping. I did manage to get into work this afternoon, though."

We stood in front of my place looking at one another. The sun was directly in Grace's face, so she hand-shielded her eyes. I realized the futility of my avoidance and said. "Grace, do you have time to come in?"

"Briefly," she answered without enthusiasm. "You look tough, Mike."

I wondered if I had alienated her, and then wondered if that mattered. "I feel tough."

We went inside. Grace hesitated momentarily on the landing, and then walked down the stairs. Her scent lingered where she had stood and I made sure I managed to inhale it all. Today, she was wearing blue calf-length Capri's, colorful sandals, and a tee with spaghetti straps. The slacks showed off her form to advantage, and my pulse quickened as my eyes followed her movement.

I lumbered down the stairs behind her.

"Would you like to sit in or out?" I asked.

"Is in okay with you?"

"Fine."

"You see, I wanted to talk."

"Want anything to drink?" I asked.

"Just water."

"Sure."

I went to the kitchen and returned with two waters. I could wait a bit to start my hard drinking. I gave Grace her water, removed my suit jacket and tie and opened my collar. I took a seat opposite Grace with a coffee table in between.

I was looking her up and down when she spoke. "Look, Mike, I know there's nothing between us, but I'm thinking of leaving town, and I was wondering if there was a reason I should be staying?"

The implication was there, and I had no immediate answer for her. I was not prepared for that question. Marshall had not even been buried yet, and here she was with what appeared to be a full court press. I was uncertain what to say. Maybe I had it wrong.

Finally, I spoke, "I'm glad you came over, Grace. We haven't seen much of one another since the reunion. We really need to talk."

She was looking at me with those big blue eyes, and I wanted to go over, throw her on the floor, and ravish her. I had managed to control myself so far, but for how long I wasn't sure.

When she didn't answer, I said, "You look very nice today, Grace."

"Thank you, Mike. It's been hard to think of that sort of thing these last two weeks, and now with Marshall gone . . ."

Grace tried to control herself, but her voice caught and then tears formed in her eyes, before yielding to a flood of emotion.

"Oh, Mike. I don't know what I'm going to do."

I capitulated to weakness and went over to her. Sitting next to her, I put my arm over her shoulders. Grace buried her head in my chest and held tightly onto my shirt. I rubbed her back lightly with one hand and her arm with the other. She was supple and warm.

Her hair was fragrant and soft against my cheek. It must have been freshly washed. I decided some women just always look good no matter what. Grace was one of those. Grace lifted her head. Tears were trickling down her face, while my shirt was wet from the earlier flood.

My heart was pounding and my loins were demanding release. A bulge had expanded my pant leg. Grace wiped the tears from her cheeks with a finger, and said, "Sorry, Mike. I need to show more control."

I knew if we kept talking, the mood would end. That was what needed to happen, but was it what I wanted to happen? She no longer was married, but she was vulnerable. Ah, shit. I bent my head and brushed her lips with mine. Her's attacked mine with fervor.

The die was cast. The dam had burst. There was no going back. I reached down and pulled her right leg onto my lap. My pant leg bulged higher from the contact. Our mouths were open and exploring. There was no temperance in sight. We both were committed wholly.

The bedroom was too distant and our need too great, so the floor becomes our love platform. The simple act of removing a woman's top held an eroticism of its own, the exposed breasts a suitable reward. Our bodies ground together in a frantic dance. Grace's back was arched, as she worked to achieve maximum pleasure. Her breasts had become pink from my mauling of them. Then it was over.

We lay together, she on top, as we waited for my exit. I was exhausted from my effort, feeling less the man for that, but not sorry for the experience. I ran my fingers over the small of her back and traced them over her butt. I placed one hand on each side and pulled her tighter against me. Then I released her and relaxed.

Grace's face rested against mine, and she raised her head just enough to kiss me. She then pushed herself away, stood and started to get dressed.

This was the awkward time for me and perhaps for her as well. I wondered what her expectations had been? Were we going to have a talk? Was Grace going to ask for some kind of a commitment? I waited. Then I stood and pulled on my pants. I wanted to approach her and hold her in my arms, but she appeared to be thinking, and I did not want to disturb her.

Finally, she looked me straight in the eye and said. "Mike, I'm thinking of leaving Excelsior, moving back to Texas. Not in any rush, but I'd like to make a decision soon. Maybe you can help me with that decision."

I began to feel flushed. What was I getting into? I said to her, "I can do that. It's an important decision, one that needs discussion. Let's not rush it. There's the funeral, your kids. Can you wait, at least until after the funeral?"

"That makes sense," Grace said. "I think they'll release the body soon. I'm considering cremation. Since we're new in town and don't know that many people, maybe a private service."

I nodded. "Okay."

Grace bit her lower lip. "I'd better get home. I have no idea what the kids are doing. I'll call you real soon." She stepped toward me and gave me a kiss on the mouth. "Bye, Mike."

"Bye."

I walked up the stairs following her to the door. Closing it after her, I stood for a moment and exhaled. What a night.

Downstairs, I picked up and made myself a drink. Then I went outside onto my deck, leaving the patio door wide open. I sat looking at the lake and sipped my scotch. Without the sun, I felt chilled and shivered. After getting a sweatshirt I sat back down and tried to relax, but it didn't come easy. I stretched my neck by circling my head, and then I rubbed each side of my neck with my fingertips. It felt like a headache might be on the horizon. I lit a cigar, which usually relaxed me. I would try anything right now.

It appeared certain Grace had thrown herself at me. There was no other way to state it. She had made it plain that she might consider staying here rather than going to Texas. It was obvious to me that decision rested on my answer, and that answer would be for us to be a couple. Was that not what I had wanted, or had I been hiding behind the safety of her marriage and unavailability? It was easy to want something when you know you cannot have it.

Was I ready for a change? I had been alone a long time. I was set in my ways. Why change everything now? Would I even be considering it for anyone else but Grace? There were a lot of questions to answer.

On the practical side, we couldn't live here. I only had the two bedrooms. Neither child was of college age, so they would both be here. Three bedrooms would be a must. Shit, I did not want to leave my place here. I was on the lake, had a boat, just a short walk to work.

Then there was work. I did not make enough to raise a family. I would have to expand my practice, get out of my comfort zone, and take on the public.

None of that would be easy, but it involved Grace. Three weeks ago, if it had been proposed, the decision would have been a snap. Now that it was a real possibility, it was a whole different ball game. No, it wasn't going to be an easy decision.

I remained outside on the deck until I became one with the evening shadows. I had forgotten about my plans to watch the ball game. Somehow it was not important enough at this point to watch, but I had to do something to occupy my mind, so finally I did tune to the game. I found myself paying attention for a while and then my thoughts drifted off once again to consider my future with Grace.

Later, I decided to sleep on it and take a fresh look in the morning. I was sure things would look clearer then.

Chapter Twenty-Eight
Missing

After a restless night, I woke to find the same problems confronting me that had bewildered me the previous evening. Inaction seemed to be my mantra, and I lay in bed looking up at the slowly moving ceiling fan, mesmerized by its motion. Maybe it was a metaphor for my current life, round and round and round.

My head was clogged with so much competing information I had not been able to think straight. I felt like a dog chasing its tail, always seeming to end up back where I had started. I did not remember a time in my life when I had been so irresolute.

Sitting up on the side of my bed, I attempted to jumpstart my day. My body felt like it was still asleep, and what I needed was a good jolt to get me moving. Grace, Grace, Grace. I was hoping that, over time, my thoughts would clear on the subject of the two of us, and I could reconcile my conflicting goals. Then and only then would I be able to make a commitment. I hoped that Grace would give me that time.

I needed to make coffee at home because today I needed something to get myself going. I made a quick trip downstairs to start the pot. Returning upstairs, I shaved and brushed my teeth. The shower beckoned me, and I lingered there, trying to limber my muscles. The hot water felt good, and I let the force of the water beat against the back of my neck. Then, while still under the running water, I did some minor stretches to complete the effort. My neck has felt awfully tight. Tension will do that. My ribs felt better even without the protective wrap from the hospital.

The thought of breakfast held little appeal, but I did go ahead and make a lunch. I packed an extra sandwich just in case I got hungry early. My menu held little variety, as I stayed with the basics. One last cup of coffee and I was done.

Then I was off to work, seeking the familiarity of the office and its routine to get my mind settled. People take a lot for granted, and one of those was the comfort derived from a good job or career. Lately I had been learning to appreciate mine.

The weatherman had said it was going to be a warm day. The sun already was up and the sky nearly cloudless. A soft southerly breeze beckoned me, but I met my obligation and arrived at the office as promised. The first thing I did was to pour myself another cup of java. Then I dove into work.

I took a call from Grace mid-afternoon. It was a welcome diversion, though I wished I had the freedom to call her. We had agreed last night she would call me whenever she was free and had the time. I was relieved when she sought no commitment from me during this current conversation.

Grace's call was to inform me the police had released Marshall's body, and the funeral home was scheduled to pick it up. She said she was using a Minneapolis home that did cremations, and Marshall's now was scheduled. Once the cremation was complete, the family would have a prayer service. There'd be no public announcement or visitation.

I didn't have a lot of experience with funerals, but Grace's decision seemed singular in its approach. It wasn't for me to say, though, and at least I had been informed of her plans. I was left wondering how I felt not to be included. At least my participation at the service was not mentioned. I felt like an insider on the outside. Grace constantly dangled a relationship before me and then seemingly pulled it away. Maybe that was because I never committed.

It was surprising, but after the brief phone contact from Grace I felt better. Some of the lethargy seemed to have disappeared. If just hearing her voice could do that for me, why was I dithering in my decision to spend the rest of my life with her? I think that was what she wanted.

I made it through the remainder of the afternoon. On my walk home I wondered if Grace and I would talk tonight. I decided probably not, since she had called me earlier. If we did talk later, then it would be a bonus.

Instead of sitting around doing nothing, I decided to spend the evening doing a financial analysis of my life, looking at my meager assets, and seeing what I might garner from the sale of my home. It was not what I wanted to do, but I did think I should explore my options.

The activity caused me to sleep better.

Two days later I was toiling away at work wondering when I'd hear again from Grace. I knew she was very busy right now, and I had agreed not to call her unless it was important. I was disappointed I had not heard from her the previous night. I was of the belief I needed to hear her voice to help me make my decision on what to do with my life from there on out.

It was nearly noon, and I was hungry, so I removed my lunch from the mini fridge in the inner office and proceeded to eat the peanut butter and banana sandwich I painstakingly had prepared that morning. Most often I ate in the office. There wasn't much to choose from in simple eateries locally, and I really didn't want to waste the time, or the money. This way I could control my diet, and go for a walk near the lake when I had finished eating.

My walks were not long ones, maybe a couple of miles. I varied the route so that I hit every street in town in a month's time. Generally I reserved my outdoor activities to the nicer weather, so winter found me less active.

The sky today was overcast and the wind had shifted to the northwest, but that was still better than sitting inside all day. If I got cold, I could always cut my walk short. We closed the office over the noon hour, and Janet sometimes was gone as well.

I grabbed an apple and said good-bye to Janet, as I headed out the door for my stroll. I hadn't gone five feet when Bill Rehms pulled up in his squad. He opened his window and leaned out.

"Got a minute, Mike?"

"Um, okay."

"Can we go inside and talk?"

"Sure."

I was hoping this would not take too long. Then I looked up at the sky and wondered if maybe I should maybe just skip the walk today. Suddenly I was feeling fatigued. I looked at my apple and then turned and led the way back inside.

Once in my office, I said. "What's up?"

"Mind if we sit?"

"No, go ahead," I said as I motioned to one of the two visitor chairs. Apparently this was going to take a while.

Bill took one chair and I the other.

"Have you talked to Mrs. Adams lately?" Bill asked. "I understand you know her pretty well."

I sat not answering for a moment, as I wondered what he meant by his statement. Then I ignored any implications he may have inferred and said. "Let's see, I got a call from her . . . yes it was day before yesterday. She advised me of the funeral arrangements for her husband."

"What are they?"

"Cremation and private prayer."

"You going?" Bill asked.

"I wasn't invited," I replied in an even tone. "I don't even know when it is."

That statement caused Bill to raise his eyebrows in surprise. "Very private, then," he said.

I tried to guess the inference of Bill's statement, but failed. I answered. "I guess." Then I waited to hear the point of Bill's questioning.

Finally, he spoke. "Mr. Brooks said you knew her."

I nodded.

"I've been trying to reach her."

Now I begin to be concerned what Bill was leading up to. I waited.

Bill watched my face, as he said. "No one answered the home phone, and when I went there, no one was there."

I still waited, wondering what this had to do with me.

"Do you know if they planned to leave town?" he asked as his right hand picked at the chair.

"No, why?" I questioned, surprised at the suggestion.

"Because the place was empty."

"What place?" I asked.

"Their house."

"What do you mean empty?" I asked. It didn't make sense.

"Just that. Furniture moved out, nothing left."

My face must have shown the surprise I was feeling.

"You had no idea?" he asked me.

"No. You sure you got the right place?"

"It's the address I got from Mr. Brooks."

I thought for a minute. "Did they own or rent?" I asked.

"Rented," Bill replied.

I thought a bit longer, and then said. "Maybe they moved."

Bill laughed. "Obviously, but why and to where?"

I was unable to answer either question. I was as stumped as Bill must have been.

"I have a cell number," I offered.

"Could I have that?"

"Sure."

I went over to my desk and retrieved my cell. Scrolling down the phone list I gave him the number.

"Why are you trying to reach her?" I asked.

Bill hesitated, then said, "I needed to ask her some questions."

"Okay, fair enough. Do you want me to have her call you if I hear from her?"

"Are you expecting to?"

"No, but I have occasionally in the past."

"Yes. Have her call me. I need to tie up some loose ends."

I changed topics. "Have you found out who the dead woman was?"

Bill hesitated once again. Then answered, "Yes."

"Who is she?"

"That's privileged information, Mike."

"Privileged! Shit, the woman tried to kill me for Christ's sake. I think that gives me a few rights."

I had raised my voice and Janet who was still in the office, looked my way through the glass partition. I waved at her, telling her everything was okay.

Bill contemplated and then said. "All right, but it goes no further."

"Right."

"Her name is Maria Gomez. She has a rap sheet. Mostly minor stuff from her teen years. Nothing recent."

"That's it?"

"So far."

"How'd she die?"

"You were there."

"I tried not to look."

Bill looked at me quizzically. "A single gunshot to the back of the head."

"I wonder why?" I mused.

"Why what?"

"Why would someone shoot her? If my thinking is right, she tried to kill Marshall the night of the fire and then again in the hospital."

"But, what if someone beat her to it?" Bill said.

I wasn't listening closely," I went on. "She was there in the room with opportunity. I just can't figure out how she did the spray thing so quickly."

Bill smiled. "I read the report, and if your timing is correct, then she couldn't have committed the murder. So are you correct in what you said you saw, and with your timetable?"

I got out of the chair and wandered around the room, thinking. I reviewed in my head what I did at the hospital, and what I had reported. Then I said. "I suppose if she had the can in her hand as she entered the room, and walked right up to the patient, shoved it into his nose or mouth, it would take three or four seconds to expel enough liquid to do the job. Then three or four more seconds to do the other orifice. I never saw a can, though."

Bill answered. "That timetable would work, but the fact is that the foam was too well set up to have been done in that timeframe. According to the report, the foam already had hardened by the time staff tried resuscitation."

"You have all that?" I questioned.

"Yes. I'm coordinating with Minneapolis. There's obviously a connection between the deaths of Marshall and Gomez. I just don't know what it is."

A thought popped into my head. Revenge. Did Grace kill the woman because the woman killed Marshall? No wait, Bill said the woman could not have killed Marshall, and Grace would never do it. Keep quiet or I would get someone hung for something they never did.

Instead, I said. "If that woman, you said her name was what?"

"Maria Gomez."

"Right, Maria. If Maria didn't kill Marshall, then who?"

"Yes, that's the question. The report says there was ten minutes after you left the room until you returned. Is that correct?"

"Maybe. Probably not more than ten. Maybe a little more. I never timed it."

"That's a lot of time for someone to go in, kill him and just walk away."

"No photo surveillance?" I asked.

"Not there. So many visitors in that damn place, there's no way to identify and check on them all."

I mulled that over. Then I asked. "What about motive?"

"See," Bill replied, "that's where it all comes back to here."

"You mean back to the first attempt on Marshall?"

"Yes. I need to figure out why they, whoever that is, wanted him dead."

"It must have something to do with the art fraud."

"What art fraud?" Bill asked, perplexed.

I told Bill as briefly as I could about what John and I had discovered with the duplicated paintings.

"Is someone looking into that?" Bill asked.

"Yes, but I don't know who. John is probably up to date on that, but we haven't conversed on it lately.

"That angle might be helpful," Bill said. "I think I'll go over and see Mr. Brooks."

"Can I come?"

"Why?"

"I want to hear where we are on that end. It'll save John the trouble of repeating himself to me later. Besides, we also might be able to figure out where Mrs. Adams is."

Bill acquiesced.

"Before we go, try that cell number, will you?" Bill instructed.

I complied, but received no answer. The call went to voicemail and I left a message asking Grace to give me a call. Then I told Janet where I was going and hitched a ride over to John's in the squad.

Chapter Twenty-Nine
New Information

When we arrived at John Brook's office, John was surprised to see us, but stopped what he was doing and invited us into his office. We each took a seat in front of John's desk. He walked around behind and sat.

"It's probably too late for coffee," John said.

"It is for me," I answered.

"None for me," Bill answered.

"So, what's up?" John asked.

I looked at Bill and then said to John, "I was filling in officer Rehms on the investigation you've been doing with the insurance company over the art thefts."

John nodded.

"I thought you might be able to update him," I said.

"Where should I start?" John asked.

Bill answered here. "Mike's explained to me what you suspected and what the insurance company has been looking into. Have they dropped their investigation, are they still looking, or have they turned it over to some other authority?"

John began. "Lloyds New York office determined that the paintings in question that had been ransomed were indeed forgeries, very good forgeries. Essentially, those paintings are worthless. Lloyds informed the primary carrier they would be dropping coverage, and I assume the primary did likewise.

"Then Lloyds turned the matter over to the F.B.I. My understanding is that currently the F.B.I. is conducting an investigation."

"Mr. Brooks, are you informed of the F.B.I.'s intentions?" Bill asked.

"Of what?"

"Have they made a connection in their investigation to the situation here in Excelsior?"

"Not that I know of. No one's spoken to me. How about you, Mike?"

"No, I've heard nothing," I replied. "I didn't even know the F.B.I. was involved."

"So, neither of you have been contacted. You both were the first to have suspicions about this. Explain," Bill said.

John and I looked at one another, and then I nodded to John.

He said. "Mike saw a work of art being copied that will soon be shown at the Walker in Minneapolis."

"A Goya," I interjected.

John hesitated and then continued, "Mike tumbled to the concept that someone might try to do a switch. Then he found out something like that already had been done to a museum in Chicago.

"I really don't remember how, but we decided this racket might also involve fire losses and stolen paintings. Since I had insurance contacts, I began researching losses and came up with potential frauds."

Bill was paying close attention and didn't interrupt.

John continued. "When we informed the underwriter of our suspicions, they checked and saw through the scam. It really was Mike's idea. I just got lucky on my end."

"Have either of you wondered about the attempt on the gallery owner's life?" Bill asked.

"A lot," I said.

"Certainly," John seconded.

"Any conclusions?" Bill looked from one to the other.

"It's probably stupid," John said.

"Nothing's stupid," Bill answered. "What is it?"

"It's just that here we think they have this scam running. It's been going on for a while, right?"

"Seems like, " I said. Bill looked from John to me.

John absentmindedly scratched the side of his head while he organized his thoughts. "They move to town here. Adams has to be part of it. I mean how can they be copying paintings without him knowing. He may even have been the painter."

Here I interrupted, "I had similar suspicions, so I discreetly asked his wife about her husband's art talent. She told me he's a frustrated artist. He studied art, tried his hand, but never was very good. He gave up serious painting, but got into the gallery business. That's how they met. She could have been lying, of course, but then she'd have to be implicated as well. Mrs. Adams didn't know why I had asked, so I see no reason for her to lie."

"So, for the moment we'll say Marshall didn't do the work," Bill said. "Then who was doing the painting? Any thoughts there?"

John looked at me, and I nodded for him to continue, "It could have been anyone, but let's think of opportunity. According to what I learned from the underwriter, this scam has been going on for years, long before Grace married Marshall, so I don't think Grace did the painting. Yet, it had to be someone who didn't raise suspicion when going up into that apartment over the gallery.

"I thought that it probably was that Ray Singer fellow. He disappeared right after the fire and at the same time the stuff from upstairs went missing. I asked myself why he'd disappear. He should have been here helping out, since he's an employee of the store. And why did that upstairs stuff get moved out ahead of the main store's works? Because someone didn't want it to be seen.

"You see, I don't think they knew Mike and I already had seen that work. We never told anyone." John paused to take a breath, and then said, "Now I know I don't have the kind of proof that's needed in court, but that's a tie in that doesn't pass the smell test for me."

Bill said, "But why would they kill Adams?"

Here I jumped in. "Maybe Adams is on okay guy. He gets sucked into a get rich scheme, not knowing everything that's involved.

He's newly married to a hot wife and wants to do right by her. Has a chance to move her to her hometown and jumps at it. That may have been one of the enticements, to open a gallery in her hometown. Later he finds out things aren't on the up and up and wants out. Can he walk away from the mob?"

John was excited now and he spoke up. "That's just what I was thinking too. He seemed like a mild sort the few times I interacted with him. I could see him not liking the deal if it was playing out the way we think it was."

"Is his wife from Excelsior?" Bill asked.

"Yes, she lived here growing up," I said.

"Did you fellows know her then?"

"I did," I answered. "We dated in high school."

"You never told me that," Bill said crossly.

"I did. Don't you remember?" John said.

Bill looked taken aback. "I guess not. It hadn't seemed relevant."

"How's it relevant?" I said. "You're getting off track here."

"All right, where were we?" Bill asked.

John said, "Marshall wants out, and they decide to let him out, but permanently. When the first try fails, they have to eliminate him quickly before he talks. The only problem is that he's in I.C.U. and how do they reach him?"

"That's why they try as soon as he's sent to a regular room," I interjected.

"Right," John says.

"You've really thought this out, John," I said.

John blushed. "Well, it makes sense, doesn't it?"

"Yes, it does," Bill said. "Except for the part where the Maria woman gets whacked. Explain that."

Neither of us could.

I headed back to the office and tried to concentrate, but I was all worked up over the murder discussion. On top of that, I could not understand what was going on with Grace. She had not called, and now she apparently had gone. I just did not comprehend.

Chapter Thirty
A Review

I excused myself rather abruptly from the discussion with Bill Rehms and John Brooks to exit John's office. The look on John's face as I stood to leave told me I was not acting in character. After all, this had been my deal as much as it had been his, but I did not care what he thought. At the moment I was feeling overwhelmed, and all of a sudden everything seemed to be closing in on me, maybe not because of the discussions of the murders, but probably from the revelation that Grace was nowhere to be found. I just could not understand what was happening there. Being in the dark was maddening.

I began to walk the main drag back toward my office, while thinking about everything discussed at John's place. It was finally dawning on me something was amiss with Grace, or at least with her actions. I needed time to sort things, to rethink everything that had happened since the reunion and my reuniting with my old lover.

One quandary was whether Grace somehow had been involved in this whole art mess all along, or, god forbid, had someone also hurt her? I think the realization of the last possibility was what had me unbalanced. There already had been two deaths I knew of, and I didn't know how I could survive if something also had happened to Grace.

There was no way for me, or anyone else, to tell what had taken place with this whole art thing, or her apparent move out of town without me talking to her. It was unsettling to me to think that if she were not involved, then why would she choose to disappear? Was that action as damning for her as it now appeared?

Shit, I was really frustrated. Nothing was making sense about this whole messed up deal. I bit my lip, as I tried to think. John was afraid for his family, and I hadn't heard from Grace. Two major concerns, but that was not all that was troubling me. Not communicating daily is what I had expected since she was busy after all, and she had said she would call when she had the time.

What shook me up was Bill making the statement that Grace appeared to have moved. Holy shit, what was that all about? In fairness, she had talked about moving, yes, but never gave me any indication it would be anytime soon. Were we not supposed to discuss that together?

I was shaking my head in disbelief as I talked to myself. I chuckled. Maybe that was why I was getting those sideway glances from people I passed by. They must have thought I was taking over for Jimmy, our town character.

I hoped on the one hand Bill's information about the move was correct, because if Grace had not moved, her whereabouts would cause me needless anxiety. On the other hand, if Bill was right, and she had moved, what did that mean? Moved where?

When he mentioned it, Rehms had not seemed concerned by his inability to reach Grace, but how sharp was he? What did he care anyway? He hadn't appeared to be getting anywhere with either that first attack against Marshall or the murder of the Maria Gomez woman. I know this was not TV, but I would have thought he would have been making more progress by now.

Ah, shit, was I being fair to the man? He did find out the gal's name, but how hard was that? John and I had to give him everything else on deep background. So far, all Bill knew on his own was that the woman was whacked with a .22 and died sometime the night before she was found, and that information was handed to him by the M.E.

I was damn frustrated with the whole affair and was quite willing to take it out on anyone and everyone, so I had better watch myself. Walking on, I racked my brain trying to come up with the logical reason for Grace's disappearance. Could she have been afraid for her safety, for that of her children? Perhaps, but I certainly did not recall anything in her actions or what she had said that would indicate a need for that level of concern.

What then?

Grace had said she was thinking of moving to Texas, I do remember that. Thinking was not the same as planning, though, or did she say planning? I thought she was waiting for me to help with that decision. Why else come over to my place and discuss it? What game was she playing?

I was daydreaming now and nearly walked into a woman who has stopped to window shop. Stopping short at the last moment, I apologized to her and then continued on my aimless wandering.

What had I been thinking just then? That's right, Grace's moving. So why come over to discuss her moving with me if she already had made up her mind to do it? It surely didn't make any sense to me. Damn, none of this had made any sense. Grace almost would have had to be packed up and ready to leave the night she visited me. No, no sense at all.

She had been using me. That was all I could come up with. Could she have been using me? I guess, but why, for what? Sex? I initiated it the first time, or had I? The second time I thought maybe for her it had been an escape from grief. Could she have been using me? Again, why? Grace was not like that, or was she? I just did not get it. None of it made any sense at all. I was going nuts over this.

She threw herself at me, wanted me to help her decide to stay, and the next thing I find out is that she was gone. Or was she really, really gone? Maybe she was living in a motel or maybe they moved to another place, because she wanted the kids to be in another school district? Yes, that was a possibility. That could have been arranged well before the latest drama unfolded.

But then, why was she not answering my calls? Why had she not communicated with me? Had my actions told her I did not want a future with her? Damn it, she was gone. I wished I knew how to reach her sister.

I leaned my forearm against a light pole and rested my forehead against it. I wanted to cry. Everything had become so blessed complicated.

A man talking into my ear startled me. "You okay, mister?"

I looked up, and then realized where I was.

"Are you hurt?" he asked.

My face was still colored from the beating I had suffered, so I must have looked like I was in trouble. I swallowed, and managed to say. "Hey, thanks. No, I'm okay. Just resting."

I walked away, leaving the Good Samaritan bewildered.

When I reached the office, I had no idea what to do. I could tell myself over and over to forget Grace, but that was not going to happen anytime soon. If I could talk to her, at least I would feel better, even if she had left. It was not knowing anything that was killing me.

I decided to call her cell number and leave a message. "Grace, it's me, Mike. I'm worried about you. Honey, please call and tell me you're all right." I decided not to say more. What more could I do? Nothing.

I missed my walk at lunch and now I had work to do. Somehow I managed to keep focused for more than two hours before an idea popped into my head. I thought about the discussion between John, Bill, and myself earlier at John's office. It was now clear to me that there was little or no coordination taking place between the east coast F.B.I. unit on their fraud investigation, Minneapolis on Marshall's murder, and Excelsior on the Gomez killing. Since Gomez apparently had not killed Adams, what did Minneapolis care about that case, they had enough murders to deal with. I did not see how anything could get done without something or someone pulling it all together.

My faith lay with the F.B.I., so I decided to call the F.B.I. office in Minneapolis. After being shuttled around to various people, I finally found someone who was willing to listen.

While I was waiting to speak with that someone, I decided to keep my story simple. Therefore, when my call was answered, I told the agent that I had information dealing with an art fraud case I believed was being run out of New York.

The agent took my name and number and said she would gather as much information as possible and call me back. I give her the names of the local police officer and that of the officer in Minneapolis that I said were involved on a periphery basis. She was on her own with contacting the F.B.I. office in New York.

I figured the F.B.I. had stiffed me, when I had not heard from anyone for two days. Then surprisingly an agent by the name of Walt Sirene called me, asking to make an appointment. It was ten-thirty in the morning when he called, and he said he could make it out to visit with me early that same afternoon if it worked for me. I told him it would work fine for me. I actually was happy that someone had returned my call.

Now all I needed was to get a message from Grace telling me she was all right, and my mind would be at peace. I had not heard a word from her for several days, and I was concerned she had given me the bum's rush. I instinctively knew it was over between us. There had been a window of opportunity with her for me, and I had missed it. Shaking my head, I chastised myself and wondered how I could have been so naive.

I remained on pins and needles for the next few hours, but the clock eventually moved on. Then later that day when Agent Sirene entered my office, I knew I was in the presence of someone with authority. I could tell from his demeanor. The agent stood a couple of inches shorter than I was and had a thinner build, but he looked to be in top physical condition. His thin face was anchored by a strong jaw and topped with light, almost white hair—unusual for a man who could not be much over thirty. Dark eyes stood out from his other features. He was attired in a dark pinstriped suit with a red tie, lending him to look very professional.

I welcomed him and we sat. Agent Sirene declined coffee but accepted a glass of water.

"Mr. Connelly, I am very much interested in hearing from you. Could you start at the very beginning with your story? Just tell me the whole thing, everything you know. You don't mind if I record our conversation, do you?"

I said I didn't, and I began to talk. An hour later, I had finished without interruption.

Agent Sirene turned off his recorder and placed it into his case. He tapped his hand on the arm of his chair as he said, "I've a much better understanding of things now. There were several questions I had before I came out here, but your story has helped me with those. You have done well."

"You don't think I'm nuts, then?" I asked.

Agent Sirene laughed. "No, not at all. Everything makes sense. We just need to tie up some loose ends."

You think you know what's going on?"

"Not entirely yet, but we will. You can count on that."

His confidence lifted my spirits. It even led me to believe he could help me with finding Grace.

We said our goodbyes. After the agent left, I sat back and reflected on what he had said to me. It comforted me that he understood what had taken place. Meanwhile, I understood nothing. That was the difference between us, I guess.

I was left to wonder what the F.B.I. would be able to accomplish, and I had no idea when I once again would hear from them. I could only sit and wait.

As the days went by, I realized there was little I could do but wait. I had no control over the events that troubled me the most, and I understood little of what had happened to the situation with me and Grace. That is why I was shocked when I picked up my ringing cell phone one evening during the following week.

"Hello," I had said without screening the call.

"Mike." The voice was soft and tentative.

I recognized the voice, though there was something different about it. "Grace? Is that you?"

"Yes, Mike, it's me. How are you?"

"Me? How are you? Where are you? Are you okay?"

There was a pause. Then, "Mike, I can't answer those questions just now, but I have one for you."

"Me?" I answered with a tremor in my voice. There were a million questions I had wanted to ask Grace during my reflections over the past days, but now I was dumbfounded by the surprise call. I could not think of what to say.

"Mike, you still there?"

I choked out, "Yes, I'm still here."

"Mike, I love you. I want you to believe that. I've always loved you. I think you love me too. Do you think you would want to come away with me?"

"Come with you? Where Grace, honey?" My head was spinning and my ears were ringing. I quickly found a chair and sat before I collapsed. For a moment I thought I might faint. Everything was happening so fast. I needed time to think, to decide.

"Does it matter where, Mike, as long as we're together?"

"No, honey, but where are you?" I blurted out. I listened for her response, but none was forthcoming. "Grace are you there?"

There was no answer and then the phone went to dial tone indicating the call was lost. I pulled up the number that had called me and hit redial. The phone rang and rang without being answered. I was beside myself now. What had happened? Had Grace hung up? Why would she? I had never given her an answer. Perhaps her battery had died. I had been so close. Close to Gracie. Just hearing her voice was stimulating. What had happened?

I sat up all night waiting for her to call back. She never did.

Chapter Thirty-One
Time Moves On

Summer moved to fall without complaint, and life for me went on. Excelsior became a different city this time of the year. Gone were the weekend lake dwellers, since the water temperatures were less inviting. The beaches were empty now, the children in school. A few boat dinner cruises still embarked, but there were fewer landlubbers to watch their departure. The ice cream store had closed for the winter, and the streets generally were quiet after six o'clock.

It has been a long three months for me, now that we were in the middle of October. It had been said that time healed all wounds and that may be true, but for me it seemed to be taking a long time. When someone lost a loved one through death, time slowly heals the pain. In my case I paralleled that, as I slowly regained my equilibrium after my too brief encounter with Grace.

I was settling back into my routine, my normal, everyday, humdrum life, and that was the way I liked it. There was something comforting about continuity and regularity. Yes, I thought of the woman plenty, and what might have been, but I realized with reflection that it would not have worked. I liked my life just the way it was. That ship with Gracie sailed many years ago. There was no turning back the clock.

That was why I was not prepared when Agent Walt Sirene called me at my office one October workday. I hadn't heard from him since our initial meeting in late July, and I'd given up the inquiry for lost.

Agent Sirene told me he had some information on the investigation and wondered if he could stop by sometime to talk. We settled on the next afternoon, and as soon as I had hung up, I regretted not finding out more of what he knew. I was left wondering what this was all about, what he had to tell me. Had they found Gracie? If they had, would they tell me where she was now living? Did I really want to know?

The next afternoon, Agent Sirene arrived at my office at one-fifteen. I suggested we walk to my home to talk. With no sunshine, my living room was dark and somber. To combat this, I turned on all the lights and those in the kitchen as well. It helped. Then I cracked the patio door to let in a modicum of fresh air.

"Take a seat, Agent Sirene."

"He sat on the couch and placed his case on the coffee table.

"Well, Mr. Connelly, I suppose you've been wondering where our investigation has headed."

"I guess I'd kinda lost track of it," I said. "I haven't heard anything on the local front either."

Agent Sirene nodded.

Then I remembered my manners. "Would you like something to drink?" I asked.

"Water would be nice, thanks."

I went into the kitchen and returned with two glasses of ice water.

Agent Sirene had opened a thin case and had removed a packet of papers in a binder.

He thanked me for the water and said, "Normally we wouldn't disclose any of this to a single individual, but you, along with Mr. Brooks, did bring the case to us, and we felt you deserved to know something of our progress. I'll tell you where we're at today, but let me begin at the beginning, okay?"

"Fine."

I realized I was becoming nervous. I really wanted to put this to bed, but was uncertain if I needed to hear any of this. Perhaps it would help bring closure for me. I just wished it had come sooner when I really was hurting more.

"Mr. Connelly, I'm going to take you back to Louisiana where Grace Adams lived while married to her first husband, Bill Johnson."

I listened, trying to pay close attention.

"The Johnsons lived in a small town near the coast. Bill Johnson worked for an oilrig company. Grace stayed home and cared for the children—two, a boy and a girl. They didn't have a lot of money, but life in the Deep South wasn't that expensive. They got by.

"Mr. Johnson would be away for extended periods because of the work schedule on the rig, which left Grace with time on her hands. Like I said, it was a really small town with little to do, so she began to visit the Mississippi casinos along the coast for some social life. She was a very attractive woman. Over time, she developed a friendship with an underworld figure by the name of Jim Collatta, who was loosely tied to the casino business. This friendship would later come into play."

I had not known any of this, and I was struggling to take it all in, not knowing if it was important.

Sirene continued, "After twelve years of marriage, Bill was killed in a rig accident, leaving Grace adrift—no job and two kids to feed."

Here I interrupted. "Was that that big deep-water disaster?"

"No, just an everyday accident. The rig didn't explode or anything, just an industrial accident. Anyway, Grace moved to Houston, Texas, where an old college roommate was living. Once in Houston, she got an apartment and a job and tried supporting her two kids.

"She had gotten a small compensation payout from the rig company of five thousand dollars, and her husband had a ten grand insurance policy, but they didn't go far after the funeral expenses. So, she was hard up to say the least.

"After a while, her college friend introduced her at a party to an art dealer by the name of Marshall Adams. Apparently, Grace put on the full court press, and soon after they got married. They continued to live in Houston. They lived there for a couple more years, but she became restless.

"Marshall had this dream of owning his own gallery. The problem was he didn't have the money and didn't really have the experience running such an operation."

I sipped my water, wondering what the relevance of all this was.

Agent Sirene continued, "This is where Mrs. Adams's former association with Collatta came in. About two years later, Marshall moves the family to Excelsior where he opens his own gallery. The best information we have is that Mrs. Adams used her connections with Collatta to get the front money for it. The quid pro quo was that Adams would be required to do some things for the organization."

"You mean, like the mob? Grace was tied up with the mob?"

Sirene nodded. "I'll get to that. Unbeknown to Adams, the organization was looking for a front in the upper Midwest for the Goya deal they were planning. Adam's gallery was perfect. The Goya caper was long planned. Once the fake painting was complete, the switch would be made. The store could have been anywhere, Chicago being the first choice, but with Mrs. Adams, having lived in Excelsior, they came here."

"So Grace was in on the deal?"

"Well, to some degree, maybe only in that she knew where to go to get the money for Marshall's dream. We don't know if she ever knew what went on behind the scenes. She was going to have more money now, and also the benefit of moving somewhere she knew. That's probably all she cared about."

"Do you know how the theft was to be made?" I interjected.

"Yes. In fact, we stopped it when they tried. Got them red handed, so to speak. The organization has ties to the trucking company transporting the painting from the airport to the museum. The delivery truck had a false panel in the front of the rear storage area. Once the truck was underway, the false panel was opened and the fake painting was taken out. Then, the crate containing the original was opened, the switch made, and the real painting hidden behind the fake panel. It was a gifted plan really."

"Who made the switch?

Two guards riding in the back of the truck."

"Too bad they didn't have surveillance in the back."

"They did, but with a phony tape loop showing nothing but the guards sitting inside with the painting the whole time."

"So, they got away with it?" I asked.

"No. Thanks to you and your friend, John Brooks, they were arrested once they reached the museum."

"Wow." Now I was feeling really proud for a change.

"Wow, indeed," Sirene said. "But the Goya wasn't the only fraud being perpetrated by the group. Singer also was making copies of obscure paintings to be shipped to galleries in different parts of the country and sold for high prices as originals These paintings commanded high prices because the gallery owners touted them as deserving them. All those gallery owners were in on the game and got a piece of the pie. This fraud was bringing in good money.

"You tumbled onto that scheme, Mike, when you noticed the three copies of Zola Jimenez work upstairs above the gallery the day after the fire. No one had been expected to enter that apartment, so Singer hadn't removed either those or the partially completed Goya, at least not until after you'd seen and photographed them."

I nodded. "Just as I suspected, then," I said.

"Yes. You were on the money there, and your suspicions and the subsequent follow up you fellows made with Lloyds exposed further scams they were running with the fake insurance claims for fire, and theft losses. This discovery totally dismantled the mob's plans."

I thought for a moment, "Gee, that's great."

"Yes it is."

Sirene continued his story, "As I said, apparently Marshall Adams had always wanted a gallery of his own, but didn't have the resources to begin. Now he had the money and the backing necessary. He jumped at the chance. Only later, when he saw what was taking place did he get cold feet. Wanted out, according to Singer."

"You got Singer, then?"

"Oh, yeah. He was able to fill in a lot of the blanks. We cut him a deal. And that gets us to where you came in. Any questions so far?"

"You said Adams wanted out? They wouldn't let him. Is that why he was killed?"

"Don't get ahead of things," Sirene said.

I nodded.

"Okay, good. Now the fire," he said.

Agent Sirene went over the entire episode of the fire and what I had seen and thought I'd seen. Then he said, "You had everything right except for one thing."

He paused, and I asked, "What?"

"The lady you saw behind the store was Maria Gomez, but she hadn't come out of the gallery. She had come out of the adjacent door from the upstairs apartment. She had been meeting with Ray Singer, working out the details of the switch of the Goya at the Walker."

"She didn't start the fire?" I asked.

"No, she knew nothing about it."

"Singer was up in the apartment when everything happened?"

"Apparently, but didn't know anything about the fire either until all hell broke loose. He took off through the front entrance when the first fire squad arrived."

"Who started the fire, then?" I asked.

Agent Sirene said, "We'll get to that. When Adams was attacked, everything looked like it was to get him out of the way. But that's not how these boys operate. If they wanted Adams gone, he'd merely disappear. No, that attempt on his life was pretty amateurish.

"When it failed, it was necessary to try again, and that next attempt had to come in the hospital. But since no one could get to him in I.C.U., they had to wait until he was moved to a regular room. They had to move quickly, though, before he could tell anyone who had tried to kill him. Fortunately for the killer, they succeeded before Marshall had recovered enough to talk."

"Wasn't it the Gomez woman?" I interrupted.

Sirene smiled. "No. Remember, she was upstairs with Singer at the time the fire began."

"But in the hospital, that was her. I saw her. Fought with her."

"Oh, she was there, but not to kill Adams. Actually, she was there to find out who had attacked him at the store. The organization wanted to find out what was going on. Their entire plan potentially was in jeopardy, and they didn't know who was causing the problems."

"But she attacked me."

"Did she? Or was she merely defending herself? Maybe from Adams assailant. Think about what happened."

I thought for a minute, then said. "I walked in and she was leaning over the bed."

"And?"

"And when she tried to leave, I stopped her."

"Why?"

"I thought she was doing something to Marshall."

"Right. You grabbed her by the hair and dragged her to the ground. She was being brutally assaulted by a stranger and fought back. Then she escaped and reported to her bosses. They suspected you as Adams's attacker."

"She was holding a pillow."

"Yes. She took it from under the victim's head when she saw he wasn't breathing. She was about to attempt CPR and call for help when you showed up.

"As it turns out though, Adams was already dead when the two of you were fighting in the room. He had been killed minutes earlier when someone injected foam insulation into his airways. Neither of you had anything to do with that."

Sirene paused and waited as I tried to assimilate everything he had just told me.

"Then who killed Gomez?" I whined.

"The same person who killed Adams."

The look of confusion on my face must have pleased Sirene, because he sat there and watched me.

He waited before dropping the bombshell, "Mrs. Adams."

"What, Grace?"

"Yes. She killed them both."

Chapter Thirty-Two
Closure

So, that was that then, the final straw. As I sat in my large overstuffed chair facing the F.B.I. agent, I felt all the energy bleed from my body. My mind tried to comprehend what agent Sirene had said. How could it have been Grace? I sat there and shook my head. No way, not my Grace.

I gripped the two arms of the chair tightly and asked. "Have you arrested her?" I looked down at my hands, as I awaited the answer. My knuckles were white from the pressure. The sound of his voice grabbed me.

"No, we haven't found her," he said. He hesitated for a moment, and then followed up with, "We want you to contact us if you hear from her. That is why I had the okay to fill you in on these details."

My body relaxed somewhat. "I just can't believe it," I said.

"I understand how you feel. It must be a great shock, but there appears to have been a strong motive."

"What?"

"Life insurance—a half-million-dollar policy taken out against Marshall's life," Sirene said. "Grace was the beneficiary. That's a lot of incentive."

He began putting his file back into his case.

"I need a drink," I said. "You want anything?"

He shook his head. "No, but you go ahead."

I stumbled into the kitchen, holding onto the counter for support. I felt lightheaded. I took a tumbler off the shelf, filled it with ice and then with Crown Royal. Then, I wove my way back into the living room and sat. Taking a big drink, I asked, "She did it for the insurance?"

The smooth liquid burned my throat as it descended. I didn't care. I needed it, and probably much more.

"It appears so," Sirene answered.

"You can't trace her with that information?" I asked. I wondered why an organization as big as the F.B.I. couldn't find her.

Here agent Sirene hesitated. Then he said, "She never filed a claim."

The alcohol was doing its work and my feeble brain already was dulled when I asked, "That's odd, isn't it?"

"Seems so."

"Any ideas?"

"Yes," Sirene stated.

"Care to share?"

There was silence for a full minute, but I waited it out.

"She's maybe dead," he said softly.

I thought those words would cause me to collapse, but I think I had anticipated them.

"What about the children?" I asked.

Sirene shook his head.

"Who would have killed them, all of them, and why?" I asked, as I took another stiff drink. My hand shook and I barely got the glass to my mouth without spilling its contents.

"The organization doesn't like double crossers. She cost them a lot of money and a long-term setup. Plus she was a really loose cannon. But we don't know she's dead. Maybe they're living somewhere in South America."

I appreciated his attempt to mollify me. "We probably blew the setup," I said.

"Yes, but they didn't know that at the time. Maybe they wouldn't have cared if she had killed her husband, but for them killing Gomez probably crossed the line."

"Why do you think she did that?" I asked.

Sirene shrugged, and then offered, "Gomez may have realized at the hospital that Marshall already was dead, and after inquiring, discovered that only the wife could have done it."

"But how could she have done it? I was there."

"Didn't you say that the two of you left the room together to go to the lounge?"

"Yes."

"And that she went back for her purse?"

"Yeah." I was trying to remember. The booze was making my mind lazy.

"That's when," Sirene said.

I thought about what he said, and then whined. "She wasn't gone very long, just a couple of minutes total."

"That's all it took. Take the can, shoot the liquid into the airways and it expands and hardens all by itself over the next few minutes."

Suddenly, I had a thought that blew the whole thing out of the water. "Ah ha," I said. "It couldn't have been her. She had an alibi the night of the fire."

Sirene smiled, and I knew I was trumped.

"She did all that too, but earlier. Then she set up a delayed fire to cover her tracks."

"How'd she do that?"

"The Fire Marshall thinks a candle was used. It's an old trick. You light the candle in the midst of combustible materials. When the candle burns down far enough, the fire starts. By the time the fire started, the alibi was established. If you hadn't tripped over the scene, who knows, maybe the whole building would have gone up."

"Yeah, I know, the water was turned off."

There was nothing more to tell. Sirene left and I chose not to walk him back to his car. I called the office and told Janet I would not be back today. Then I cried.

Winter came and with the cold came a sense of closure for me. This time of the year I walked to work until the temperatures got below zero, and then too unless the wind was blowing hard. It was only two blocks. The cold seemed to purify me.

It had taken time, but I had begun to forget Gracie for the most part. Sometimes it would be three or four days in a row when I had not thought of her. Realizing what kind of person she really was had made it easier. Now I believed I could move on. It was not easy though. One day at a time.

As my little six-year-old nephew Henry said, "I didn't know life was going to be this hard."

Neither did I, Henry. Neither did I.